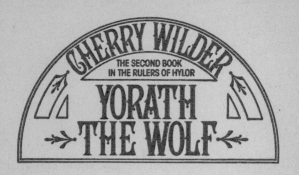

CHERRY WILDER

THE SECOND BOOK
IN THE RULERS OF HYLOR

YORATH
THE WOLF

D0639896

BREN
fantasy
BOOKS

YORATH THE WOLF

This is a work of fiction. All the characters and events portrayed in this book are fictional, and any resemblance to real people or incidents is purely coincidental.

A Baen Book

Baen Enterprises
8-10 West 36 Street
New York, N.Y. 10018

First Baen printing, October 1985

ISBN: 0-671-55987-7

Cover art by Stephen Hickman

Printed in the United States of America

Distributed by
SIMON & SCHUSTER
MASS MERCHANDISE SALES COMPANY
1230 Avenue of the Americas
New York, N.Y. 10020

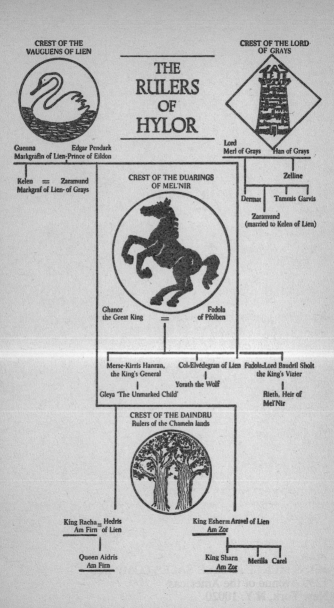

THE RULERS OF HYLOR

CREST OF THE VAUGUENS OF LIEN

CREST OF THE LORD OF GRAYS

Guenna
Markgräfin of Lien

Edgar Pendark
Prince of Eildon

Lord Merl of Grays

Han of Grays

Kelen = Zaramund
Markgraf of Lien- of Grays

CREST OF THE DUARINGS OF MEL'NIR

Zelline

Dermat

Tammis Garvis

Zaramund
(married to Kelen of Lien)

Ghanor
the Great King

=

Fadola
of Pfolben

Merse-Kirris Hanran,
the King's General

Col-Elvédegran of Lien

Fadola-Lord Baudril Sholt
the King's Vizier

Yorath the Wolf

Gleya 'The Unmarked Child'

Rieth, Heir of
Mel'Nir

CREST OF THE DAINDRU
Rulers of the Chameln lands

King Racha _ Hedris
Am Firn of Lien

King Esher = Aravel of Lien
Am Zor

Queen Aidris
Am Firn

King Sharn
Am Zor

Merilla

Carel

CHAPTER

I

AFTER A LABOR OF FOUR DAYS AND NIGHTS THE FAIR young Princess Elvédegran of Lien, wife of Gol, the prince of Mel'Nir, gave birth to a monster. It was myself. The prince, my father, a handsome man, turned aside from my mother's blood-stained bed and vomited. He rinsed his mouth out with wine, turned back and cursed my mother. She was in no condition to reply, but her old nurse, Caco, who feared neither men nor demons, cursed him back. Gol kicked the old woman; he fell into that raging frenzy that it pleases the men of Mel'Nir to call god-rage. Half a dozen nobles who were packed into the tower room watching the birth restrained him. Hagnild, the physician, had the place cleared at last. The prince was dragged out struggling followed by the rout of his court. Women screamed; dwarfs and greddles were trodden underfoot.

Outside, the chronicles will tell you, a black

heap of storm clouds rolled up over the Dannermere and bolts of godlight tore at the doomed land of Mel'Nir. The winds howled, and I, the misshapen harbinger of the Great King's fall, writhed and shrieked upon the blood-stained bed. In fact it was not so; I cried feebly, the day was misty and dank. There *were* portents, and Hagnild knew them, but his present concern was the health of his patients. He let Caco bind up my faint princess mother, and meanwhile he examined me. I was, he has assured me, a revolting sight; but when he had wiped me clean and removed my caul, he found me healthy if not straight. One shoulder was twisted. I had a line of hair down my back and a rudimentary tail, which he removed at once, sealing the small wound. A deformed male child.

There was a precedent to be followed in such cases. I would be presently displayed to the Great King himself, then slain. Ghanor had had four grandchildren put down already, as casually as puppies. He struck in vain, Hagnild believed, at an hereditary defect that lay in the blood of the Duarings, the royal house of Mel'Nir. A crook-back king, a poor wry-necked princess, these things had been known to occur in every generation. There were other accidents—a skull moulded strangely at birth, a blood-colored mark—that were not hereditary. Of the four unfortunates, the children of the Great King's daughters, Merse and Fadola, Hagnild had sadly approved the death of two, one a birth injury, the other a serious case of the family crookedness, a hunchback. The others, superficially marked, might have lived healthy and sound, but he had no power against the combined unreason of Ghanor and the chroniclers.

The curse of the royal house and a wish to be free of their tyrannical masters had brought the scribes who worked upon the *Scroll of Vill*, the *Dathsa* and the *Book of the Farfarers* to agree firmly on one point. The Great King would lie in jeopardy from a marked child of his own house. It was not difficult to find a mark on any newborn child. Only the insistence of the seers and chroniclers that the danger lay in the second generation had protected the Great King's daughters and Gol, his son. Now here I lay, Gol's first-born, marked beyond hope; I should follow my hapless cousins to the steps of the throne. The creature Drey who lived in the folds of the King's robe crept out with a stinging knife to dispatch such victims.

And yet . . . Hagnild carried me to the window, searching for a sign. It was autumn, early in the Thornmoon. He looked out over the hunting preserves of the king that lay about the Palace Fortress and over a bay of the inland sea, the Dannermere. In a patch of clear water a last swan sailed into view and took to the air. Hagnild saw that it had one black wing. It was enough. He knew that I must live.

He had not much time to do his working. My mother, Elvédegran, whispered from the bed, "Show me the child . . ."

Hagnild met Caco's burning gaze, but he stepped up and laid me for the first and last time in my mother's arms. She was brave; the torments she had suffered since she left the warmth and security of her mother's house had not dimmed her spirit. She was the youngest of the three lovely swans of Lien and, some said, the most beautiful. The Markgrafin Guenna of Lien had striven passionately to protect her daughters: two she had saved ... they were given in marriage to the Daindru, the rulers of the Chameln lands, good but ill-fated men. The third swan she could not save. Intrigue and stupidity, this time in the persons of Rosmer, the Vizier, and Kelen, the young Markgraf, had triumphed, as they often did in the glittering realm of Lien. When Guenna was broken and disgraced, Kelen ruled; he gave his youngest sister, at seventeen, into the tender keeping of Prince Gol of Mel'Nir.

Elvédegran knew well that at this moment her life was ebbing away. If she did not die from the ordeal of the birth, then Ghanor might have her killed. She examined my body, wrapped me again in the princely cloth that had been waiting to receive me, and said a prayer to the Goddess. With Caco's help she placed around my neck the silver swan, token of the house of Lien.

"He could grow," she whispered.

"No doubt," said Hagnild.

"Does my word have any power?" she asked.

"As a princess ... ?" asked the magician sadly.

"By no means," she said, "though I am one. My power might come from the fact that I am dying."

She lay back upon the bed pale as the mist that swirled up to the ramparts of the Palace Fortress. Hagnild was impressed. Death might assist his working, even though time was short. The word had been brought by now to the Great King himself, and Drey was sharpening his sting. Hagnild made his decision and swept about the chamber repeating a simple fastening upon the doors and windows. Then he placed me, wrapped as I was, in Caco's arms.

"Bid farewell to your mistress," he said. "She is for the Halls of the Goddess. Swear fealty to the child!"

Caco did as she was bid, and Hagnild said impatiently to my mother:

"Name the child!"

"Yorath," whispered the princess. "Call him Yorath."

It is the name of a king's son who was hidden in a wolf's skin. Hagnild signed the name on my breast and gave Caco instructions:

"Go down the little stair to the second postern gate. The guards will not be able to see you. Take my mare Selmis, tethered by the horse trough just beyond the gate. Ride with the child to the crossroads by the dolmen and stay my coming. If I am not there by nightfall, go on into the marsh and find out Finn's smithy. Wait with the smith and his goodwife until I come."

Heavy footsteps sounded in the passage, and there was a pounding at the door of the tower room. Hagnild shouted, "Stay clear! We are bewitched!"

He spoke to my mother, giving her certain words of power. He unfastened the door to the little stair and recited the spell for the guards at the second postern gate.

"Wait . . ." he said.

He stripped off the old woman's grey shawl and replaced it with a velvet cloak belonging to the princess.

"Now go!"

Caco held me tightly, bobbed one last time to her poor young mistress and went down the stair. Hagnild made fast the door and hurried on with his ritual. The hammering on the main door of the tower room began again.

"Master Hagnild!"

It was the voice of Pulk, the Captain of the Guard.

"Open up! We must have the newborn creature!"

Hagnild took my mother's limp white hand and kissed it.

"Now!"

He gestured, and the door flew open. The room was lit with snapping darts of blue fire; the men at arms staggered in with a roaring in their ears. Elvédegran gave a thin, high scream, and they saw it: A scaly creature perched upon the bed, a twisted body that glowed dull green, murderous eyes glittering above a horny beak. The air in the chamber was foetid with the demon's breath.

Hagnild, backed against the wall, cried out, "Be gone!"

Three times he conjured the evil thing, and at last it unfurled leathern wings. A whirlwind tore at the hangings, the room was plunged into darkness, the round window was shattered: the demon was gone.

When the mists cleared, Pulk and his shaken men at arms found no sign of the monstrous child. Caco, the old woman, had also been spirited away, leaving only a shawl half burnt to ashes. Hagnild the Thaumaturge still reeled against the wall, pale from his ordeal. Clearly, Pulk explained to the king, he had rid the palace of a changeling, a monstrous demon sent to work ill on the royal house of Mel'Nir.

The Princess Elvédegran, innocent vessel of misfortune, lay dead upon her charred and blood-stained bed. Women came and removed her body while Hagnild instructed the house servants in the purification of the chamber.

The princess was borne on a flowered bier into the great hall of the Palace Fortress. Prince Gol, sobered and guilty, walked by her side. He could not take his eyes from her pale face; there was something in her death smile that mocked him and struck terror to his heart. She was borne to the steps of the high throne, called Azure; a single trumpet sounded her own fanfare, a call of the house of Lien. Gol looked up in the torchlight at the Great King, his father, Ghanor of Mel'Nir, Lord of the High Plateau, conqueror of the Danmark and the Westland, scourge of the war-lords.

The king sat brooding, his iron-tipped staff resting across his massive knees. The folds of his robe were encrusted with rough rubies in filigree, thick as blood. His bearded face in the torchlight shone red and black, the carved face of a savage god. His old eyes, always bloodshot, were hooded like the eyes of a huge bird. Hagnild was in attendance, easing back through the silent ranks of warriors and courtiers, anxious to take his leave. Outside the palace a storm rolled up at last and broke in sudden fury over the dark waters of the Dannermere.

I lay safe and warm in Finn's smithy; Caco warmed her hands at the fire in the smith's house among the cooking smells and tumbling brown children. I took my first meal, I am told, at the breast of Erda, Finn's wife, who was nursing her ninth child. Beyond the house lay the marsh and beyond that the reaches of Nightwood. A light shone out from the smithy where Finn still worked, hammering with great art at horseshoes and at weapons.

* * *

I grew in Nightwood. Hagnild knew, and now I know, the ways that penetrate that forest's awful shade. There is a clearing in the very midst of the wood where the trees advance or retreat at a word, where the sky is visible, where the weather can be a matter of craft. There Hagnild had a secret house, a brown house with low walls and a towering conical thatched roof. I grew there on goats' milk and Caco's devotion and long evenings with Hagnild over the books. My earliest memories are firelight on the hearth; a huge book bound in smooth brown fur; snow falling. Did Hagnild draw down snow for me one winter's day?

At three years old I was lost for a day and brought home by two hunters of the Kelshin, the pygmy race who live in Nightwood. I do not remember these patient hunters, guiding the stout lump of a child, taller than themselves, but I have one memory from this time. A tiny little woman in a leather apron is scolding me. I can see her hood, her white hair in intricate braids, her sharp features and black eyes.

I grew in Nightwood. Those who live thereabouts, in the marsh or the forest, enter into a conspiracy with the place: they preserve its legend and do not dispel the fears of outsiders. Nightwood is much feared and sometimes with good reason. Its ways can be dark and treacherous; in a hard winter the wolf packs range beyond the marsh and ford the river Kress to hunt the King's game. Ribur, the last of the great grey bears in the wood, lives in a rocky chasm topped by a hazel grove. He is old and almost toothless but still a danger to men.

Those who fear Nightwood think of dark magic,

not of swift-flowing rivers, impassable thickets, the morass or the wild beasts. The magic I saw in the wood was mainly that imposed by Hagnild, therefore benign or designed to scare off intruders. The paraphernalia of clutching trees, shifting darkness, howling or whispering of the wind, these are mostly his doing. Yet there are ancient districts of the wood where all mortals feel like trespassers. Worse still, there are haunted places where even I would not go willingly. There is a certain ash tree that bears strange gallows fruit. In a grove far to the east, down by the shore of the Dannermere, a pale fetch comes hopping, hopping through the long grass, eyeless, with a carrion stink.

As a child I hid from strangers. I played and fought with my milk-brother Arn, ninth child of Finn, the Smith, and was welcome in the smith's house. I throve on barefoot summers, climbing those slippery customers the forest trees, trolling for fish in the Kress and in the channels of the marsh. Arn and I had a favorite tree, an oak, on the forest side of the river, where we sat hidden, watching the courtiers and soldiers of the king ride to hunt in the broad acres of parkland on the far bank.

The Palace Fortress enveloped its squat hill a little way to the west. Further off was the neglected town of Lort, struggling to become a city, the capital of Mel'Nir. There were traces in the masonry of the fortress and the town of a former race of builders in stone, neither the men of Mel'Nir nor the darker, sturdier race they had displaced in the land.

I had been saved by Hagnild, but I was kept alive and succored by Caco. She "licked me into

shape" as she-wolves and bears were supposed to
do with their cubs. By this I mean that she moulded
and massaged my twisted body so that I grew up
straighter than might have been expected.

I have often thought of Caco's strange fate. She
was a farmer's wife of Lien, taken into the service
of the Markgrafin Guenna on her country estate,
beautiful Alldene. She was wet nurse to the royal
children and raised six children of her own. When
she was widowed, at an age when she might have
settled to being a grandmother, she elected to stay
with the youngest princess. Elvédegran went from
the silken captivity of her brother's palace in Balufir
to the Palace Fortress of Mel'Nir and the rough
embraces of Prince Gol.

When Caco was eight and fifty years, she found
herself bereaved of her young mistress, alone,
among strangers, with a newborn child to rear. She
did this without faltering; Nightwood and the
marsh became her territory, just as they were mine.
She made friends: Erda, the Smith's wife; an old
woman, Uraly, the reed-gatherer.

Caco had developed a boundless contempt for
the so-called high estates, for royal personages and
nobles. Palaces were for her places of discomfort
and misery; princes were by nature cruel, stupid
and unreliable; courtiers were vicious and self-
serving. She had no difficulty in concealing from
me the circumstances of my birth. I was the child,
she said, of Vida, a lady of Lien, and Nils, a soldier
of Mel'Nir, both dead. She had a deep hatred for
my true father, Prince Gol, and she invented in
Nils a father who resembled her eldest son, a member of the palace guard in faraway Balufir. If any
asked, she told me as soon as I could speak, I must

say that I lived with my grandam in the marsh; but I knew from the first that she was not my blood kin.

So I was Yorath Nilson, and when I was grown, and if I was good—if I wore my shoes, came in for supper, went to bed without fuss, let myself be scrubbed clean and did the exercises in reading, writing, ciphering that Master Hagnild had set— then one day I might make something of myself. I might become a merchant, or a scholar, or, yes, with a sigh Caco must admit it, a soldier.

I was born in the year 305 of the Farfaring, in the twenty-first year of the reign of Ghanor, the Great King, and in the third year of the Long Peace, also called the King's Peace. Yet the whole purpose of life as it appeared in the chronicles and sagas and in the life of palace and town was the making of war and the practice of arms. The men of Mel'Nir are tall and strong; in the chronicles of the other lands of Hylor, they are very often described not only as giants but as "giant warriors." The cult of size and strength, of steely temper, aptness to command, courage in the face of pain and death, is drummed into all the children of Mel'Nir and pursues them beyond the frost fields to that adopted heaven. Not one but a whole troop of White Warriors usher them into the Halls of Victory, the dwelling of the Goddess. Even with my curious upbringing, between Nightwood and the books and scrolls, I had very little chance of being anything else but a soldier, and Hagnild must have known it.

Nevertheless he tried to put off the evil day ... and so did other parents and guardians. The threat

of soldiering made me an outlaw for the first time
when I was twelve years old.

The season was high summer. Arn and I went
down to fish in the Dannermere and watched a
barge being laden with men and horses at the
king's wharf by Kressmouth, a sleepy watchpost
that was likely to turn into a harbor village since
Mel'Nir had made a protectorate of the Chameln
lands. Then we wandered through the woods along
our bank of the river. A man sat fishing in the
curve of the Kress with a basket of apples by his
side. We watched him from the trees: he reached
out now and then and ate an apple in two or three
bites. They sounded wonderfully crisp.

Presently he turned his head, shaded his eyes,
and said, "Are you there, then? Come out and have
an apple!"

We came out. I saw that the fisherman was dark,
undersized and dressed in worn leather.

"Two lads," he said, "and well grown. Eat
hearty."

We sat beside the apple basket and polished off
a couple. I saw that he fished very carelessly and
without a good float. The man's face was leathery
and brown as his tunic. Presently he said that his
name was Medgor. He asked our names and we
gave them, pat answers both: Arn, son of Finn, at
the smithy, Yorath Nilson, lives with his grandam
in the marsh. By the time he asked how tall we
were and guessed our ages, I took fright. I gripped
Arn's wrist. We took two more apples, muttered
our thanks and ran off into the forest. But the
damage had been done. Medgor was a scout for
the longhouse where the soldiers of the Great King
were trained; an intake of young lads was due in

autumn, in the Hazelmoon. So much Hagnild found out when he heard of our apple-friend.

The remedy was for Arn and Yorath to be sent away until the recruiting officers had gone through. The people of Nightwood and the marsh were few, and some of them were wanderers like the tinker woman or the brothers who caught birds and taught them to talk. If two boys listed by Medgor were not to be found, time would not be spent searching for them. Arn, son of Finn, would be "apprenticed to a sword-maker in the west"; Yorath and his grandam would have gone away, disappeared into the mist. Arn and I felt a great adventure brewing. Where would we go? I had hardly left the marsh, had been east to the port of Ranke on the Danner-mere but west not even as far as Lort. I am sure Hagnild and Caco suffered qualms and wondered how it would continue with the hiding of a great lump of a boy.

Hagnild thought at first of sending us to his family home at Nesbath, that lovely watery town, built at the confluence of the Bal and the Ringist where both these rivers flow out of the Dannermere and spread out to embrace the fabulous land of Lien. But Hagnild's parents were long dead, his brother, of whom he seldom spoke, was on his travels. The House of Healing where he had grown up was given over to the care of ancient servants.

At last it was decided that the two fugitives would go to the west, to the brother of Erda, the smith's wife, who was indeed a swordmaker and a man of substance in the town of Krail. The Great King's officers did not go about in Krail: it was capital of the territory of Valko, Lord of Val'Nur, Valko the Thunderer, Valko Firehammer, in short

the most powerful war-lord in Mel'Nir. The King's
Peace was in effect a truce between Ghanor and
Valko; both rulers seemed to be enjoying the respite. The Great King took the opportunity to an-
nex the Chameln lands when the Daindru, the two
kings, died untimely. Valko kept his lesser lords to
heel and built roads and forts.

Arn and I set out for the west with Roke the
Carrier, another man of the marsh, who trundled
reed baskets, fish, salt, rope, mushrooms and truf-
fles through Lort to the west and came back with
butter, orchard fruit, wine and mutton. We sat
inside his small wagon as we went through Lort,
pretending more danger than there was. No one
challenged Roke. Through slits in the canvas we
saw that Lort was a square, yellowish town, built
of stone and brick around the garrison fort and the
old walls, built by the ancient masons. The scale
of these old walls and the Ox Gate, with its mighty,
weathered carvings of two bulls, showed that these
builders, gone so long that their names and the
names of their kings and cities were forgotten, had
indeed built like giants. The men of Mel'Nir built
painstaking solid forts and houses that were like
forts.

When the town was passed we came out of hiding and sat beside Roke. In late summer the road
was dry but not too dusty. We had come uphill a
little and could look back to the Palace Fortress
and to Nightwood and the marsh. The endless
vistas, the wild beauty of the land of Mel'Nir held
us spellbound. This is not the ordered beauty of
Lien or of Athron, nor the wildness of forest and
lake and plain to be seen in the Chameln lands.
Rather Mel'Nir is a land uncultivated, waiting to

be smoothed or tilled. To the northwest, beyond the palace, green hills and groves of trees rolled to the skirts of the border forest, in the far blue distance, and to the banks of the Bal, the border with Lien. To our left, as Roke's old brown warhorse plodded up the hill, we could see the High Plateau, a country full of mist and magic, like our own Nightwood. Over the brow of the hill was the Westland, where we were going.

When we reached the crest of this hill, Roke turned the cart aside to the banks of a thin stream, unhitched the old horse, and sent us to fetch firewood. We made a fire, and Roke hung a black pot over it with a rich stew of hare, turnips and mushrooms. I had eyes only for the old round tower that stood on the hilltop, again a work from an earlier time. It was a watchtower, now no more than a shell of blackened brick, but I wondered if it could be climbed inside. When we had eaten, Roke settled down in the shade against a wild plum tree with his straw hat shading his eyes and his wooden leg stretched out comfortably. Arn dozed too; he opened one eye and said he would follow by and by. I went through the trees to the road and entered the tower alone.

Inside it was cool and dark; the tower was still in use as a watchtower: the old curving stair had been mended with yellow stone and had a wooden balustrade. I ran up and stood on the platform at the top, feeling the wind in my face and looking for miles in every direction. Far down the hill to the west, the way that we must travel, there grew a small dust cloud.

I continued to look about; and when I looked to the west again, the dust cloud was a troop of

galloping horsemen. The chargers in their cotton
covers pounded along in impressive style, but a
lithe black horse drew away more and more from
the troop. The black horse came on, swift as a
bird; and I saw that there were two riders upon it.
What I was witnessing was a pursuit. The two
fugitives were now far ahead. I looked down and
saw that the black horse had been brought in close
to the base of the tower. It swung round the big,
drooping cedar tree at the doorway, then on down
the hill. I saw it come into view again and take the
right hand path at a crossroads, the road to Lort.
At the same moment I heard light footsteps climbing the steps of the tower.

Perhaps it was the lightness of those steps that
made me go to meet the newcomer. We faced each
other on the stairs in a shaft of light pouring down
from above. The fugitive who had slipped from the
black horse and entered the tower was a woman—I
would have said a lady or more of a lady than I
had ever beheld. She was tall and slender and
pale-skinned; her hair was black, held with a band;
her lips and cheeks were red or reddened; her
wide eyes were a striking light brown. She wore
riding breeches of green leather with the overskirt
swung back like a train. Her impact was one of
startling beauty. I felt her looks like a blow in the
face. I knew beauty's power.

We simply stared at each other as the troop of
horses drew near, with a sound like thunder. The
lady, the lady in distress—I had read many scrolls
from Eildon and from Lien—moistened her lips
and said in a low voice that did not tremble, *"They
will kill me!"*

I believed her at once. I said or croaked, "I will
go out . . ."

We knew what I meant. I would go out and put
off her pursuers, lie for her. I came down the stair
and had to squeeze past her; I was twelve years
old and nearly six feet tall, but I was still childish
and undeveloped. Yet this moment was one I recalled as I grew older and reenacted in various
ways in my dreams.

She spoke once more: "What is your name?"

"Yorath Nilson . . ."

The riders were outside the tower, and they had
checked. Above me she drew in her breath. I ran
down the remaining stairs, dashed into the sunlight and cried, pointing down the hill, "They took
the road towards Lort!"

The leader of the troop, a young ensign, waved
his hand; three of the riders plunged on down the
hill, the other three, including the officer, drew
rein. I saw one man on a brown charger who was
distressed for want of breath; he was middle-aged
and wore a jewelled baldric across his surcoat.
The ensign drew in close and supported him in the
saddle. The third man was altogether a civilian,
riding a red horse from the plateau; he was sharp-
featured, swarthy and bearded.

"Shall I fetch water for the lord?" I asked.

The sick man took two more long gasping breaths
and smiled at me.

"No need, lad. I have some."

He drank from his water bottle. The ensign said,
"Where did you spring from? The tower?"

"Yes, Captain." I upped his rank.

"Name!"

If I had been older it would have been "Name and rank!"

"Yorath Nilson. Travelling to Krail. See, my party was camped yonder by the stream."

I saw Arn and Old Roke coming uncertainly up to the road through the trees.

"Captain," I asked, "were those bond-breakers that you were chasing? Or thieves?"

"Both!" said the ensign angrily. "They have committed great crimes against our lord Thilon of Val'Nur and his noble brother."

The dark man came up suddenly on his red horse and said, "You, boy, what did you see? You were in the tower!"

"I saw the chase," I said, "and heard the black horse go by, then I saw them turn off on the road to Lort."

"Something may be foul here, Lord Thilon!" cried the dark man. "We may have lost the one we seek. Is the boy telling the truth?"

"I think he is," said the sick man, Thilon, smiling at me again. "You are too harsh, Geshtar. Do you think he has been bewitched?"

"A moment, I pray you, Lord," said Geshtar. "Boy, can you describe the riders?"

"No sir," I said, hanging my head. "Just two men on a black horse."

Hem Thilon and the ensign laughed indulgently; I had outfoxed Geshtar. I sensed another reason why they believed me: we were of one flesh. They were tall, fair men, big-built, with hair of the sun-colors . . . red, tawny . . . and I was one of their kind.

"Yorath," said Hem Thilon, "one of those riders was a woman, an accursed witch, Gundril Chawn, the Owlwife. She stole from me . . ."

He was wracked by a fit of coughing, and he spat phlegm streaked with blood into the grass at the roadside. Geshtar came up and fed his master some draught; I saw that he was a healer. The ensign gave me a smile and a salute.

"Beware of witches!" he said.

When Hem Thilon had been treated, they rode on slowly down the hill. Roke and Arn hurried across, questioning eagerly, and I told them all I had told the lord and his men. At last Arn and I went into the tower again. It was quite empty, as I knew it would be. Magic might have been the answer, but the doorway was well screened by the cedar tree, and a bold fugitive could have come out and made off into the bushes that grew at the tower's base. We climbed up. I went ahead of Arn, and on the topmost step I found two brown feathers arranged so that they made the first letter of my name. I gathered them up and hid them away in my tunic. From that time the Owlwife flew through the forests of my dreams.

So we travelled on into the west, sleeping in Roke's wagon, until we came to the town of Krail and the forge of Bülarn, the Swordmaker. There was great excitement when we came into the yard. The master came from the forge, the mistress from the house, the two pretty girl children came out with their nursemaid. The whole family embraced Arn, their nephew and cousin, and carried him off indoors. He looked back and pointed me out, and a glance was cast in my direction. Roke and I waited, and when the Master emerged, Roke delivered the sealed letter from Hagnild asking the family to care for me. Bülarn turned the letter over in his hands and sent me off to the apprentices' barrack, by the forge. He went on his way.

"Well, there it is, lad," said Roke. "You are not his kin. Take your bundle. I'll come by in the spring."

There it was indeed. I spent a miserable six months in Bülarn's yard and learned what it was to have no kin. I hardly knew how ill I was treated, but felt it all like a dumb animal, a dog, hardly able to protest. When Arn, poor fellow, tried to bring me into the kitchen, the cook shooed me away "because I had no place there." When the apprentices ate, I was served last and grudgingly as an extra mouth to feed. I worked at odd jobs in the yard and watched all that was done at the forge. I was able to walk about in the town and even steal away with Arn to the meadows and do some fishing. We were late back for supper and the master knocked me down for taking Arn away, then drew his dear nephew back into the house. I felt all the time that Bülarn and his family treated me so ill because I was almost invisible to them. They never seemed to know my name or remember me from one day to the next. Arn did what he could, but the treatment *he* received would have turned the head of any boy, let alone one who had grown up as a ninth child.

Although I did not like to think of my time in Krail for years afterwards, I did store up some good memories of that time. The town was a fine place, with fruit markets bathed in the golden light of autumn. On the High Bridge over the river Demmis there were shops and booths full of weapons, metalwork, leathergoods, cotton cloth and . . . best of all for me in my loneliness . . . books, scrolls, inks and pens. Here I met the only person who could be called my friend in Krail.

One afternoon as I wandered away from the baskets in front of the bookshop, a hand plucked at my sleeve. He seemed to be crouching between the leather mantles of an old clothes merchant. His face was dreadfully twisted; on the right side, where his mouth was drawn down, the skin was thickened and fiery red. A pair of large liquid eyes peered out of this face; it was impossible not to think of a mask.

"Boy. . . ." The voice was soft but penetrating, "You are not straight."

I gulped, staring down at him. I could see now that he was a beggar with a single crutch and a begging bowl held to his grotesquely twisted body.

"No," I said. "My shoulder is twisted. But it is growing out."

"You will help me," he said. "You have silver. Go to the scribes' shop again and get me two bunches of wooden pens, dirt cheap, half a groat."

When I gasped out a question, he said, "I have no money, and I have a copying work ordered. I am quick enough, but too slow for the shopkeeper. She knows me too well, even gave me tick once or twice. I cannot steal the pens."

Of course I did what he asked. I went back and bought the pens and then went down a certain stair off the bridge and sat on a stone coping beside the river. A bent shape, a bundle of rags whisked out of the shadows of the bridge piers and sat beside me.

"My name is Forbian," said my new friend. "Some call me Flink. Yes, these will do very well.

And on the bridge do not keep your belongings in an outside pocket."

He handed me the contents of one of my pockets: a small knife, a filthy kerchief, a particularly fine horse chestnut—a conker, threaded on a thong. We talked, and Forbian the copyist, was a mine of interesting information. We watched the river and the tall, golden citadel rising above the town, the stronghold of Valko Firehammer. I heard all the exploits and attributes of this great lord in the measured, acrid tones of one of the least of his subjects. By and large Forbian approved of Valko. He not only gave generous handouts to the poor and the dispossessed, the beggars or self-styled "veterans," he gave them a sort of territory of their own: Darktown, a warren of crooked streets and cavernous cellars beneath the Old Bridge, further downstream.

On one of the days when we sat by the river and shared some food, we saw a troop of cavalry ride by. They were well turned out and mounted on fine wirey horses from the Plateau. These were the Sword Lilies, a chosen troop of tall battlemaids in Valko's service. The kind of coarse remarks passed about such a troop I had already heard in the swordmaker's yard.

"Make no mistake," said Forbian, spitting pips into the river. "Those gals are well-trained and dangerous in battle, like all true kedran. They must do more because they live among men, who are generally taller, with more muscle. They make up their lack of weight with swiftness and ferocity. They are taught to go for the face and the throat. They can whirl about and reform on their horses while the troopers are wondering what hit them in the first charge."

Forbian had a gift for imparting information, and he was just as good at getting it out of others. He had my whole history from me in an hour or so ... Nightwood, Hagnild, Caco, my supposed parents, my present miserable state at the swordmakers.

"You will go for a soldier," he said, "like your father, this Nils. I am a good judge of bones. I even know the shape of my own bones and have pledged them long ago to a collector of curiosities. You will top seven feet and thicken in proportion. The shoulder will not grow quite straight, but it will not hinder you. In fact it will make you more terrible and frightening to look upon. No hindrance in a warrior. Have you never wondered, boy, who you might be?"

I hardly understood the question.

"Think a bit," said Forbian. "This Master Healer, from the king's court, raises you in Nightwood with the aid of an old Lienish woman. I think, saving your presence, my dear Yorath, that you are the bastard of some noble lord or noble lady. A child of the bower, as they say, borne in shame. You must come to some kin, my lad. Ask your guardian when you are older."

The long autumn in Krail came slowly to an end. I was still a child, and in some ways a mollycoddled child; I did not know how to look after myself. By the time the wind blew cold through the swordmaker's yard and the end of year furlough for the apprentices drew near, I was a sorry sight. I was afraid of the winter, afraid of the time when the forge would be put out, when the four heavy-handed apprentices would go to their homes and I would be left alone in the barracks. When the first snow fell, I shovelled it from the entries of the house. Arn and his two girl cousins went out to skate and ride their sleds. I was allowed at last to come indoors, into the kitchen.

It was the largest room in the house, in fact the largest room I had ever been in. The big blazing hearth had three fires upon it, with spits and cauldrons. The kitchen was divided into work places; it was shadowy and dim, with piled sacks and barrels; flitches of bacon, plaits of herbs, bunches of onions, hung from blackened hooks in the roof. This was the domain ruled over by the cook, a huge truculent woman called Mistress Trok. She had a maid of all work and two scullions to help her; one servingman and the nursemaid worked above stairs.

The day was divided into periods of hectic shouting, steaming activity and times when everyone lay about exhausted, waiting to prepare the next meal for the family. There were frightful accidents: burns, scalds, knife wounds. The servants had one regular meal in the evening, the rest of the time they ate on the run, snatching bites and sups from the ends and crusts and leftovers on a certain table. I spent most of the time hiding in the shadows until the cook shouted for "That boy . . . the sweeper . . . where's he?" if she needed an extra hand.

At supper I sat at the foot of the trestle table on a pickle barrel. The warmest places at the hearth and in the chimney corner were taken for sleeping purposes by the maid, poor creature, who had a built in bed in a sort of cupboard, and two scul-

lions who slept on a long settle before the hearth.
The cook had a room near the locked pantry; the
manservant and the nurserymaid slept above stairs.
I was glad to have a choice of warm sleeping
places: under a table, among the meal sacks, or
best of all, on bread days, I had a place in an outer
room, between the woodpile and the warm plaster
wall of the baker's oven.

On some special day the servants dressed in
their best to receive the swordmaker and his family. The cook and the little maid perceived at last
that I was filthy and neglected. I was given a bath
in the laundry copper, for the washerwoman had
been in, and my clothes were put to rights.

Bülarn and his goodwife appeared; gifts were
exchanged, glasses of spirit were drunk. The two
girl children came in with Arn, all fancily dressed.
I hardly recognised my old companion from Nightwood and the Marsh. I recalled Forbian's notion
that Bülarn wished, perhaps, to adopt Arn and
make him his heir. Yet Arn himself did not seem
to have changed very much; he found me out in
my shadow and gave me a box of sweetmeats. We
laughed and elbowed each other as we always did.
Suddenly Bülarn called me out into the light. He
had had many glasses of schnapps that day, and
when, for the first time, he tried to fix his attention on me he could not focus perfectly.

"You there, boy," he said, "you're speaking with
my nephew, Arn."

"Yes sir."

"You know him," he said. "Do we know you?"

"I came out of Nightwood with Arn," I said.
"My name is Yorath Nilson."

"Out of Nightwood," he said. "Do you work?

Do you work in my yard? We give no charity here!"

"My guardian is the Healer of Nightwood," I said. "Roke gave you his letter when we came here, Master Bülarn . . ."

"Master Bülarn . . ." he said, mimicking my speech. "A letter was it? And what should we do with a letter?"

"My guardian asked you to take me in," I said. "He put a gold piece under the seal of the letter for my keep."

Bülarn goggled at me. His drunkenness vanished away in one belch.

"Under the seal!" he said.

He gave a curse, shouted for the family and bustled them out of the kitchen. Everyone stood in silence, and into the silence came the sound of cupboards being ransacked, boxes thrown aside. Bülarn was in his counting-house looking for that unopened letter. Suddenly all the servants burst out laughing; they wheezed and shrieked and roared. The cook's eyes streamed with tears, the stiff serving man clapped me on the back and gave me a glass of hot punch.

I learned a fact of life: servants do not love their masters. I had made a fool of the swordmaker, and for that they loved *me*. I asked the cook, later, how Bülarn could be a master swordmaker in Krail and not know how to read.

"No trouble," she said. "He can count and reckon pretty well, be sure of that. He has a hired scribe who comes in."

"I could have read the letter for him," I said in all innocence.

"To tell the truth, Yorath, so could I," said Mistress Trok, her raisin-brown eyes beaming shrewdly, "but he wouldn't thank us for the offer."

To give Bülarn his due, he tried to make up for his neglect a little. I was given a second settle before the kitchen fire and permitted to go with Arn to see the New Year bonfires lit. A horde of beggars danced about the square below the citadel allowing themselves to be touched or even kissed to ward off ill-fortune in the coming year. I spoke with Forbian Flink, and we exchanged gifts. I gave him my small knife to sharpen his pens, and he gave me a small leather pouch stamped with a wolf's head.

"Come back," he said. "Go to the Plantation, Valko's longhouse, and train for the guard. Over the fence the Sword Lilies grow . . ."

He was gone, with an appalling wink.

When the spring came, I kept my eye open. The moment Roke's wagon trundled into the yard I was aboard, with my bundle.

"As bad as that?" he asked.

II

I went back thankfully to Nightwood and the marsh. Arn stayed at the swordmakers for almost another half year and continued to make visits there. I was reunited with Hagnild and Caco; I continued to live and more especially to grow, in Nightwood. Hagnild provided diversions and training for me. I learned to ride on the retired chargers kept by the tinker woman; I was taught the rudiments of sword play by Finn and Roke.

Hagnild was still putting off the evil day. He knew that I must one day go out into the world. He tried to make up for my lack of experience of any places outside the forest and the marsh with travellers' tales, with book-learning. He taught me a good deal of recent history of the continent of Hylor and of the ruling houses of its lands. I became familiar with the Vauguens, the ruling house of Lien; the Firn and the Zor who ruled the Chameln lands; and the Menvirs of Athron. I already knew the Duarings of Mel'Nir and their life in the Palace Fortress. With the aid of his scrying stones, Hagnild and I looked together into its somber halls, bright bowers and lofty chambers. I saw the Great King upon his throne, I saw Prince Gol and his second wife, the Princess Artetha, from the distant Southland. I saw the Princess Merse and her husband, Kirris Hanran, Kirris the Lynx, and the Princess Fadola, married to Baudril Sholt, the vizier of the kingdom, whom Hagnild found intolerably stupid. Sholt the Dolt was his kindest name for the man.

Then, unexpectedly, in my fifteenth year, the great world came to us. One summer's night as I came in late from hunting I saw the mare, Selmis, tethered in the clearing. I ran the last hundred yards and bent down to enter the house. Hagnild, contained and pale as ever in his plain dark robe, sat reading in his favorite chair. The beloved room sprang up before me in the warm light of a forest summer. It was rough hewn and comfortable, the round table groaning with books and scrolls. Caco began to dish up game stew: venison and wild boar with boiled greens and dumplings. Hagnild raised his eyes from his book and stared at me so keenly that I wondered what it was he saw.

"We will have company," he said softly.

"Someone coming here? To this house?"

I saw that he was moved in his own way and that Caco was full of excitement, her black eyes twinkling.

"My brother," said Hagnild. "My brother Jalmar has had a falling out with Kelen, the Markgraf of Lien."

"He is coming to Nightwood?"

"He is sending his two sons to me. My nephews Pinga and Raff Raiz."

"Two boys!" I said. "But that is fine . . ."

"Psst!" he said. "Remember what I have told you. Raff must be about nineteen years old; his mother, Caria Masur was a lady of Balufir. Poor Pinga, the elder, is a greddle . . ."

"What is the cause of that?" I asked. "*Why* is he dwarfish?"

"The changes in the body I cannot understand," said Hagnild, "but I was about to say that this dwarfishness is hereditary."

He leaned over and plucked leaves from my shoulders as I sat on the sheepskin rug before the hearth.

"It is hereditary in the family of Jalmar's first young wife, who was a Cather of Nesbath."

"Two boys from Lien!" burst out Caco. "Oh bless the Goddess . . . what I must do to prepare for them. Yorath, you must go beyond the marsh to Beck village and buy salt and salad in the market there."

"Hush, old woman," said Hagnild. "You with your salt and salad. Find a honey tree, Yorath. That is what they will like."

"When will they come? How were you called?"

"Tomorrow night," said Hagnild. "Jalmar used an old family scrying stone. I have not seen its light or felt its soft influence for many years."

"Master," I said, "surely he is not so well versed in magic as you are . . ."

"In some ways more so," said Hagnild. "He had great gifts. He belonged to the world; he was and is a worldly man. He would have made an excellent vizier or chancellor to some monarch. I do not think he will ever attain this now."

Next day I scoured Nightwood and the surrounding districts for provisions and found myself hanging back, deliberately returning late to our house so that the visitors would be there when I returned. The nightly chill that settled on the forest even in summer had come down. I came in and there they were, settled by Caco's fire. I do not know what they thought of me, poor monster, but I had never met anyone to compare with them.

Pinga, clad in a fine child-sized tunic and hose of grey figured stuff, perched on our settle, his tiny feet in their green boots swinging merrily. The contrast between this greddle, well-proportioned, though marked with the scaly skin and thin hair of his kind, and the awful deformity I recalled in my poor friend Forbian, was enough to make him seem good to look upon. His wide, bright brown eyes were those of a very intelligent child, for in spite of his years and his quick wits Pinga remained childlike. I never had the feeling, as I had with Forbian and with the Kelshin, that I was speaking to a small adult.

Raff Raiz lounged on the settle in the outlandish clothes of Lien, with slashed sleeves and a short grey cloak lined with apricot silk. He straightened up and smiled at me. His thick, fine golden hair hung about his ears in a round cut; he had a player's face, long and mobile, with a wide, humorous mouth and fine eyes of a distinctive dark blue. He was one of the most attractive human beings who ever lived. He had a physical charm, a gaiety, wit and gentleness that captivated all who knew him. This was Raff Raiz, who went on to love a queen and to lose her love because he played the king, the False Sharn, who raised the Chameln against Mel'Nir and held the city of Dechar. This was Raff Raiz, who sailed to the lands below the world and, so it was said, returned in another guise altogether. Already he had Caco eating out of his hand with tales of Lien, of the fashions and follies of Balufir, of the extravagances of the royal house.

I sat down with them at the fireside, after I had set down my pack, and listened to the tales told by our visitors.

"Truly," said Raff, "the Markgraf Kelen would put aside his lovely Zaramund for she is barren, but he dare not do so. Her mother was a Denwick, her father is the Lord of Grays. The poor lady Markgrafin is thirty years old; she has a few years of potions and pilgrimages to look forward to, before hope is gone. Last spring it was believed suddenly that larks might be the answer. The court, the whole city dined on larks. The woods and fields were scoured for the poor little birds, there was hardly a lark to be had for gold the length and breadth of Lien. And there was an awful dearth of sparrows and finches and other lark-sized birds ..."

"Alas poor child, poor Zaramund," said Caco

with a sigh. "Tell me, young Master Raiz, are the rose gardens still so beautiful?"

"Lovelier than ever. They are wonders of the world. In summer they perfume the whole city. Besides the wheels and rounds with red roses and white and yellow, they have bred pink and white, apricot, flame and orange roses. There is a special park called the Wilderness for climbing roses of every kind from the sweet briars of the hedgerow to ramblers, creepers, strange roselike plants from the lands below the world. They grow upon fake ruins, crumbling towers and portals made of brick and plaster, with pleasant grottos and groves in between."

"A place for picnics," said Pinga. "At the gates there are candy booths where you can buy roses of sugar and marzipan."

"I can promise you some fine picnics here in Nightwood and the marsh," I said, "but our sweetmeats are not sugar roses!"

"Mother Caco can make dainties just as fine!" piped the greddle, taking another hot cake spread with honey.

"Oh my brave boys!" cried Caco. "What a joy to cook for those with good appetite. What a summer this will be . . ."

The old woman was right. It was a summer never to be forgotten, and it lives in memory the more keenly because it was the last peaceful summer that I spent in Nightwood. We roamed the forest and the marsh and hunted a little. Arn was home again from his uncle's house in Krail; it was his last summer before he became the swordmaker's heir and his apprentice. Childhood's end. A boy of Mel'Nir is brought abruptly from childhood to manhood; indeed those lads in the training schools or longhouses have less childhood than we did. We went about with Raff Raiz, slightly older, much more experienced. We spoke of many things, but women and soldiering loomed large. I had found no middle ground between the love, the sweetness, the gallantry of some of the books I had read and the appalling coarseness of the swordmaker's yard and the kitchens. Raff Raiz was a model of tact and kindness; his bawdy stories were not cruel; he never boasted.

Pinga and Raff and I had a favorite game or fantasy that we were a troupe of strolling players. In a certain glade where the Kelshin hung about overhead in the trees to watch, we practised our tricks. Raff and his brother tumbled and danced, and I was, naturally enough, the strong man, the base of the pyramid. Pinga stood on my head, gripping on with his little scaly bare feet, then dove off into Raff's arms. I spread my arms wide, and Pinga walked across from one hand to the other. Now, I suppose, I could do the trick with Raff himself, but I guess he has put on weight, too, though he is one person it is hard to think of as an older man. In all our play there was the hint of longing to be free. The brothers would be free of their father and his intrigues; I wanted to be free of Nightwood, to be about in the great world with two good companions such as these.

The only road through the marsh is an ancient causeway that runs past Finn's smithy; there is a track leading off into the forest to a certain twisted thorn tree with a pool at its base that is known to grant wishes. We went there towards the end of our summer and made our wishes in a complicated ritual that Raff had borrowed from his father. We all wished twice, once secretly, once out loud. Then one by one we looked into the pool for a sign and told what we saw.

Pinga wished first, and his second wish was simple: he wished that we might all three meet again and speak of our forest summer.

Then I wished and secretly I wished to come to some kin, to find my family, and aloud I wished, "I wish to meet again the one who gave me this token!"

I held in my clenched fist over the pool the two brown feathers of the Owlwife, a proof that I was growing up and also that I could keep a secret, for I had told no one in the world of this encounter.

Then Raff Raiz wished, and aloud he said, "I wish that my father would find his heart's desire!"

So then we looked for signs, in the same order, and Pinga cried out:

"I see a tall ship, a merchant ship, with sun and stars upon its mainsail!"

We puzzled at this, wondering if we might all go sailing together. When I gazed into the pool, I saw nothing for a moment and was disappointed. Then the clear water glowed, as if a beam of light had fallen upon it, and I saw green fields and two wooded hills and between the hills a building between a keep or fortress and a manor house. It had a distinctive round tower with a cone roof, at one corner, and two, three little turrets, decorated with plaster and wood, like a half-timbered house. Tall, old trees grew up to the sides of the little keep, and the whole scene was very peaceful, bathed in sunlight. I could hardly convey what I had seen, but said, "I see a small keep with a tower, in green fields ..."

Raff Raiz asked if it answered any of my wishes, but I could not tell. I wondered if the Owlwife lived in such a place, or if some of my kin lived there. Already Raff was looking into the pool for his sign, and he said at last, "A white horse! I see a white horse drinking at a pool!"

Then before we could speak further, Arn came to join us. I did not want him to feel left out, and Raff Raiz understood this. He explained the game to Arn, and my milk brother, a broad-shouldered, dark-haired youth, with a look of his uncle, Bülarn, the Swordmaker, grinned and did as he was told. His spoken wish was as follows: "I wish that the gods of the Farfarers would protect my family while I am absent."

Then he gazed into the pool, obviously not expecting too much, and he gave a cry: "I see a man, a mighty warrior in armor, mounted upon a black horse!"

When Raff questioned him a little, he shook his head shyly and could not tell us any more.

The summer came to an end. There were a few days when poor Pinga stayed indoors with a head cold and Caco spoiled him with honey-cakes. Raff Raiz changed a little at this time, he was not quite so carefree, and I thought it must be anxiety for his brother's health. At last they sailed away to meet Jalmar Raiz again in the Chameln land across the Dannermere, and at the very last, as I helped them into their boat, Raff Raiz shook me by the hand and clapped me on the shoulder.

"Long life, Yorath," he said, "and death to all your foes!"

It was a bluff farewell of the sort we had used, but it struck home to me and so did the expression of mingled fear and curiosity in his blue eyes. At night, when Hagnild came to our house in the wood, I had been thinking back most carefully about Raff and his strange silences in the last days.

I waited until that hour of the night when we talked best; Caco had left mulled wine for us upon the hearth and gone to her room in the back of the house. The fire burned blue and green by Hagnild's art. There was an autumn chill falling upon the forest and the marsh. He drew out from his sleeve one of the scrying stones in which we had seen so many wonders. It was a certain yellow stone called Little Eye, which he used for scenes of the present, near at hand.

This time as the mists cleared I saw a lofty chamber with green hangings painted with hunting scenes; I knew it for a certain bower in the Palace Fortress. A girl child about ten years old was alone in the chamber playing with a puppy. I knew her, too, it was the unmarked child, Princess Gleya; and now her mother, the Princess Merse, came in and sent her to bed. Merse had a strong dark face. I could not tell why, but the scene warmed my heart; Princess Merse's face was moving, familiar. I thought of my mother, that "lady of Lien," although Caco had told me often enough that she had died young and she had had hair like spun gold.

"It is the child's birthday," said Hagnild. "The puppy is her birthday gift."

"It is hard to believe that they are the child and grandchild of Ghanor," I said.

I had often seen the awful lineaments of the Great King in the scrying stones.

"Wheesht," said Hagnild. "I remember a time when Ghanor was a warrior in the prime of life. The time when the Princess Merse was beautiful as springtime . . ."

I knew that he had made this princess his liege lady. His love for her had determined the course of his life. The restlessness that had grown upon me this last summer could not be stilled.

"Sir," I said, "what is my parentage?"

Hagnild controlled himself; his fine, high brow wrinkled, he had a pinched look about the nostrils. He had, perhaps, been expecting the question.

"Your mother was a lady of Lien, as Caco has told you," he said, "and your father was also well-born. But more I dare not say at this hour, Yorath."

"Dare not?" I asked.

I was angry and frustrated at the way he put me off.

"Master," I said, "is it some question of bastardy . . . or . . . or incest? Am I a 'child of the bower'? For the Goddess's sake, dear Master, give me something to lay hold of! Am I to spend the rest of my life in Nightwood for the sake of something my parents did?"

"Why do you ask this now?" he demanded. "Has something been said . . . by my nephews?"

"No, but Raff has behaved strangely to me, as if he were half-afraid. And it is since he saw my silver amulet, the one Caco gave me to wear upon my birthday, last Thornmoon."

"Lien is full of silver swans." Hagnild smiled. "Just as Mel'Nir is full of animal crests and the

Chameln lands are full of oak leaves made into amulets."

I was silent, knowing he would not tell me. Hagnild said again, "Next year in the autumn we will travel to Nesbath together. I will have the old house put to rights and find you a tutor and a master-at-arms. Perhaps Pinga and Raff could join you there . . ."

It was a tempting offer and one that satisfied a boy because it did not look too far ahead. But before the next autumn came there was a violent end to our peaceful life in the wood, and I took up arms for the first time.

After eighteen years the King's Peace had worn thin; Ghanor was seized with a burst of his former energy. He swept his court and his armies off on a long rambling progress to Balbank, the border with Lien. The Red Hundreds of the Great King poured forth from the Palace Fortress, from the longhouse and from the manors of the local lords and made a series of violent and exhausting manoeuvers in the royal domains, penetrating as far as the forest border with Cayl. His territories were wide, he seemed to be saying, but not wide enough to contain him. He menaced the land of Lien and the land of Val'Nur. He was about to cross the inland sea into the Chameln lands but his health failed, and it was Hagnild who persuaded him to forgo this journey.

Yet suppose the king had crossed the water? Would he have felt the lure of the plains where his countrymen gathered estates and so loved the land that some forswore their King and Mel'Nir? Would he have brought the Chameln so firmly under his yoke that they would never have broken free? Would he have given respite to that most troubled of his true servants Hem Werris, the Protector in Achamar, battling a surly half-conquered folk and a tyrannous bunch of Mel'Nir landlords? Would Ghanor have died, far from his Palace Fortress, and plunged Mel'Nir into anarchy? This last was what Hagnild feared most and with good reason.

The moment the Great King's back was turned, so to speak, the war lords of the east of Mel'Nir, especially Huarik of Barkdon, the Wild Boar himself, began to ravage the land. Raids in old style left a trail of burning villages all down the fertile strip of the East Mark, between the High Plateau and the White Mountains. Sharpening his tusks the Boar scoured the eastern edges of the plateau, drove into the horse farms, reaching into the preserves of Valko Firehammer. He dared to spread his bane even in Nightwood and the marsh, in the domain of the Great King, on the shores of the Dannermere.

CHAPTER

II

THE AUTUMN WOODS WERE DARK AND WILD, AND AS I came up to the smithy I heard shouting and the clash of arms. It was not the first time; the men of the Boar and parties of brigands and outlaws had made inroads into our peaceful domain. I ran to the smith's yard. Four swordsmen, lightly armed but quick and fierce, had attacked a tall shieldman in full armor who was assisted by his bearer. I looked about for Finn and saw him where he had been caught and held by the open doorway of the forge. A fifth warrior, dark and nimble as the rest, held a crossbow against the smith's mighty chest. His huge arms hung powerless, the fingers clenching and unclenching with strain. He had been preparing to shoe one of the shieldman's horses; the big animals stood back, fretting and stamping in their rich coverings. The smith's house was silent, but I knew from the twitch of the window coverings that Erda and the family were within, dreading the outcome of this unequal battle.

But now not so unequal. I circled the smaller loose boxes and came up on the blind side of the man who held Finn; he was not even middle-sized, he was a little man. I came from between the buildings swiftly and stealthily, and my arms were around the crossbowman, crushing. He screamed with pain and fright, the crossbow jammed his fingers and I flung him across the yard into the door of an empty loose box. Finn gave a shout of relief, picked up his hammer, which lay at his feet, and slid me the first weapon he could find. It was a swingle tree from a wagon, a metal-bound crescent of wood, trailing chains. We plunged into battle with these quick, slippery fellows, all lithe and brown, all with cropped heads and long, thin, curved swords; they had cloaks thickly wrapped around their arms in place of shields.

The shieldman, a lord by his looks, was fighting well, but his strip mail hampered him when he was on foot and his broadsword had not found its mark. He bled from a sword cut on the face, for he had removed his helm. His bearer, a tall boy with a long dagger, held his master's shield, still in its cloth cover, and moved it forward, striking from its shelter.

Finn rushed forward and poised, drawing the attention of one warrior, who side-stepped and danced towards the brawny smith, making quick, twinkling passes with his sword. Finn threw his hammer waist high with the force of a kicking stallion; it caught the swordsman under his ribs, he went down into the dirt of the yard, and Finn picked him up again and shook him like a rat.

I circled behind the three swordsmen and let out a roar and went in waving the horrible swingle tree. One turned, the chains clipped at his ears and he struck at me, fought me high and low with his thin, bright blade, but his reach was not long enough. It was a bad day for skill and craft. He slipped, I poked him in the wind, a chain wrapped round his sword arm, and I pulled until his sword dropped.

The lord, no longer so hard-pressed, cut at a swordsman with a rust-colored cloak, the leader, and sliced him badly in the leg so that he fell down. By this time the shutters of Finn's house had flown open and two of his daughters were shouting encouragement to us. The fourth swordsman suddenly broke and ran ... into the house. We were all dumbstruck by this move, then Finn gave a roar. I threw down the swingletree, snatched up a fallen dagger and ran into the house, which was ringing with shrieks.

I do not know what I expected to find. In fact there was Erda, a woman of similar shape to her goodman, beating with a stone pestle at a shrouded bundle by the hearth. The swordsman had been sent down by a washing basket hurled from the narrow stair by Vona, the fourth daughter; the two youngest boys, Till and Ofin, held a wrist that came from the bundle and were prizing the sword from the man's fingers with the aid of a lump of coal from the hearth. I felt a pang of compassion for the poor brute.

"Holy light!" cried Erda, "what a come-up! You're bleeding, Yorath. What, will you have this beggar?"

"I will take him out," I said. "He is no match for this family!"

Then Vona and her sister Fern dabbed at me here and there with a clout from the washing basket. I dragged the half senseless warrior out of the bundle and frog-marched him back into the yard, followed by a cheering tide of Finn's sons and daughters.

The place was a battlefield. Finn's man lay where he had fallen; the injured leader had cast aside his sword and was binding up his leg wound. He looked afraid, and I saw that he feared his own red blood, which might be taking his life with it. There was a clatter of hoofs on the causeway ... two of the swordsmen had run off and taken flight on their wirey horses. The lord sat on the mounting block and his bearer tended his wounds. Finn washed at the pump. I pushed my prisoner up to the shield-man.

"Bind him," said a woman's voice. "We will question him when my lord recovers."

The bearer had spoken; it was a tall woman in riding trousers. I was mildly surprised, but what was one more surprise on that day? I took the prisoner to a stall and bound him with old bridle reins and left him on the ground.

"Young sir," called the woman, "come to us, we must thank you. Are you a friend of the smith? How are you called?"

I thought her politeness a shade more than I deserved. I looked more like a wild man of the woods than a "young sir." I went and bowed to the lord and his lady.

"My name is Yorath," I said. "Yorath Nilson."

"I am Strett of Cloudhill," said the shieldman, "and this lady is my wife, Thilka. We are indebted to you and to all who helped us here."

He had a long, handsome face, rutted with age and hard outdoor work; his fair hair was streaked with grey. I knew his story. He was the natural son of the old Lord Strett of Andine, a landowner of Balbank. He had long been the lord's only child, but when he was past sixty the old Bear married for a third time and his wife bore him a son, a legitimate heir. Old Lord Strett consoled his bastard son with the family horse farm up on the plateau, and Strett of Cloudhill made its name famous for the quality of its horses even beyond the boundaries of Mel'Nir. Then at last the old Lord died, at ninety, and his heir, the new Strett of Andine meanly desired the horse farm back from his elder half-brother. Strett of Cloudhill took the matter to the Great King, and in a wise decision . . . not uninfluenced by the fact that the Bastard of Andine was an ally of Valko Val'Nur . . . Ghanor let the horse farm, the Cloudhill Stud, remain in his possession.

Now Thilka of Cloudhill took the stained cover from her lord's shield and showed his crest, a Bear's head upon a cloud.

"My lord," I asked, "were these men brigands or are you pursued by some enemy?"

"Both!" Strett laughed. "These are hired blades and I think the Boar sent them, Huarik of Barkdon himself."

"We have seen his work, even in Nightwood," I said.

Then Erda came up and bade the lady and her lord step in by the fire and drew me in after them to have my scratches attended to. I was shy but I went along and drank a cup of Finn's best wine. The smith added to my shyness.

"Well, you see, Hem Strett," he said, grinning in my direction, "we breed 'em big hereabouts, and not unhandy."

"No indeed," said Strett. "Stand up for me, young man . . ."

So, blushing, but urged on by the smith's family, I moved into the center of the chamber where I could stand upright. The Bastard of Andine rose up and walked around me as if he appraised a piece of horseflesh.

"That shoulder twist is from birth?" he asked softly.

"Yes," I said. "It has almost grown out. I have spoken with one who is a good judge of bones, and he claimed it would not quite go, but would be no hindrance in battle."

Strett had me take off my skin vest and stand in my tunic, sleeves rolled up.

"Remarkable," he said. "A true godpillar. I would be proud to have you train on my farm, Master Yorath, if you have no better offer. What d'ye say, my lady?"

"Truly, we would be honored," said Thilka.

Her smile was sweet; I thought of the Princess Merse.

I thanked them, and the lord, to prove his serious intention, gave me a silver ring marked with a rune for Cloudhill. I took my leave, explaining that I had only come to the smithy that day for my lesson in arms . . . which raised a laugh, for I had had a sharp lesson indeed.

Out in the yard I found Gradja, Finn's third child and eldest daughter, tidying up.

"One man is dead," she said, "and one bound,

and the leader is very weak. Speak to the poor devil, Yorath."

I found the man lying on a pile of straw.

"I cannot stop the bleeding," he said in a hoarse voice. "I will die unless the wound is stitched. Mercy. Have mercy . . ."

He was a dark-skinned man, one of the Danasken from the distant southland, of Chyrian stock, mixed in old time with a dark race who had come from the Burnt Lands. I could not bear to have him die.

"If I help you," I said, "you must tell all to Strett of Cloudhill and beg *his* mercy."

"I swear it," he said, "by Ara, the Great Mother."

I bound up his eyes with his bloody neckerchief and picked him up in my arms. I said to Gradja, "I will take him to the healer. He'll talk to the lord when he is treated."

She looked doubtful, but I could not wait to explain. I ran into the wood and brought the man quickly through the dark trees to our house, where I knew Hagnild was at home. I burst in, and Caco shrieked and Hagnild started up from his favorite chair.

"Leg wound!" I panted. "I think he will die . . ."

Hagnild, who had seen many emergencies of this kind, did not wait to ask questions. He snapped out instructions to Caco; we had the man laid on the big settle. Hagnild washed his hands, and Caco held the needles into the flames and quenched them and threaded them and brought them to Hagnild who stitched and tied, as I had seen him do on others and on myself. Finally, lips compressed, he laid a plaster of herbs and bone gel on the wound and bade Caco bind it up. I had taken the binder from the man's eyes; he lay still and made no sound while he was doctored.

Caco fed him a cup of broth, and at the fireside I explained what had happened in a low voice. I had helped to save a lord and at the same time brought home a brigand, a hired swordsman, in the pay, very probably, of the Boar himself. Hagnild sighed. I wondered if I should run back with the man and deliver him to Strett to tell his story.

Hagnild sighed again and walked off into his study, so called, his secret chamber, which lay towards the back of the house. I knew that he had gone to consult a scrying stone; he returned with his brow lightly creased.

"Gone away," he said. "Strett and his wife have left the smithy in great haste. I think they questioned the other survivor. Did they have no servants with them?"

"Their people had ridden on ahead along the high road to the plateau," I explained. "They did not want to bring their packhorses into this region. Strett and his lady brought the horses to be shod."

"Then they have ridden off to catch up with their folk," said Hagnild.

The Danasken assassin lay where he was for five days; we fed and cared for him and asked no questions. I believe Hagnild wished him simply to run off, once he was well, as the other survivor had done from the smithy. Our man was remarkably silent, like a man cast ashore in a strange country. His hair and beard began to grow swiftly and gave him a less haggard and dangerous appearance. On the sixth morning he was gone; Caco looked about but nothing had been stolen, though the man had eaten a piece of bread. I could see that both Hagnild and Caco were relieved to see the last of their patient. I felt foolish about the whole episode.

Hagnild was gone until late in the night attending to the Great King himself, who had an attack of gout so agonising that he half-killed two servants who attempted to move him. The healer was forced to desperate measures: he used sleep magic and drugged wine on the old tyrant, then changed his bandages and fed him medicine. At last he returned, although he might have spent the night in the Palace Fortress as he often did. He asked if anything out of the way had happened; plainly he labored under one of his forebodings.

The fire burned blue and green; it was late. Caco had just set a jug of wine to warm upon the hearth when there came a light scratching upon our door. Caco straightened up, afraid, and Hagnild motioned her aside.

"Someone has slipped through our barrier," he said.

He gestured, and the door swung open. The man of the Danasken stood in the doorway wrapped in his rust-colored cloak. He had a proud and solemn look, and he stepped in without being bidden.

"Peace to this house!" he said.

No one bade him welcome. He stood where he was and said, "I have been to the Dannermere and bathed and I have been all day meditating in this fearful wood. I owe my life to those in this house . . . to you, Master Healer, to you, good mother, and above all to this young man, Yorath."

"We need no thanks . . ." murmured Hagnild.

"I offer more than thanks," said the man, smiling for the first time. "I am a man of the Danasken, and my foremothers and forefathers came from the Burnt Lands, and we retain some of their ancient customs. I have looked into my heart, and the Great Mother, Ara, has told me what I must do in this case."

He came forward swiftly and knelt down before me, where I sat by the hearth, and stared most earnestly into my face.

"I will serve you," he said. "I have bound myself to no man's service until this hour. Now, be it known that I will serve Yorath and no other. My life is in his keeping. He will be a worthy master, and I will strive to be a worthy servant. I know he is a prince among men!"

Then he bent his head to the floor at my feet. I was embarrassed and I was also moved by the man's fervor. I turned my head and saw Caco and Hagnild both wearing expressions of shock and fear. I felt a stab of fear myself and covered it by raising the man up.

"Do not bow before me," I said. "Sit on the stool. Tell me your name."

"I will tell you my true name," he said, "my ancient family name from the Burnt Lands. I will be Ibrim, your servant."

I looked back at my two beloved guardians, and the moment had passed. Caco busied herself at the hearth, Hagnild had a keen searching expression as if he would question this Ibrim. Perhaps I had imagined their distress.

"Ibrim," said Hagnild, "how can we trust you? You came to Nightwood as a hired swordsman to kill Strett of Cloudhill!"

"The man who did that is dead," said Ibrim. "He was a desperate man who lived by the sword.

Now I am Ibrim, the servant of Yorath, and my sword will be used in his service."

Hagnild was about to speak again, but I put a hand on his arm.

"I will accept his service," I said.

I held out my hand to Ibrim, and he clasped it, smiling at me but not in any servile fashion. To my surprise there was no argument from Hagnild. Caco reached Ibrim a cup of wine and a bowl of the meat and gravy we had had for supper; he sat by the fire quietly.

Hagnild was preoccupied and not with the strange reappearance of Ibrim. He listened to the sounds of the night; then I heard it too ... voices in the forest. Hagnild uttered one of his mild oaths and made the candles go out.

"Riders!" he said.

A horse whinnied, and Selmis, the pale mare, answered from her stall. I sprang to the window and peered through a star-shaped hole in the shutter. Hagnild flicked his fingers, muttering, and I saw the thickening of the wood around our house, as if the trees moved two steps closer.

"Shall I go out?" asked Ibrim softly. "Is there a sword in the house?"

"They will pass by," said Hagnild.

He rose to his feet; the fire burned a dull green and Hagnild himself glowed with the same fire as if his scholar's robe was woven in shot silk and worked with emerald.

"Armed men of the king," he said, "pursuing a troop of Huarik's followers. Perhaps it is a good time for Yorath to have a bodyguard, Master Ibrim."

This seemed to me, too, something of an admission. Presently we went off to sleep: Caco to her small room, Hagnild to his study. Ibrim lay down on the settle before the banked fire. I climbed the narrow stair to my low but spacious quarters under the thatched roof cone and fell asleep thinking of princes.

The autumn became mild, its stormy breath was stilled. I went about Ibrim, showing him the ways of Nightwood and the marsh. Ibrim had made sure of two of the long, thin, curved blades used by his former comrades and also of his own dun-colored horse, left at the smithy. In the glade where I had played the strongman a year past with Pinga and Raff, he taught me to handle a sword. I made fair progress in this delicate art—of the thin blade, then Ibrim would stand apart and give instruction while I handled the broadsword. He was an excellent master-at-arms, demanding accuracy, timing and daily practice. He reminded me, as he sat in the grass, wrapped in his rust-colored cloak, head erect, eyes half-closed, watching me attack a fallen tree, of Hagnild, hearing my spelling. I was educated by pedants; I repaid their diligence.

I remember a warm day in that "old wives' summer" when Ibrim and I left the brown house together with Caco. She was off on a jaunt to the village of Beck with her crony Old Uraly, the reed-wife; it was market day. I meant to go fishing across the causeway in the southern channels of the marsh. We parted from the old woman at a place where the paths divided and went to the smithy to pick up some chicken giblets from Erda for our bait. We promised her any eels that we caught for her salting vats. The smith's yard, which had always seemed to me, as a child, the busiest place in the world, was quieter these days. Finn's two eldest, grown men now, were serving as army farriers in the Chameln lands; two of the girls had married and moved away to Lort; twin boys, older than Arn, had died of a fever when they were eight years old . . . I could hardly remember them . . . and now Arn had gone to Krail, to become a swordmaker.

"See here, Yorath!" called Gradja.

Finn was about to shoe a magnificent black horse, a tall, deep-chested war charger with its hooves plumed in rusty grey and a similar streaked mane and tail.

"A prize," he said. "Captured first by Huarik's rascals somewhere down east then taken from them by the captain of the king's new garrison at Beck. A ravaging bastard of an ensign brought him here yesternight. Ran him down the causeway with no decent shoes. Let's hope the captain treats him better."

The big horse was well-mannered. Gradja held its head while it was shod; Till and Ofin worked the bellows. Finn hammered with ringing strokes upon his anvil. At last I took my leave and went across the causeway to fish, with Ibrim after me, my servant, my shadow. Far down the causeway between the tall reed beds I saw two reed bonnets: Caco and Uraly going to market. I did not plunge into the marsh but took a path that wandered through the reeds and the bearded swamp oaks beside the causeway.

I have lived through this time over and over again, trying to untangle all the threads. There was the unusual warmth of the day, the pleasant, watery stink of the marsh; a crane flew up, legs dangling, and flapped away into the trees. I heard hoofbeats on the causeway and knew that there was more than one rider and that they were coming very fast. I went on without the least anxiety. Then I heard a hoarse shout, a clattering of hooves, a long, high scream, a woman's scream.

I plunged through a narrow channel of marsh water and pushed back on to the causeway through the reeds. Directly opposite stood Uraly the reed-wife shrieking aloud, and at her feet lay what looked like a bundle of brown rags. About fifty feet away were two horse troopers trying to control their chargers and a third rider, off to my right, nearer to Beck village. I ran across, flung myself down and saw Caco already dead. Her head was a bloody pulp, the iron mark of a horseshoe was across her forehead.

"Ridden down," croaked Uraly. "O my dear, O Goddess save us . . . they were racing . . ."

She sat in the reeds and keened aloud. I saw that the troopers were riding back down the causeway to the scene of the accident. They looked at the ground; I heard one, the officer, in an ensign's sash, exclaim, "There it lies!"

I stood up and went back on to the causeway. I seemed to be moving very slowly and deliberately. I looked down and saw what it was the officer was seeking . . . his whip, his heavy riding quirt, that he had let fall. I picked it up and slipped the leather loop over my wrist. As I came close to the ensign I saw a curious expression on his broad fair face. He had not noticed me as I had run across to Caco, now I had risen out of the marsh.

"You have killed the old woman!" I said.

"My whip . . ."

His voice came to me as if from a long way off. "You rode her down!" I said again.

His eyes did not leave mine; he gestured to the trooper and I heard his tone, an officer's voice, yet edged with fear. "Here's trouble," he seemed to say.

"My purse is in my saddle-bag," he said. "Let me . . ."

The world became misty and blood-stained. I reached out, seized the officer, dragged him from his saddle, lifted him high in the air and flung him face downwards on the causeway. I beat in the back of his head with the heavy bronze-tipped handle of his own whip. His charger went wild and tangled the other horse, the trooper's horse. He was still trying to draw his sword when I reached him. I seized him by his sword arm and flung him as a hammer is thrown and heard the sound as he struck a stone marker on the road-side. I drew back and the two horses went bolting down towards the smithy; I did not see the third rider. I sat down on the ground not far from Caco's body and smelled a terrible reek of blood.

Ibrim was beside me. He held a leather bottle of fiery spirits to my lips and made me drink. I drank, choked, retched once or twice, then began to come to myself.

"We have not much time," he said. "Try to stand. Their groom has ridden back to Beck garrison."

"Caco . . ."

Uraly, that true daughter of the marsh, was beside me now. She and Ibrim realised, as I had not, that I was in peril; my god-rage was irrevocable; my only hope was in flight.

"Caco is with the Goddess," said Uraly, wiping

her eyes upon her shawl. "You were all her care, Yorath. Save yourself. Respect will be paid to Caco . . . she will sleep in the Deadmarsh."

Ibrim urged me a little way down the causeway, and suddenly we were among some folk coming from the smithy. Finn took me by the arms and shook the breath out of me.

"Holy fire!" he said. "This cannot be undone. Gather your wits, boy . . . where can you go?"

I gulped the air and deliberately took another sip of Ibrim's spirits.

"Hagnild's house . . ." I said.

"No," said Finn, "I doubt it is safe even there."

"I will ride on to the plateau," I said, "if a horse can be found for me. I will ride to Cloudhill, to Strett, the Bastard of Andine."

"That may serve," he said. "We'll tell the troopers a tale of maurauding brigands. I doubt they will get much sense out of the groom who rode back."

"I must go to the house . . . leave word . . . make up a pack . . ."

"Quickly then," said Finn. "Go with Ibrim, your man, to the house, then come back to the yard. Roke and I will have horse and arms ready."

As Ibrim and I turned to run off into the wood, Old Uraly came running up. She slipped a thong over my head; it was stained with blood and held a small leather pouch.

"Caco's amulet," she said. "It will keep you free from harm."

I turned aside with a sob and ran through the wood with Ibrim at my heels. It was dreadful to be in the empty house again, to see Caco's cooking pots, her new birch broom that I had cut for her, all the reminders of that poor old woman. I climbed the stairs, wrapped clothes, a book, a writing set; I came down again in a rush and went into Hagnild's study. His presence lingered in the small room. His scrying stones were locked away but on the desk was a small skull, that of some long dead Kelshin that he had found in a barrow and used in his conjuring. I laid my hand on the smooth round and said in a low voice:

"Master . . . Caco is dead. I have done murder to avenge her death. I am riding to Cloudhill."

I came out of the study and found Ibrim strapping my blankets into a decent roll. He had filled a reed sack with provisions. As we ran back to the smithy, I saw that the weather had begun to turn round: black storm clouds were rolling up from the west.

When I came into the yard, I was seized and armed by Finn and Roke, grim-faced. They put me into a fine shirt of linkmail, a breastplate of black-painted strip mail, a mighty old-fashioned helm. Over all was a long black mantle trimmed with grey fur. They buckled on a sword belt with a dagger and slung a leather baldric across my body.

"Now lad," said Roke, "onto the block . . ."

Gradja, the smith's daughter, led out the magnificent black charger, newly shod, the prize horse that the dead ensign had brought to the forge for his captain. It had an old war saddle over dark green trappings. Finn and Roke had plundered the smith's store of arms, many of them the unredeemed pledges of poor shieldmen or troopers. I mounted up, Finn adjusted the stirrups, Roke handed me a broadsword . . . I knew that it was the sword of the ensign. I sheathed the sword. I

saw that the smith's family had come out to gape
at me, mounted upon the black steed, in my collection of armor.

"Go then," cried Finn, "ride out from Nightwood,
Yorath. Remember your friends. The Goddess give
you a soldier's blessing!"

I looked down, and in the water of the horse
trough I saw something like Arn's vision in the
wishing pool. A mighty warrior in black armor
mounted upon a black horse.

"I will do you honor!" I said. "What is the horse
called?"

"The ensign called it a strange name," said Finn.
"Something like Rashidur . . ."

Ibrim, mounted on his own wirey Kalkar and
bearing arms from Finn's store, laughed aloud.

"Reshdar!" he cried.

The great horse snorted and stamped, answering
to its name. I rode away from Nightwood half-
made, stained with blood, untried, with my wits
still reeling. I led Ibrim quickly out of the marsh
and to the crossroads by the dolmen. The thunderstorm that had come up broke over our heads and
lightning struck the top of the tall grey stone, the
godpillar. I drew rein and looked down the road
that led to the Palace Fortress.

No rider was to be seen and Ibrim made as if to
ride on, but I bade him wait. I saw a patch of mist,
a moving place where the rain seemed thick and
grey, approaching down the road. We waited and
Ibrim cried out. Hagnild appeared riding upon
Selmis, the pale mare. In this guise, almost invisible, he often travelled between the palace and
Nightwood.

"So be it," he said when he had heard my story.

"Try not to grieve for the old woman. Your god-rage is spent ... do not let it come again. Go to Cloudhill and tell the Bastard of Andine frankly what has happened here."

He handed me a purse of gold and raised a hand in blessing.

"Watch over your young liege!" he said to Ibrim.

He remained by the dolmen as we turned and took the road to the plateau: a thin-faced old man, his shock of hair snow white. When I turned one last time to look at him, he had gone; only a patch of grey mist remained.

So I came from one magic realm to another, from Nightwood to the High Plateau of Mel'Nir, from the dark trees and the channels of the marsh to the arid wastes and fertile rift valleys, to the clear air and blazing stars. We rode on for three days and nights and saw no living soul and no spirits or demons in that uncanny place. The horse, Reshdar, was patient with me and bore my weight well, and I began to understand the attachment between horse and rider.

On the second night of our journey as we sat by our campfire, I thought of Caco's amulet. Inside the leather pouch was a small square of parchment folded so that it was not much bigger than my thumbnail. It was very old and waxy, as if it were folded round an ancient seal that had melted and gummed its folds together. I could read no words on the folds but thought of a written charm, perhaps some runes for good luck. I held the thing near the fire but I was afraid it would be damaged if I tried to melt away its wax or unfold it. It needed an expert ... a scribe or one who restored old writings. So I put the amulet back in its pouch and continued to wear it, a last blessing from the old Lienish woman who had been mother and grandmother to me.

At length we came to the Great Eastern Rift and asked the way to the Cloudhill Stud. The yard was deserted when we rode in except for one groom who ran into the broad low-roofed house of yellow stone below the watchtower. It was midmorning; between the loose boxes and the barns I could see the green fields and the horses in them. I had the feeling of being watched closely from the windows of the house, and I saw a soldier on the tower, armed with a crossbow. At last Strett himself came out and stood on his back step, arms akimbo.

"By the Bear!" he said. "A mighty warrior indeed. Where in the name of the Goddess did you find Reshdar?"

I felt a pang of despair to lose my charger so soon, but I told him what had happened.

"And who rides with you?" asked the lord quietly.

"It is my man Ibrim," I said. "Once he bore another name and served other masters as a hired blade. Since I saved his life in Nightwood by bringing him to a healer he has taken me for his liege. I will answer for him."

"Yorath," said Strett, holding up a hand to his face, "you ask a great deal. I must hide a fugitive who rides on a horse stolen from me six moons past by Huarik's raiders, and your servant is a brigand who tried to kill me!"

"I will return the horse if I cannot buy him with my store of gold," I said; "and if I may not stay I will go on with Ibrim, Lord Strett."

At that moment the lady of the house, Thilka, came out wearing a blue gown and a long dark apron. She burst out laughing, and Strett joined in.

"Yorath!" she said. "Yorath, you are a sight for the gods. The helmet ... the saddle ... and Reshdar, our beautiful lost Reshdar!"

"In truth, I would give all I have to keep him," I said sadly.

"Get down, boy," said Strett wiping his eyes. "You'll have your horse, but you will pay for him. Take that ridiculous collection of ancient harness off your back. I will put you and your servant to work."

So I entered the service of my first master, Strett of Cloudhill.

II

I have had the disturbing experience of meeting some of the chroniclers who wrote down and dreamed up my own life. One was Less, Brother Less, as he liked to be called, a dark bony fellow, born in the Chameln lands and educated in Lien. He had come exploring into Mel'Nir in search of a holy revelation, and when it eluded him, he worked as a scribe in Krail and in Lort. He came at last to work upon the Great Scrolls themselves, in the archives of the Great King. No one is supposed to know the names of the scribes who do this work; the scrolls must seem to be almost god-given. No one was more human than Brother Less. He ate and drank sparingly, did not fight, for he was puny, had neither love nor liking for women, mortified his flesh with cold baths and whipping and felt uncomfortable when listening to music. He could not grasp the fact that this sort of self-denial was very human—what beast, what fairy spirit would bother with such privations?—and he stoutly denied the notion that he lived his life at second hand in retelling the exploits of so-called heroes.

He ran after me in the sunlit covered way of a country villa and begged me to sit down with him and explain parts of my life. What had I done at such and such a time? Was this rumor true? What was my favorite food? Had I killed this man or that? Could I fill in a very important gap in my valiant career, my course of glory. After I left Nightwood . . . Yes, I said, I worked on the Cloudhill Horse Farm for four years. Morning, noon and sometimes at night. I mucked out the stable yard, I mucked out the loose boxes. I learned to groom a horse, I groomed horses. I exercised horses, the largest horses in the world, the chargers of Cloud-hill. Between times I helped to plough and bring in the harvest. I trained four days in every ten in swordsmanship, drill, hurling and wrestling. I went on watch; I rode out to the boundaries of the farm to guard it against raiders. I led, in the end, a troop of Lord Strett's men-at-arms.

Brother Less found this intolerably dull. I had not found it all quite so dreary as it sounded in the telling. I cast about for something that would liven up my time at Cloudhill for the scrolls.

"There were noble youths there," I said. "The sons of great lords."

Less was pleased with noble blood; a small smile creased his lips.

"Who, my lord?"

So I named my companions. Times were hard at Cloudhill and dangerous through the Boar's depredations, so lords were less keen to send their sons for training to the Bastard of Andine. Still in my time there were four young lords. At first I met Marris Allerdon, son of the king's general, and Benro Hursth of Hurhelm in Balbank; then came Rieth of Pfolben in the Southland and Knaar of Val'Nur, second son of Valko Firehammer. Discipline was good . . . they all worked in the stable, just as I did, and we did not shirk our training.

These were my peers, the young men I might have been raised with if my body had been unmarked, if my estate had been acknowledged. As it was our upbringing had been very different. There were strange quirks in the fortunes of all these four, before our meeting and afterwards. Rieth, whose father was immensely rich and managed his peaceful southern domain with an iron hand, was a simpleton. He was tall and well-made with a golden head and a vacant blue eye. He could not read, he could barely sign his name. Between us we taught him to ride without falling off and to draw his sword without injuring himself. Benro Hursth was five feet eight inches tall and we called him the dwarf, the pygmy, the Kelshin. He was quick, dark, cruel and clever; he could ride light horses and fight as swiftly and dangerously as the kedran women. Marris Allerdon was the finest flower of a country without a knightly order. Even to our jaundiced eyes he was handsome, fair-minded, cool-headed, and wonderfully skilful in all that he did. Knaar of Val'Nur was our bane, a proud and vengeful fellow, a troublemaker, jealous of his estate, filled with a gnawing hatred of his elder brother in Krail. How would Yorath Nilson have fitted into this list and been judged by his peers? He was good enough with weapons and with horses; he was shy and stuffed with weird book-learning. Someone's bastard. One shoulder twisted.

After a few months no one would wrestle with him. In the tilt yard sweet-tempered Marris shouted, purple-faced, as I released his head from a lock, "Godlight smite you, Yorath! You are just too damned big!"

I thought, then, as I answered Brother Less, the chronicler, of the days we passed together and the years and knew them for a golden time, the days of his youth that a man remembers. Brother Less moistened his lips and put in slyly, "And were there no sweet vessels . . . no early loves . . . on the High Plateau?"

"No," I lied. "We took cold baths, Brother Less. We practiced whipping . . ."

His eyes popped.

"Fascinating!"

"Less," I said, "you are a worm, you are a cockroach. There were young women in the villages of the rift. We kept our lust within bounds. If you make a bawdy tale of the lives of my companions and of my life I will have it burnt and you with it!"

I stood up; he cowered. I was never alone in those days, and some of the officers and pages gave a look of enquiry as if they might have the pleasure of carrying out my threat. I was forced to smile upon the wretched chronicler to save his skin; we spoke again, several times.

Ah, but to think of Cloudhill. The cold, thin air of the plateau and the rime of frost upon the grass as we rode out in autumn. The wild beauty of the Great Rift spreading out before us as we took the road to Ochma village and to the manors of the rift lords, strung out to the west along the banks of the river Keddar. The walls of the valley are five hundred feet high and striated in a rainbow of dark and light earths. Strange flowers bloom in the rift and seashells lie in the river bed and scattered in clumps upon the plateau as if the whole wide plain had once lain at the bottom of the sea. I have seen the bones of a dragon, turned to stone, found in the valley wall. From an old grave pit came the bones of a man large as myself, a warrior who lay with a spear of dragon bone clasped across his breast.

As we rode out, on a day of leave, in autumn, my companions would turn off each to his own place, with his squire or body servant. Rieth, with his sorely tried squire, to a certain tavern in Ochma; then Benro, little devil, darting off into the territory of Lord Keddar, to a farm where he fathered two children. I rode on with Marris, keeping the peace, and Knaar, intent upon breaking it. When we passed another village, Cann or Cannford, Marris, mounted upon his splendid grey, Stormbird, turned to the right and crossed a bridge. An ancient building lay in a grove, a house of grey stone, brought from a different part of the plateau. There lived the dowager of a noble lord, Lady Cannen, mother of Thilka, Strett's wife; Strett's three daughters lived with their grandmother. It was not unusual for girls to be schooled away from home, but perhaps Strett was protecting his children from the young lords. He had a fine appreciation of legitimacy. Marris, the eldest of us, had sown his wild oats; now he paid court to Annhad, the eldest of Strett's daughters. We saw them walking about under the trees or riding sedately, palfrey and charger side by side, in the river fields. They were beautiful, Marris and Annhad, a pair of lovers from a Lienish idyll.

Then Knaar and I, the two youngest, rode on to a fair or a market in the lands of Paunce and of Nordlin, further down the valley. For years I had no friend, no leman, and felt myself unloved, a monster indeed, when the others boasted; but even I found a sweet friend at last. She was the widow of a man-at-arms, long since remarried, I would say. I remember her very clearly, but I will not put her in my story.

When Knaar and I were alone, he was better behaved, less quarrelsome. He spoke of Krail and of his family, and it was easier for me to see, under his fire and bluster, a shrewd intelligence that fought against the difficulties of his life. Valko Firehammer, a fierce and brilliant father, had a reputation that weighed heavily on both of his sons. The Heir of Val'Nur, Duro, had inherited Valko's looks, but his drive and energy had gone to Knaar. He was forced to over-excel, to be stormy when his brother was calm, to be devious when Duro was straightforward. He was a little devious in our years of riding together at Cloudhill; I was part of his plan for success, and he was cultivating me.

I found a question to ask Knaar concerning his

family: "Do you not have an uncle, Hem Thilon of Val'Nur?"

"I had an uncle," said Knaar shortly. "The poor devil has been dead these five years. The elder brother of my father if you see what that means . . ."

"He was the Heir of Val'Nur?"

"Stricken as a young man with a chest weakness . . . the sweating sickness, some call it. He stepped down in favor of my father."

"When I was in Krail as a boy, I heard some tale that he was troubled by a witch . . ."

"News to me," said Knaar. "Yet he was always seeking some cure or another. I would say he wanted a charm to prolong his life and some hag took advantage of him."

So I learned no more of the Owlwife.

Knaar said, after a pause, "Magic is no work for a shieldman or a soldier. Wizards and their ilk can be bought for gold."

I did not contradict him. Magic was much more familiar to me than it was to my companions, but I kept quiet about the identity of my guardian. He was simply a healer from the village of Beck; his name, if it must be given, was Nils Raiz. I saw little evidence of magic or of the Shee, the ancient fairy folk, while I was at Cloudhill—the beauty of the rift and the plateau were magic enough for me. I came no closer to any kin, but from the end of my seventeenth year I began to experience a strange recurring dream.

In the midst of the colorful life and movement of my ordinary dreams I was suddenly called . . . a voice called from a long way off: "Yorath!" Then the calling became a dream in itself. I walked in a dream wood or stood in a dim hall and heard the voice calling me. It was a woman's voice, but I knew in my dream that it was not the Owlwife. I answered sometimes in my dream and even asked who was calling my name. Sometimes the veil was lifted a little further ... I saw through a doorway or among the forest trees a hooded figure who spoke my name in the same voice, reassuring and tender.

Just as the young riders went their ways, turning off the road through the long valley, so they left Cloudhill one by one as the years passed; and at last after four years, only Knaar and I were left. Where had they gone? To be soldiers, to serve their fathers, to serve, in turn, Ghanor the Great King. Even Rieth, from distant Pfolben, went away with a magnificent escort of his father's troops, to be received at the Palace Fortress.

There was no question of Knaar fighting for the Great King, and I was personally outlawed from Ghanor's domain. The tale of maurauding brigands had not been believed by the king's troopers around Nightwood. I was described in a "wall warrant" from the garrison in Beck village, which Hagnild had acquired, as "Hunter Nilson, a lordless man, without rank or shield, about eighteen years old, seven feet high, red-haired, with light eyes and very strong. Wanted for the stealing of a prize horse, black, eighteen hands high, with grey streaked mane and hoof plumes, war-booty of Captain Rohl of the Second Home Muster in Beck, and for the cutting down of Ensign Hem Fibroll and a trooper."

I showed this parchment to my companions when it arrived more than a year after I did, and they reacted accordingly. Knaar laughed and so did

Benro, and Knaar said, "That's our lad!" Marris was uneasy and wondered how I might ever "get my name back." Rieth, like the idiot boy who works out sums, put his finger on an inaccuracy.

"You dint *cut* 'em," he said. "You said you just heave 'em around, like you do with us in the wrestling."

True. The military admitted no death but a soldier's death. I was sad now for the two men I had killed, though I would have wished for justice for their feckless killing of an old woman. Yet in the cohorts of the king they were reckoned less important than the captain's prize horse even if the ensign had been a lord or a lord's son.

Communication was bad; I had letters from Hagnild about twice a year and knew of the unrest in the Chameln lands, of the False King and the False Queen who held Dechar . . . though I did not know the true name of the False King. The Chameln campaign seemed to be dragging out, but it was not much more serious than the rumors of fighting that was always going on within reach of the blades of Mel'Nir.

Winter came early on the High Plateau. Snow lay on the ground in the first days of the Aldermoon; I went out alone with Knaar, even our servants Ibrim and Trenk were not with us. We were driving one of the heavy farm carts with a span of three veteran chargers. Knaar swore and complained because it was beneath a shieldman's dignity to ride in such an equipage; he felt like a baggage-handler. We took the road to Ochma village, by the cold river. It was so early in the morning that the risen sun was just sending its light through the mountains at our back. The leafless trees on the river bank were all traced with hoarfrost.

As we came closer to the village, the lead horse checked. I reined in the team and looked ahead; I heard Knaar give a long gasp. On the far bank of the river beside one of the bridges there was Marris Allerdon upon Stormbird. Horse and rider stood as if in a patch of sunlight; Marris wore no helm, but was clad in painted strip mail; Stormbird was caparisoned in red and blue. Marris slowly raised a hand in some gesture between a wave and a salute, then turned and rode into the grey shadow of the frozen trees.

"What are you waiting for?" said Knaar, in a low voice. "Drive to the bridge!"

"No one is there," I said.

"What did you see?"

"The same as you saw. Marris on Stormbird. It was a sending, a fetch."

"I am afraid," said Knaar. "Some evil has come to Marris."

I knew that Marris Allerdon was dead, dead in battle, and I was oppressed with fear and wonder.

"What if he has been seen by . . . others?" asked Knaar.

I knew that he meant Annhad of Andine, who waited at Cannford Old House for news of her beloved.

"We will say nothing . . ." I said.

So we rode on our errand to the village—collecting sacks of winter fodder—and went about our training. We were the last young men to be trained at Cloudhill. New recruits had often been expected but never came. They were expected again in the spring, but again they did not come. Before that time a dark cloud of sorrow had rolled over the land of Mel'Nir.

On the twentieth day of the Aldermoon, messengers of the king came to the rift, seeking men and horses from Strett and the neighbor lords. The disaster of the Adderneck Pass was known. The Red Hundreds of the king had been overwhelmed by the hordes of the Chameln in a narrow defile. Even in the long valley where not all were kings' men, the news was harrowing. Omens were seen throughout the land of Mel'Nir: flights of black birds, fiery emblems upon the clouds, spectral women who tore their hair and keened for the dead.

One of the strangest charges levelled against the people of Mel'Nir by their neighbors in the lands of Hylor is the charge that we have no gods. In fact we have many, and we pay honor to the dead. The people of the Eastern Rift hold to the gods and the death customs of the Farfarers—the men and women of Mel'Nir who crossed the cursed lands of the Svari and the Dettaren and came through the mountain passes to a new land. At Cloudhill we lit a fire in the courtyard after sundown; men and horses came out and stood around the fire in the evening light. Lady Thilka cast salt on the fire so that it burned blue, and a child was given a long spear to stir up the fire and make the sparks rise. Knaar and I stood watching the sparks fly upward: Marris, Benro, Rieth ... all three had ridden with the Red Hundreds.

A messenger brought letters from Hagnild, written in his fine straight-letter, almost a cypher. Despair and madness ruled at the Palace Fortress.

The old king's rage was not to be contained. He fell upon the first messengers of the disaster and hacked them to death. Later messengers simply deserted, news did not come, records were not kept. The escape of the general, Kirris the Lynx, the king's son-in-law, was not known for days; then, when it was known, the survivors of Adderneck were all proscribed as traitors. The Princess Merse trusted her father so little that she took her daughter, the unmarked Princess Gleya, and with Hagnild's help she fled to the Hanran keep on the borders of Cayl.

The vizier, Lord Sholt, husband of the king's second daughter, Princess Fadola, made himself busy in the palace and at last approached the king, in spite of warnings. The old man, brooding in a corner of the throne room, seemed to listen to the whisperings of Baudril Sholt. He bade him come closer, then with a roar seized the fellow by the edge of his sleeve, dragged him to his knees and tried to strangle him. Only the intervention of Hagnild and the palace guard saved the life of Hem Sholt. So the Palace Fortress and the realm waited, halls and courtyards empty, the vast kitchens idle, the dogs whimpering unfed, the servants boozing in the cellarage, the women and courtiers fled or hiding in their bedchambers. The palace guard stood close about the throne room, where their master raged, protecting the king or protecting those who might get in his way.

After more than ten days of this, Prince Gol himself came home from the wars; he had crossed the Dannermere and served with his personal followers in the army of the south, fighting against Sharn Am Zor, the young King of the Chameln.

During the years since the death of his first fair young wife, the Prince had fared badly. His second wife, Artetha, was barren and shrewish, but now he mourned her death and would not make the decision to marry another young Lienish princess. His exercise of arms was better than it had ever been, but he had no luck. His plans, his pursuit of order and independence, were all fruitless. He lacked the wit for intrigue and was a poor judge of men, giving his trust to unworthy creatures. He bore all these misfortunes with a dumb fortitude that suprised Hagnild; almost, admitted the Healer, one could say that Gol had learned some sense.

He had the sense at least to get the palace machinery working again, and he had plans for the forces of the king who remained in the Chameln lands. Those that were able should withdraw at once before the winter came down too heavily, and so cut their losses. The army of the south should come over the Dannermere, and the army of Hem Allerdon, father of Marris, the cleverest of the Generals of Mel'Nir, should retreat through the border forest to the rich mining district of the Adz, plunder it, and cross the realm of Lien. For Hem Werris in the distant capital of Achamar he saw no alternative but flight and surrender for his troops. He reckoned that the young King of the Zor and the Queen of the Firn would allow the defenders of the city to go home without reprisals.

These plans came to nothing; the king and Hem Sholt hung in a quandary of rage on the one hand and fear on the other. The winter came down, and Allerdon was forced into a long death march on the plain, then he holed up with the other forces of Mel'Nir in the central highlands. In the spring they came home depleted and dishonored, looking like the ghost horde of the Red Hundreds, risen from their graves. The stain of treachery was never removed from the poor devils; even Allerdon was accused of giving information to the Chameln that resulted in the death of his own son. Just how the ambush at Adderneck had been planned was never known. Magic was given as the answer: the Queen of the Firn, a deformed and ugly witch, had been warned and guided by spirits. The tall warriors of Mel'Nir did not raise their heads and glance up into the tops of the forest trees. There dwelt the despised folk of the Kelshin, whom the palace hunting parties sometimes shot down for sport, and they had brought word to Aidris, the Queen.

Sympathy for the king and for his beaten armies ran high throughout the lands of Mel'Nir. Ghanor was more popular than he had been since the early years of his reign, when as a young warrior he subdued the war-lords. Yet without a large army, he felt naked. When his rage subsided, he set about rebuilding his forces by every means and with a mad disregard for his people and his honor. He quickly forfeited the goodwill he had gained and raised up champions against his throne.

CHAPTER
III

I HAD EARNED MY STEED RESHDAR, A BETTER SUIT OF strip mail, a new helmet and a shield with the crest of Lord Strett of Cloudhill. The warrior that I now saw reflected in the water trough and in the eyes of certain beholders was a daunting sight. I heard Paunce, a neighbor lord of the rift, cry out to Strett, my master, riding ahead, "Godlight, Strett, that young bear you have counts as two men!"

Knaar, who rode with me and was more finely accoutered and had his own followers, was instantly jealous. His handsome high-colored face became set and still. He growled at Trenk, the big patient soldier who was his servant and standard bearer, and led his whole array to the head of our line. We were riding to Silverlode, to the meeting called The Field of the Silver Crown. Ghanor, the Great King, had made peace with Huarik, the Boar of Barkdon, war-lord of the east; now he had summoned the lesser lords of the rift, who had suffered under the Boar, to a peace table and a field for martial games. Silverlode, chosen as neutral ground, was forty miles from the rift in the center of the High Plateau.

Silverlode was a ghost town, a mining town abandoned when its store of silver and gems ran out. It stood on a broad, empty plain at the base of a tumbled hill, and the roads that led into its quiet streets were overgrown and stony. As the party from the rift rode in on the appointed day, at midday, the appointed hour, after a camp of one night on the road, we saw the royal standard of the Duarings with its prancing steed flying high above the town's roundhouse. I saw that the lists and the tilt yard behind the roundhouse were not yet ready; men in the king's livery of green and gold were working at them. I felt a painful anxiety and tried to fight it down. Strett longed for me to win the silver crown against the rift lords' followers and against the men of the Boar.

"There now," he murmured at my side. "The Boar comes well upon his hour . . ."

A trumpet sounded; a blue banner rode ahead of a dust cloud. I saw Huarik at last, a big man on a bay charger, his unpainted harness flashing in the sun and his ten followers all in the same bright armor without surcoats. The entry into the town had been carefully arranged to avoid the least suspicion of treachery. Yet the thing that had reassured the rift lords was the royal presence: Ghanor had not come, nor Prince Gol, but the Princess Fadola and her husband Baudril Sholt were our hosts in Silverlode.

Two of the rift lords, Paunce and Keddar, had brought their ladies; the fourth rift landowner was a woman, Arlies From of Nordlin, a tall old woman in a white cloak, mounted upon a white horse. Now she led off, dipping her standard with the device of white birds to Huarik and to her neighbors and rode into Silverlode. We followed when our turn came. Knaar went ahead of the other rift lords, soon after Huarik himself. The presence of Valko Firehammer's second son was a further proof of the security and peaceful intentions of all concerned. As we rode in and went to our quarters in the empty stone buildings, houses or storehouses, grouped around the little square, I felt the bleakness and sadness of a ghost town, which all the trappings of the meeting could not hide.

We stabled our horses. The Cloudhill sergeant was pleased, saying that the horses were better housed here than men or their lords. Trumpets called us into the square; the princess and her consort, the vizier, stood before the massive doors of the impressive stone roundhouse, the largest building in Silverlode. Fadola, the king's youngest child, was five and thirty, a blonde, stately woman, tall enough to be a "sword lily"; she was finely dressed, her golden robe flowed down over the steps of the roundhouse, her jewels blazed in the sunlight. She swayed a little and smiled, reaching out her hands to the rift lords and their followers. Baudril Sholt, in green from head to foot, tried to take his wife's hand, missed, came down a step, stumbling. I thought, smiling, of Hagnild's nickname, "Sholt the Dolt," then wondered if the man simply could not see very well. He had a bland face with a fine moustache. Fadola had uttered a few words of welcome, a wish for a speedy peace, further good wishes for the pursuit of the silver crown. The handsome pair stood nodding at our cheers like two huge dolls.

I had no pressing duties. Strett and the other lords, including Knaar, were making themselves fine for the ceremonial banquet. I strolled with Ibrim to look at the tilt yard. There was too much work still to be done; the royal servants, hammering dutifully, would have to stay at it all night by torchlight. Men of all the rift lords came up to me in a bluff, half-fierce way that was part of the ritual approach to feats of arms. We grinned, showing our teeth; patted arms and shoulders. I noticed that none of Huarik's men had come out of their quarters ... perhaps they felt themselves outnumbered. Two pages or esquires stood by the Boar's baggage wagon; they wore blue tabards, one had black hair in a long snood of silver netting. I strode on, then stopped dead so that Ibrim trod on my heels.

The dark-haired page saw how I stared, put a bundle back into the wagon and looked away with a weary smile, as if to say: "Oh yes, I *am* a woman ... I make no secret of it ..." Then as I stared longer, she took a step in my direction; I moved too, feeling my heart pound, and my breath caught in my chest. I managed to sketch a bow and croak out my name.

"Yorath!"

She came right up to me with an expression of wonder; again her beauty almost stifled me.

"Eight years!" said the Owlwife. "How you have grown!"

"We meet again," I said. "The Goddess has granted my dearest wish."

For me the town of Silverlode, the whole world had vanished away. I felt that I stood alone with Gundril Chawn.

"I thank you for saving my life," she said.

"What became of your companion?" I asked. "The rider on the black horse who went towards Lort?"

"He was not so lucky," she said. "Thilon had him thrashed and imprisoned. He was a servant and pleaded bewitchment."

She reached out and touched my ensign's sash.

"You serve Strett of Cloudhill," she said. "I think you are that 'young bear' they talk of at the tiltyard."

"If you wish me well, I know I cannot fail to win the silver crown!"

She would not raise her head to look me in the face. I thought she must have a loyalty to Huarik or his house.

"I will repay my debt," she said slowly.

Still without raising her eyes, she took my right hand and looked into the palm for a long moment. Then she stepped back and gazed at me with a kind of terror. At that moment the trumpets sounded for the entry to the banquet; Gundril turned and ran off. I went with Ibrim to watch the lords and ladies go into dinner. He grinned at me warily and said, "Do you know that lady is a witch?"

"I do indeed," I said. "How can you tell? Have you heard her name?"

"The air burns around her head," he replied. "She is a witch."

"I am bewitched then," I said, "for I find her very beautiful . . ."

The trumpeters beside the steps of the round-house blew the call of every lord who went in to the banquet. They were stripped of their armor and wore fine robes; it was a time of peace. Each lord or noble pair was permitted one servant, a cup-bearer perhaps or a waiting woman. Strett was preceded by a page, the young curly-headed son of Keddar, another rift lord; and I saw Keddar's lady smiling proudly upon her son. Knaar went in first with a kedran, one of his escort from Krail. Last of all came Huarik, I saw him up close for the first time. He was much younger than I expected, a powerful man in his early thirties with a scarred face and a head of thick brown hair that grew back from his broad forehead in a peak. His cup-bearer was Gundril Chawn. So they walked into the roundhouse, and the doors were shut. I saw, hardly noticing, the other page of Huarik edging through the crowd; he stopped by Ibrim, then went on his way.

Ibrim, smiling, pressed an object into my hand. I thought it was a folded paper, but as I quietly and privately unfolded it I saw that it was a pa-pery leaf, five-fingered, of a clear golden yellow. I looked down into my palm and read the message on the leaf and at once the leaf curled in my hand, turning brown. But its message burned in my brain. *Treachery. Do not drink. Save yourself.*

I crushed the leaf in my hand and looked over the heads of the crowd, stretching my neck a little. The armed followers of the rift lords were walking slowly to their quarters; still no followers of Huarik were among them. The royal herald, standing with two guard officers of Fadola's escort before the doors of the roundhouse, spoke up.

"Come then, lads . . . back to your alloted quarters, remember the orders of the day. Time to take your ease while the princess and the lords and dames are feasting. Look at our cookhouse yonder, filled with bakemeats and ale for your pleasure . . . but it must be served in your quarters . . ."

I bent down to Ibrim.

"Go at once, spy out the quarters of the Boar's men. Bring me word!"

He was slipping like a shadow through the crowd. I looked about in the press of soldiers for one I could trust. I saw the roundhouse as if for the first time, a place with no second entry, a prison. I saw the cookhouse, a smaller roundhouse directly across from the larger one, and the stone houses that were our quarters; I saw the pitiful numbers . . . forty soldiers. I seized the arm of a man going by.

"Trenk," I said, "walk with me. Do not cry out. Listen to me.

We went towards our quarters which both lay on the west side of the square.

"Ransom!" said Trenk in a hoarse whisper. "Lord Knaar will be ransomed, by the Goddess, and maybe the princess too. This must all be the bloody Boar's doing."

"Do *you* know of any second entry to the roundhouse?" I asked.

He shook his head.

"They have their own kitchens inside . . . it is built like a keep," he said.

"Remember . . . do not drink," I said. "Hold the drink carriers. Start no outcry."

So I stepped into the small stone house that served as our quarters and looked at the nine men of Cloudhill, old Sergeant Wayl and his eight companions, men picked for looks and strength. They sat there thirstily at an old round board. I told them, and they stared at me fearfully as if I had lost my wits.

The sergeant sprang to a narrow window and said, "Carriers coming. Two to a mess."

We waited and presently two men in the livery of the king came in with two small barrels of ale already tapped, carried upon a trestle. They were very cheerful, doling out pottery jugs, and when the first creamy draught of ale had been drawn I seized one man, the larger, about the body, and the sergeant took the other.

"Good cheer indeed," I said. "So drink, friend!"

The man I held was dark-skinned, fat; he turned pale. His younger companion began to whimper.

"Drink!"

I held the jug of ale to the fat man's lips, and he writhed and spat.

"No . . . have mercy . . . I am sick . . ."

"What is it? Tell me or you'll drink indeed. Would it kill?"

"No, no, sweet gods, no," he whispered. "Sleeping draught, I swear it. I saw it done. Sleep."

I nodded to a soldier called Slyke.

"Warn the others. Try to keep them still." Slyke went out; the sergeant let his wretched servant fall, and two of the men seized him at once and poured a jug of ale into him. He sat on the floor gasping, and they watched him.

Ibrim came in and said, "Empty except for a

couple of servants. Huarik's men have gone from their quarters."

"We have not done," I said to the fat man, tightening my grip. "Where have the Boar's men gone? How shall we come into the roundhouse?"

"Underground," he said quickly. "Passages lead from their quarters . . . from our cookhouse in the square. Let me loose, lord, my ribs are gone. Underground, a nest of caverns, cellars . . ."

"How many men has the Boar down there?"

He shook his head, and I squeezed him.

"Fifty, sixty, didn't count. Spare my life, lord!"

"Lead us in secretly, friend . . ."

"Joost," he said. "I am Joost, journeyman cook. I can lead you in. I can take you round the Boar's men!"

"Joost, if we are discovered, you will be the first to die!"

"I can do it," he said. "I swear it . . ."

With a sigh the other servant keeled over on his side; his sleep looked as ugly as it was sudden. I wondered if some might not wake after this sleeping draught.

There was a sudden commotion in the yard, and Slyke came running back in.

"Too late, Ensign Yorath," he said. "The Old Lady's folk from Nordlin, half down. The rest have run mad, trying to get the door to the citadel open!"

We went out and saw twenty men and servants from the rift lords battering at the door. They held the royal herald fast and the guards. I met Trenk and the ensign of Knaar's men, furious and afraid.

"Keep this up," I said to the ensign. "Batter at

the doors. I will go in with my company and get the door open from within."

"The king," panted the ensign. "These are the king's men. If Lord Knaar is harmed, by the gods, Valko will have the king, once and for all!"

"The Boar has conspired with the king," I said. "We know too little. I will go in!"

I pushed Joost, my fat guide, and ran with Ibrim and the nine men of Cloudhill to the second round-house. There was a little food and a few servants all in the livery of the king. We snatched some food up and some wine the servants were drinking. There was no protest but some heads were broken; I snatched back one young lad who had run to a big open trapdoor behind a stack of barrels.

Joost led the way down a comfortable flight of stone steps and into a roomy, well-made brick underpass. He pointed to a torch on the wall and the sergeant took it. We turned off at once into a narrow, dark tunnel; I pushed the fat man along in frantic haste and squeezed through after him. We came to a crossroads and heard the murmur of voices. The hidden soldiers of the Boar, armed and tense, were packed into a round chamber doing nothing, waiting for the word. I saw that they were nothing like the soldiers of his escort in their polished armor. These fellows were shabby veterans in worn boots; I wondered where Huarik had such creatures.

The fat man still knew where to go and felt my dagger in his ribs. We took a short tunnel then a flight of steps that wound up and up.

"Where . . . ?" I whispered in his ear.

"We come out on a gallery over the hall, lord," he

said. "No guards . . . just the musicians. You'll see you'll see . . . I did all you asked . . ."

So we went on, panting up the little winding stair and came to a small door that I sometimes see even now, in my dreams. I stretched an arm over the guide's shoulder and pushed out the door a crack. I saw the yellow, dusty daylight inside the roundhouse and part of a wooden balcony. I heard a scream, a single wailing cry, so wild and terrible that it told me we had come too late. I pushed Joost ahead of me through the door, and we fell out onto the wooden gallery above the hall. We were in shadow, unseen except by a few cowering musicians, who could not know or care whose men we were.

We looked down; the high table faced us and on the left was a long serving table. The scene was laid out for us, without disorder or riot, like a painted picture or a tapestry. On either side of the two thronelike chairs set for Princess Fadola and Hem Sholt three rift lords sprawled in their death agony. Keddar had fallen forwards on the white cloth, blood pouring from his throat wound; I saw Strett, my loved master, lying in the same attitude in a pool of dark blood, and Paunce, canted back in his chair, the blood still pulsing from several wounds. The old woman, Arlies of Nordlin, was nowhere to be seen; Knaar was still living, held fast by two of Huarik's escort. The Boar himself had stripped off his robe of silver grey with its scarlet lining and stood in his tunic of linked mail between Strett and Keddar. His dagger was in his hand, his arm red to the elbow, even his face bespattered with blood.

I could not tell who had screamed. The women

had been dragged or driven back behind the high table in a heap against the wall of the roundhouse, tapestried for the meeting. Now the young wife of Paunce ran mad, flung herself past the men of the Boar, scratching and tearing at them, and came to the side of her lord and clasped him about the body. Huarik wiped his dagger on the long sleeve of Strett's robe and strode round to the front of the high table. He gave an order and the servants from the banquet and two of his officers began to wrap and carry the bodies. The serving dishes were twitched to the ground with a clatter and the rift lords laid out upon the trestle. In the midst of this scene of carnage the princess and Baudril Sholt still sat in their high chairs. They clung to each other and Fadola had pulled up the long train of her golden robe to cover her face.

I saw where wooden stairs ran down right and left from the gallery.

"Get down to the main doors," I said aloud to Sergeant Wayl. "Have them open. Where will the Boar's men come up from the cellar?"

"Kitchen," said Joost. "See, yonder on the right."

"Dead!" said the sergeant. "Our good lord Strett is dead!"

"Hold fast!" I said.

"All is over . . ." said the sergeant, his voice trembling.

One of the nine men, the youngest besides myself, began to retch, clutching his belly.

"Hold fast!" I shouted angrily. "There is work to do!"

I went to the rail of the gallery and looked down. It was a ten foot drop into a patch of shadow.

"Get to that door, you hearts," I said to the men

of Cloudhill. "You can come there quickly, unseen behind the drawn arras. I will do what I must . . . and at the worst it will give you time to let the rift men in."

I saw that they still had no idea of what I intended. There was a murmuring and wailing below in the hall.

I stood at the gallery rail and cried out in a loud voice, "Huarik! Huarik of Barkdon!"

My voice rang out strangely in the hall, echoing from the heavy roof beams and broken slates overhead.

Huarik called, "Who speaks?"

He nodded to his soldiers and they began to look about, sword in hand.

"A champion!" I cried. "A champion for Strett of Cloudhill and for all the lords of the rift. Fight me, Huarik . . . will you fight?"

"Who speaks?"

"I challenge you, Huarik, I challenge you to single combat. Are you a coward as well as a foul murderer? Is treachery your only skill?"

Then Huarik gave a snort of rage and held out his hand for a sword. I went over the gallery rail and dropped down lightly into a patch of shadow. I drew my sword and strode out into the dusty yellow sunlight that came from the holes in the roof. I checked my back but no one lurked behind me under the gallery except Ibrim who had scrambled down after me. I heard a faint gasp or groan arise from those watching in the hall. A champion had arisen. Then I saw no one living or dead in all that company except Huarik.

Huarik should have won the fight; he was experienced, skilful and ruthless. I had a slight advantage in reach and height, a greater advantage in youth. He rushed at me with a dreadful shout before I was set on my feet, and as I clumsily dodged and parried his first mighty blow, I knew that he was the better swordsman. I set myself to tire him out, running, dodging, tempting him to blows that fell short as I drew back, then striking before he could recover. I was absolutely unafraid; I had no fear of death because I could not conceive of dying. He caught my hip a glancing blow, and I caught him a sharp showy thrust on the left arm, piercing his mail so that blood flowed. His face was a demon mask, purple with effort, his hair erect like the bristles of a boar, his pale lips drawn back over his teeth. He began to sweat and to pant and tried to conceal his weariness. He became more reckless, and his blows, every one, were so fierce that they would have hacked off a limb or cleft my body to the backbone if they had landed.

Still I went on, shouting, parrying, striking, in good, even very good, tiltyard style. Unlike Huarik, I said no words, made no taunts. The Boar wasted his breath. I believe it was his awful deed, his treachery, that killed him. After a long time, he came in more terribly than ever, cursing me for a crookbacked misbirth, and slipped on spilt blood, coming to one knee. Nothing held me back, I was ruthless as my opponent. I saw the blow, and I made the blow, one to win the silver crown, one for Strett of Cloudhill. I brought my broadsword through very true, flat and steady, with such power that I was carried almost in a circle. I heard a small, dull sound as if a clay pitcher had fallen onto a floor covered with rushes. I struck off the head of Huarik of Barkdon.

So he lay, divided, and I leaned on my sword, panting, surprised that the great war engine that had charged and charged at me did not fly together again and rush in on me once more. Then a loud cheer arose.

Ibrim came to my side, wiped my brow and handed me a beaker of water to drink. I looked about at last. I saw the banquet chamber crowded to right and left with the men of the rift come through the open doors and the men of the Boar, the shabby men from underground, crowded in the kitchen doorway. Some of them had cheered, too. I saw that Knaar had been released. All of Huarik's officers had the look of men beaten and beheaded. They had changed the world for the men of the rift by killing their lords, and now I had changed it for them by killing the Boar.

I raised my voice.

"Let some men of Barkdon tend to the body of Huarik the Boar!"

Two officers ran to do so, and a third, a man with a knot of dark hair, flew into a god-rage. He roared with grief and pain and struck about him. I saw the rift soldiers gripping their swords, but before it could come to a free-for-all the madman was punched to the ground by his own comrades.

I said again, "Take out the bodies. Lay them in the shade, in the old longhouse by the eastern gate. Let no one leave Silverlode. I proclaim truce until all is declared!"

I caught the eye of Wayl, the Cloudhill Sergeant, and he began the work. A movement caught my eye beyond the high table: a newly hung tapestry with the royal arms swung aside, and the old woman Arlies of Nordlin stepped forth unharmed.

Behind her came Gundril Chawn, whose gift for survival always seemed magical. Now she wore a long dark cloak with a hood; there was no trace of the cup-bearer of Huarik the Boar. She had a solemn look. Under the cloak, clinging to her, dazed and pale, was the curly-haired boy, the Heir of Keddar, who had served Strett.

"I stand by that truce!" cried Old Arlies. "Praise to the Gods of the Farfaring that a champion has arisen for the rift lords and their true heirs. I will go out with the slain, Ensign Yorath, and see that due respect is paid to them and the truce kept."

So the crowd of soldiers parted to let her follow the carriers, and she took along the Heir of Keddar and the mourning wives. When she had gone, I strode or staggered a few paces to the high table. Not daring to look at the bloody wreckage of the banquet, I spoke to Princess Fadola and Hem Sholt. He was on his feet, blood-bespattered, gaping at me.

"Highness," I said, "take your ladies and go at once to your bower, your tiring room in this place. Hem Sholt, I pray you, go with your lady wife . . ."

"Who . . ." croaked Sholt. "Who are you?"

"My name is Yorath," I said. "Ensign of Strett of Cloudhill."

The princess could not speak. She was half-fainting; Sholt lifted her up, called for her women. I saw him shepherd them through a door beyond the kitchen.

I turned away from the high table; the crowd in the roundhouse had dispersed. In the few moments that had passed, I had acquired a court, eager to advise or to do my bidding. There stood Knaar, my ally, and Gundril Chawn in her dark cloak, even Joost, the fat kitchen steward, who had been our guide.

Knaar gripped my hand.

"While I was swearing vengeance, you came and took it!" he said. "By the Goddess, Yorath . . ."

"This is a vile business," I said, "and the king has done it. Who are these men that the Boar kept hidden? Men of Barkdon?"

"They are yours!" said Knaar in a hoarse whisper. "Take them!"

As I turned to stare at the ranks of the "hidden men" I caught a dark glance from the Owlwife that said "He is right!" I saw that many of these men had their swords in their hands, sheathed, with the baldric folded, ready to perform an act of submission. Others had torn the sashes and shoulder-knots of blue from their uniforms.

I went forward and said, "I will speak to your officers!"

Two men pushed out of the kitchen of the roundhouse. They were strapping fellows, one middle-aged, one hardly older than myself, and they bore the marks of hard combat. The younger officer had a curious burnt patch on the side of his blond head; the other carried his left arm in a sling. Worse than these scars of battle was their curious hangdog look, half-sorrowing, half-resentful, like prisoners or men under a curse.

"Who are you?" I demanded. "Are you men of Barkdon? Where did you win these scars?"

"Lord Yorath," said the burnt captain, "we were promised pardon if we took part in a raid for Huarik of Barkdon. Yet we are betrayed, we are more deeply mired in dishonor than before . . ."

"We fought in the Chameln lands," said the older

man, answering my question. "Some of us were at Adderneck. Some surrendered on the plains or at Ledler fortress and were sent back."

"By the Goddess," I said, "who shall say that such brave men lack honor, having fought for Mel'Nir?"

Then the young captain fell down at my feet and offered me his sword and so did others of the troop.

"I am a landless man," I said; "but if you follow me and give me your allegiance, we will form a free company. We will come to honor and to just rewards. We will protect the heirs of the rift lords, so foully murdered here at Silverlode, and give our services to Valko of Val'Nur, Great Lord of the West, and to Knaar, his son, who stands here at my side, my brother in arms."

Then they all cheered and knelt down, and I had fifty veteran soldiers, a span in army jargon. They cast off their allegiance to the Boar and their blue badges.

I said to Ibrim, pointing, "Fetch me that heap of cloth, yonder!"

I could see well enough what it was: Huarik's handsome robe of silver-grey velvet, lined with scarlet silk, spattered with blood in places.

Gundril Chawn murmured, *"It is your wolf skin, Yorath . . ."*

I slipped off the broad grey and scarlet belt attached to the robe and twisted it about my arm. I flung the robe to the captains of my new troop.

"Divide it!" I said. "Let each man have a shoulder knot or a sash. These shall be my colors. A banner will be made. You serve Yorath the Wolf!"

* * *

This then was my part in the Bloody Banquet of Silverlode. Knaar rode out with his escort before sunset, westward to his father's citadel at Krail. Before midnight, when I quit the ghost town, I had sorted the plans of dead Huarik, and I knew that the rift must be protected with all speed.

The Great King's part in this treachery was plain. I went alone to the bower inside the roundhouse and spoke to the princess and Hem Sholt. I had seen these two often enough, but the source of all my knowledge, Hagnild and his scrying stones, must be kept secret.

The room, like every room in the horrid town, was hastily prepared with new tapestries scraping upon the stone walls. The princess lay upon a long chair, her thick, golden hair unbound, her bodice unlaced. Hem Sholt stood in a plain tunic staring out of an arrow slit at the arid streets. I signed to the two royal waiting women, and they ran out as if a demon warrior had appeared. I bowed low to the two royal personages and deliberately took a seat. Sholt came at once and sat down; Fadola laid a hand across her face.

"Highness," I said, "pray you, do not swoon. I know you are a strong woman. I will offer you every courtesy, but I will have answers to my questions."

Hem Sholt had not taken his eyes from my face.

"Killed him . . ." he blurted. "Killed the pig with a single blow. Botched the plan somewhat . . ."

"Be still," said Fadola wearily.

She sat up on the long chair.

"What do you want to know, Hem Yorath?" Hem, the old title from before the Farfaring, was a useful one, meaning *lord* or *liege* ... and I was a liege, even although I had only fifty liegemen.

"Was this the king's plan?" I demanded.

Sholt nodded.

Ghanor's daughter said, "Yes, but Huarik found Silverlode and made his bargain."

"The rift and its rulers in exchange for a new army?" I guessed.

"Something of that," she said.

"We were d-deluded," said Sholt. "He spoke nothing of this awful killing at table. We believed the lords would be held for ransom."

"I expected some kind of skirmish," said the princess, "but not this. Truly not this ..."

She drooped against the chair back, her face pale, and Sholt fussed over her, fetched a goblet of wine for her to sip.

"Should not have brought you here," he murmured. "Goddess help me ... I am to blame, dearest love."

"Hush ... it will pass ..."

I sensed a true closeness, a bond of love between them; they stared at me like conspirators.

"You have won all, young man," said Baudril Sholt. "The veterans have joined you to become a free company."

He left his wife, at her whispered command, and fetched two more goblets and poured wine for us all.

"What will be done with us?" asked Fadola.

There was only one thing to be done with them; they must be sent back to the Palace Fortress with their servants. The idea of ransom had been quickly dismissed even by Knaar: it was too great a provocation of the king.

Before I could answer Sholt said, "Some neutral p-place . . ."

I realised what the poor creatures wanted me to do. They longed to be free of the Palace Fortress; they did not wish to be sent home.

"I have means," said Fadola. "I brought many jewels."

She directed her gaze to the family rubies and emeralds blazing in a heap upon a stool. I did not see that I was being offered this booty.

"What place would be considered neutral?" I asked.

It was a good question. The lands of Barkdon, the towns of the Eastmark were unsuitable, and so were the lands of Val'Nur in the west. The rift was no place for these two.

"I was named for the late queen, my mother, Fadola of Pfolben," said the Princess. "The Lord Pfolben of the Southland is my cousin and a good friend to our house."

They clasped hands and waited as if I were a judge pronouncing sentence.

"So be it!" I said sternly. "You will go to the Southland, and it will be known for an act of banishment for what has passed here. You must remain here for a day before you travel. We will leave only enough horses for yourselves and a few followers. The other royal servants must walk home to the Palace Fortress."

They could barely control their looks of relief and pleasure. We drank our wine. I said, "Highness, the king has made a grave error here today. It will be paid for with blood and suffering."

"The king is old," whispered Fadola. "His temper is very uncertain. Even our good healer despairs ..."

When I took my leave, Baudril Sholt followed me to the door of the chamber.

"Take this, lad," he said. "Go on ... take it. You have a free company to feed and house. Never liked that bastard Huarik ..."

He pressed upon me a golden collar of the Duarings with huge emeralds; I took it and thrust it into the "fodder pocket" of my surcoat. I went down with Ibrim, who had waited at the door, and plunged back into the hurly-burly of pickets and brawls over precedence. The sun had just set and Silverlode was still in twilight. No man from the rift or from my new company would eat in the newly scrubbed roundhouse hall though the cold forced them to sleep there an hour or so later. Now they had bivouacked in the courtyard with campfires. I checked the order of march with my two captains and had them sent to the leaders of the rift men. I sent an officer to Arlies of Nordlin giving my respects and telling the arrangements for the princess.

I sent Ibrim on an errand and came to my headquarters, the small cottage where I had sat down to dine with the men of Cloudhill. Now it was mine alone. Presently Ibrim came with light and a writing case conjured up from the Goddess knew where. I sat alone as the commanding officer often sits, in his tent, and wrote a letter to Hagnild. A thread of sound came through the gathering darkness. In the longhouse by the eastern gate women were raising the keen for the rift lords who lay there.

I wrote down all that had taken place as plainly

as I could and came to the purpose of my letter. I begged Hagnild to leave the service of Ghanor the Great King, who had committed this act of treachery. I begged him to do so for his honor and for his own safety. War was looming between Ghanor and Valko Firehammer, that was certain, and now I was in Valko's service, together with my new company. I folded the letter and sealed it with red wax and the silver ring that I had been given by my dear master, Strett of Cloudhill. I thought of the fight in the stableyard at Finn's smithy. I was homesick for my old ways, for Nightwood and the marsh, for the brown house in the forest and Caco stirring a cauldron at the hearth while Hagnild sat over his books.

The Owlwife came in like smoke. She sat on a stool just beyond the circle of light from the lamp on my table. I saw the gleam of her dark eyes, the soft cloud of her hair when her hood fell back.

"See what I have . . ." she said quietly.

It rattled upon the tabletop, a circle of pale metal worked into roundels.

"So there was a silver crown," I said.

"It is of base metal, painted with silver-gilt," she said. "Huarik and the king knew there would be no contest."

"You served Huarik?"

"I was his scribe," she said, smiling. "I read and wrote for him. I knew more or less what he planned."

"You were his friend?"

"No," she said, "neither his friend nor his lover. Huarik, in the end, had no friends. He was too much feared."

"Who is his heir? Surely he had a wife . . ."

"A wife and an infant son. She will go home to her father, Lovill of the Eastmark. There will be wrangling about the captured lands and goods of the Boar but no movement to uphold the House of Barkdon."

"His generals served him well. Out there on the plateau or beyond he still has an army, moving to attack the rift. You know we have sent out kedran on swift horses to Nordlin, bringing the evil tidings and giving warning!"

"Neither of the generals, neither Breckan nor Thrane, will make a war lord. Lesser lords mustered into the Boar's service will take their men home. Huarik was unbeloved."

"And the Great King?"

"He comes of a noble house," said Gundril Chawn, "and the Duarings may rule long in Mel'Nir. But this act of treachery will cost Ghanor the last of his goodwill. Even the glamor of his kingship will fade. I see that his near kin have reason to fear Ghanor."

"You have heard that the princess goes to the Southland."

"I know why she goes," said the Owlwife. "She is with child. You may be saving the life of some heir of the Duarings."

"Well, Goddess be praised," I said. "I hope Fadola's child grows up unmarked and unharmed by that vile old man."

She smiled at me; I felt that we were true friends.

"You saved my life," I said. "You say that I saved your life, eight years ago, when I was a child. What will you do now, Gundril Chawn? Will you stay with me and be my scribe? Will you work magic for me?"

"You will need it," she said. "You are still a child. You are strong as the wind itself and tall as a tree and you have done your training well at Cloudhill, but you are a child and tender-hearted."

"Must I be cruel to prove that I am not a child?"

"Yes," she said. "You will learn to be cruel."

"What did you see in my hand that frightened you?" I demanded.

"The same as I saw in Huarik's hand," she said. "A fight to the death, and for you . . . a long life thereafter. I knew he would not survive this wretched journey to Silverlode. Suddenly I found the instrument of his death."

Outside, in the darkness, the watch, pacing between the hour-posts, called the time of night.

"We must sleep," I said. "We ride to the rift at midnight. Will you stay here in my quarters?"

"Will you send me away, Yorath?"

"I am not such a child as you think!"

I stood up to take her in my arms and hit my head on the roof of the cottage. I sat down in a heap and pulled the Owlwife across my knees . . . we were both laughing.

"No one will come in," I said.

We kissed, and I was lost utterly and forever. I fled back into my dreams, and my dreams were nothing to the warmth of her presence.

"*Can* you . . . ?" she whispered.

I knew that she meant, "Can you at this time? Can you make love after this frightful killing?"

"Yes," I said. "I must!"

We spread my cloak upon the floor of the cottage and lay down. When I drifted into sleep, I was marvelling at the ease and kindness of my dark lady, who took all my clumsiness away. I dreamed of a woodland glade and the beating of wings among the trees and a brown owl with yellow eyes that sat overhead. Then I was awake, aching in every limb from the floor boards. The Owlwife stood by the table, and Ibrim tapped upon the door ready to put on my armor. I thought of the letter that lay beside the lamp.

"You must trust me, Yorath," said Gundril.

"I do trust you!"

I clambered up to the stool, calling for Ibrim who came in with a smile to see the pair of us.

"Let me deliver your letter," she said.

She had found the point of my mistrust. I wondered if she had powers to read the letter. I staggered to the crock of water that Ibrim had brought and splashed my face.

"Take it then," I said wearily.

I wrote on the folded paper: "To Master Hagnild Raiz, Healer, by Finn's smithy in the marsh, at Nightwood on the Dannermere."

"With all speed!" I said. "It is a long way over the plateau. Come to me again in the rift."

Gundril Chawn reached up and kissed my cheek.

"I will find you out," she said.

She was gone into the darkness.

Soon afterwards I rode out of Silverlode under a starry sky at the head of my own free company. I had begun to learn the names and histories of all my men. My head was full of quartermasters' lists and the spoils of war, from the emerald collar of the princess to the arms and horses of Huarik's officers. I have a clear memory of the awful sense of power and well-being that grew upon me as I rode on good Reshdar through the undark summer night.

Behind us in the ghost town certain of the rift soldiers waited with Arlies of Nordlin to bring home the bodies of the slain lords. I do not know if any officers of the Boar survived. They were young, picked men of arrogant temper, a war lord's brood. For the first time I saw men who were incapable of docility even if their lives were at stake. Three became enraged and were promptly killed by men of the rift. One hostage rode with us, taken for ransom and as an informer.

When the princess and her consort headed south with a small escort, the remaining servants of the king—cooks, carpenters, grooms, armorers, who had set up the town of Silverlode for the Bloody Banquet—walked home to the Palace Fortress across the wastes of the High Plateau. Or so it was for some. When the sun rose upon my own troop, I found that we had acquired a number of faithful servants trailing along in half a dozen extra baggage wagons drawn by mules still in the trappings of the royal house. Joost, the fat steward, was among these renegades. His life had been changed utterly by the chance that he brought a barrel of drugged ale to the quarters of the men of Cloudhill. He served me from that time forward.

In the light of dawn I rode in the van with the young burnt captain, Wilm Gorrie of Balbank, and my old sergeant, Wayl of Cloudhill. Behind us came other men who still served the rift lords or their heirs and among them our hostage. We had covered a good distance in the hours of darkness, taking up all the treeless, unprotected miles that lay between Silverlode and the wooded lands that edged the rift. We were glad to come into the shelter of the trees and pressed on in silence until I gave the word to halt and make breakfast.

Our high spirits had gone; we were all cast down and thoughtful. There was no way for me to turn my thoughts without coming to something melancholy . . . the way we had ridden out so bravely to The Field of the Silver Crown, the change in fortune so many had suffered. It was on the tip of my tongue to ask Gorrie how it had been at the Adderneck, but this was another tale too painful for telling. Wayl came up with the ensign of the dead lord Paunce and said, "Now we will see if that Boar's man values his hide!"

The hostage sat alone picking at his hunk of bread. He had not been trusted with a knife and his legs were hobbled while we were all dismounted. I recognised him suddenly as the darkhaired man who had broken out in a rage soon after Huarik's death and been punched to the ground by his companions. I wondered if his wits had been scrambled, if he had suffered what Hagnild called a brain-shaking. He had spoken freely of Huarik's plans, and Gundril Chawn had marked him out as worth a ransom.

When we rode on I had the hostage brought up beside me. I noticed that he had kept his own horse, a strong and splendid bay, and wondered if love of this creature had made him so biddable. We had come through the woodland to a flattened knoll close to the edge of the rift. It was called the Green Fort, for its ancient Chyrian earthworks. Here there would be a strange encounter: Huarik had named this meeting place to his generals when he planned the treacherous overthrow of the rift lords at

Silverlode. If the hostage had not lied, we would soon meet a party of the men of Barkdon ready to greet their victorious lord and bring him news of the battle for the rift. As we drew up at the foot of the knoll, below the green maze of walls and ditches, tangled with briars, the weather had turned round. The clear morning had darkened; the sky was heavy with cloud and a mist was gathering.

"Divide here as we planned, Captain," I said. "Go round the base in two wings. Keep a sharp lookout."

Gorrie soothed his grey; all the horses were restless.

"This is an uncanny place, Lord," he said. "I am not used to the Plateau."

He gave the order. I took the bridle of Chandor, the hostage.

"Come," I said. "I see a way to the top of this Green Fort. We will try for a view of the rift."

He gave me a startled look; we rode up a path between the briars and the tumbled stones netted with green grass. The mist had thickened, but we came to the top of the hillock. Chandor made some sound, and his horse whinnied and was echoed by Reshdar. My good black steed was not what one would have called a fanciful horse. We stood still, two men and two horses with the circle of green turf on the hilltop; we were surrounded by a thick wall of white mist. The world had retreated from us; we had come into another place.

I seized Chandor's bridle again, drew the hostage and his steed closer to me. The man's teeth were chattering with cold and with fear.

"Stand firm!" I said. "They will not harm us!"

I was afraid and outraged at this sudden fear.

There came a crackling of the air overhead and a burst of sound that could have been the wind or strange voices howling in the wind. A patch of light grew in the misty wall that surrounded us. A young man was in the circle with us. He was slender, short, at least by the standards of Mel'Nir, brown-haired and fine-featured. He wore a russet tunic of dressed leather and I had the impression of jewels . . . a chain of gold, a ring.

He cried out distinctly, "Hold! Are you dark or light who come to us?"

It made no sense; it was a riddle. I strained to understand, and in a rush I did understand. My years with Hagnild had not been wasted. I answered, choking at first, then more clearly:

"You see what we are! We are dark. We are mortal men."

The young man lifted his head proudly and turned it a little aside, as if he sniffed the air and found it tainted by our presence.

"Dark indeed!" he said in the same bell-like tone. "You stink of death. You are trespassers."

"Let us go then," I said. "Show us the way out of your domain. You are light. You are one of the Eilif lords of the Shee. Give us leave to go!"

"You are bold as you are tall!" said the young man. "I will have some toll from you. I will take your boldness or your wit or your love for your fellow mortals . . ."

I was afraid, but I was impatient with the mocking fellow.

"No!" I said. "We have done nothing to earn such punishment. I can pay you with silver or gold. Do not say that the Eilif lords scorn such things."

"I will take your soul . . ." said the young man smiling. "I will take the soul of that man riding next to you. He is very sick, he is cut to the brains, he has seen the death of his liege. I can empty the tower and send in . . . another!"

"No, by the Goddess!" I cried. "This is a most cruel injustice. The man is my prisoner! I forbid you to harm him, Shee!"

Chandor drooped in his saddle; I feared for his life. The being laughed aloud.

"Go your ways, Yorath," he said. "You speak well enough for a member of your grandsire's house."

I did not reply, but trembled and would not ask what I eagerly desired to know.

"We will meet again," said the Eilif lord, "and then you will know your parentage."

A gap had appeared in the wall of mist I urged Reshdar forward and dragged on the bridle of the bay. We rode breakneck out of the circle and were plunging down a path to the foot of the knoll. I drew rein and looked into the drawn face of the hostage, Chandor. I saw only the young Captain of Barkdon, sick and haunted, in the hands of his enemies.

"What cheer, man?" I whispered. "Chandor?"

"I am here," he said hoarsely. "I am still here, Hem Yorath. What was that we saw?"

"A damned, tormenting fairy creature," I burst out. "Pray you, say nothing of this meeting. I will see that you are well treated."

"You are brave to speak to it," he said. "I have to thank you for my very soul."

We rode on more slowly down the hill, and for the first time I did get a clear view down into the rift. I saw a signal fire, which told that the rift was up in arms, defending itself against the men of Barkdon. A hail came up from the side of the hill:

"Small body of riders approaching!"

I sensed that no time had passed since we rode up on to the hilltop: my new men had seen nothing. I came to a broad grassy trench above the road and stood there with Chandor, lightly screened by a brake of alders. We watched the riders come up with their banner of the Boar snapping in the morning wind.

Ten, twelve high-ranking officers and their attendants rode confidently to the meeting with their lord. Chandor had not lied. He saw them coming and said one word: "Thrane." One of Huarik's generals was leading the party. They had come to this secret meeting without any support. My men were wary of being outnumbered, but no larger body of troops lurked about. Thrane and his companions began a ritual cheer, crying out the name of Huarik, as they saw that soldiers were waiting. I had no wish to prolong the suffering; I came out from my alderbrake on to a natural platform above the road.

"General Thrane!" I cried out in a loud voice. "Stand and parley!"

Thrane was an old man, heavy and grey-bearded, the image of a war lord.

"Who's that?" he cried. "Where's the Lord Huarik? Do you lead the moles that the king sent, the underground men?"

"My name is Yorath," I said, "and I do lead the veterans. The news I bring you from Silverlode is bad. How is the fighting in the rift?"

"They are prepared and will give us heavy work,"

said Thrane. "What's amiss? Did the rift lords give trouble?"

"The rift lords are dead," I replied, "all save Dame Arlies of Nordlin. But before you rejoice, hear this. Huarik of Barkdon is dead, too. He was killed in single combat. Your liege has been struck down."

I saw the news fall upon them like a blow. They were Huarik's own veterans, not the picked and showy young officers who had gone with him to The Field of the Silver Crown. They stirred and cursed, blistering the air, and found their way was barred. They were surrounded by armed troopers. This told them the news might be true.

"Who did it? Who could strike down the Boar?" growled one man.

I laid a hand on my sword and rode forward a little on my green dais. One of my own men cried out, "See where he stands!"

Then there were cheers for "Yorath!" and "Yorath the Wolf!" round about.

"I killed the Boar," I cried, "to avenge my dear master, Strett of Cloudhill. Now these men follow me. We are the Free Company of the Wolf."

Thrane and his brother officers looked dark, very dark and downcast, and whispered together.

"Thrane!" I cried again, "you have no liege and no reason to fight in the rift. There are men here from the manor of Cloudhill, Pauncelain and Keddar ready to kill you where you stand to avenge your lord's foul treachery, the bloody banquet he prepared for us at Silverlode."

"The king!" howled Thrane suddenly. "The Great King is to blame . . ."

"Maybe," I replied. "The Great King is an old

man, half out of his wits from the defeat in the Chameln lands. Where is the army he was promised?"

Thrane made no answer, but another man, more greedy for life, cried out, "Breckan has them, lord. Breckan leads them down the Eastmark, ready to go into the king's service."

"Thrane, you have one chance," I said. "Surrender at once! Lay down your arms, surrender to me and come down under flag of truce to call off your army in the rift."

I saw the old man wagging his head from side to side and cursing still. "Come sir," I said. "What is it to be? Men are dying down in the valley."

Thrane made some gesture I did not understand; he looked at the sky and touched his lips. Then he stood up tall in his stirrups, drew his sword and shouted aloud, "Be damned to you, landless bastard!"

He rushed upon the soldiers nearest him and I raised my hand. It was all over in a few minutes. Two of the officers tried to climb up and attack me; I struck one down with a boot in the face, unhorsed him, saw him trampled. A pair of attendants, lightly mounted, got free and rode back the way they had come. A few others dismounted and surrendered. The rest were killed on the spot.

We did not wait to be found out by the Boar's army; our way led down into the rift by a green road, a track through the trees. We came down into the valley in two hours and were at Cannford Old House, midway down the rift. We rode up through its orchards and passed the word of our arrival to a company of kedran riding to the front, which was at Cloudhill. I told my men to make camp in the orchard.

I went on foot through the barns and the stable-yard and came to the front of the house. A figure in a black and green mourning hood stood upon the steps of the house; other women looked from the windows. Thilka came towards me. We said no word, but she saw from my face that all that had been told to her was true. Strett of Cloudhill was dead. I knelt before her on the path, and she came and rested her hands upon my shoulders. We were both weeping.

CHAPTER
IV

Summer wore out in the rift, a disturbed and dismal time. Only the weather was fine, the perfect days blue with the smoke of funeral pyres. Huarik's force that had attacked the rich valley fell back leaderless, yet the folk of the rift could not believe that raiders would not come again. Men and women of every estate lived in anxiety since the death of their lords at Silverlode. They spoiled the men of my company, plying them with all that the valley had to offer, begging them to stay and almost in the same breath calling them brigands, freebooters.

Still we stayed and might have stayed forever. The quartermaster, Münch, a spare and watchful man who had served the Great King for thirty years in peace and in war, turned all his talents to procuring and salting away provisions. We were outfitted in fine uniforms, our banners were sewn by the ladies of the rift and their daughters.

I was offered the greatest inducement to stay. I remained at Cannford Old House with my men encamped in the orchard. I lived like a lord, a rift lord, in the family of Strett of Cloudhill. Thilka and her three daughters, Annhad, Pearl and Perine, kept back their grief to give me pleasant entertainment. Between one long, sweet summer evening and the next I understood what was being offered. There was fair Annhad walking with her sisters in the park or riding under the trees on her palfrey as she had done with Marris a year or so ago. Thilka stood beside me at a window; she murmured of Strett, how he had regarded me as a son, his finest pupil.

I looked out into the rift and saw the little river and looked south to Cloudhill, where the mares were in foal. Lords' sons would come again and I would be Lord of Cloudhill, Annhad's husband, a permanent bulwark for the whole valley with my veterans. Yet I could not stay. Thilka left me alone on another evening and sent fair Annhad herself, fine-boned, shy, tender, a mate for Marris but not for Yorath.

We seemed to understand one another. I saw that she was really prepared to give herself as a wife. Perhaps the feelings of friendship, admiration, suitability, mutual benefit, were the usual reasons for marriage. I felt love and longing for a different woman, and she, Annhad, still loved a perfect knight who had died at the Adderneck under a hail of Chameln arrows.

These things need not have hindered us. I had outgrown the rift, that was true reason for my going. I kissed the hand of fair Annhad and wished her a happy life when her time of mourning was ended. I sent my captains the order to pack. I thought with despair of the Owlwife, but knew she would find out wherever I might be. I sent a rider westward to Krail with a message to Knaar of Val'Nur.

We rode out westward down the valley among cheering crowds. We stopped at Nordlin, and Old Arlies kissed my cheek.

"The best for you," she said shrewdly. "You are too large for this place, friend Yorath!"

So we rode out, the Free Company of the Wolf, fifty troopers and forty servants and camp followers. The word had no disreputable meaning in Mel'Nir; some of the wives of my veterans had come over the plateau to find their husbands; I had performed marriage ceremonies between my men and girls from the rift. We might have enlisted many young men in our company, but we would not do so. Chandor, the hostage, came along, still quiet, still unransomed. His family in the east sent pleading letters; they said they had no money. He stayed by me; I used him as my standard-bearer.

We rode on unsleeping under the stars, camped three times by the wayside and saw the descent into the Westmark before us. Our scouts reported a small body of men approaching through the meadows as we came down off the plateau the next evening. I rode out with Gorrie and Chandor and men with torches.

The leader of the party had dismounted, and I cried out, "Knaar! Here is your wolf-pack!"

"Knaar is not here!" came the deep reply.

More torches were lit, and I saw the leader in their golden light, which made his armor give off a ruddy glow so that he was clothed all in gold. I had thought of all fathers as old men, but Valko Firehammer was in the prime of life, massive and handsome, with fire-gold hair and a noble beard, a sign of privilege, marking him out from the soldiery. There was power in his face, a look of concentration, of searching wit, that compelled my spirit. I knew why he had come. I dismounted, my standard was dipped. I walked into the circle of light before the lord of Val'Nur, knelt down, and made submission to him, offering my sheathed sword.

"Yorath, called the Wolf," I said, "offering his sword in your service, lord, and the swords of this free company."

"I accept your service," said Valko of Val'Nur.

He had a deep voice and a look that was half smiling. He waved a welcoming hand to my men, and I gave a call; they cheered for Val'Nur. We mounted up together; his steed was cream colored, simply caparisoned. The light and the dark horses rode on towards the lights of the city. We were approaching the east bank of the river Demmis, which ran down from the plateau further north. Before we came to the citadel, Valko had put many questions, even toned, in the half darkness as we rode along. I had told him the state of the rift, the news from the Eastmark, the exact capacity of my troop and details of the stores we carried.

When we entered the courtyard, there was little ceremony but all was firmly ordered. The lord went his way through a certain door, a marshall sorted the men to their stabling and quarters. Dinner was being sounded in the lower hall within the hour; we would all lodge in the citadel overnight.

Ibrim and myself were plucked from the crowd by a houseman and led in through another door and up a carpeted stair. Valko dined in one hour in the Old Armory. My bath steamed before the fire in a rich, shadowy tower room. Boots, murmured the houseman, were not worn on the upper floors of the citadel unless they were soft-soled. Purselings or twales, the fashionable slippers, were even more suitable.

We laughed aloud when the fellow had gone; clearly we had come to a palace. The air of my room was not only perfumed but full of curious drafts and currents, lifting the thick hangings that were embroidered with scenes of the four seasons. I could hardly picture Knaar creeping about in purselings through carpeted halls. As I voiced something of this, Ibrim held a finger to his lips.

"Speaking vents," he whispered. "We can be overheard, Master!"

I curbed an urge to send him looking behind all the hangings. I dressed in my second best robe, glanced into a long glass, which cut me off at the neck, drew on a pair of good soft boots sewn by the ladies of Cloudhill and went to dinner feeling like a courtier. A page, knee-high, in yellow livery and tasselled twales, waited to guide me to the Old Armory.

We had come to so fine a household that I was anxious about my troop even though they were moderate in their habits.

"Take word to Gorrie," I told Ibrim. "Any man unseemly drunk will be fined!"

The page trotted ahead, and I followed through spacious corridors. The wooden floors and plain hangings of Cannford Old House, even the arrang-

ments of the Palace Fortress that I had seen, were
eclipsed by the citadel. It was a place smoothed
and made comfortable so that traces of the origi-
nal fortress were almost gone. It was light and soft
and decorated, with winding stairs leading off,
small bowers where music played, even an open
court with flowering plants and a fountain all in
the midst of the keep.

Liveried servants, waiting women, a few guards
were to be seen. Two pretty girls fled away, gig-
gling, then turned back to stare, and I gave them a
wink.

I heard them speaking, and in a few paces I
realised that one had said, "No one can be so tall
. . . he is a conjuring . . ."

And the other had replied, "My dear, they are all
giants!"

The accents of Lien. The garments of Lien, elab-
orate, lowcut, the most restricting but some would
say the most enhancing for a pretty woman. But
Lien? What had Lien to do with the city of Krail
and Valko of Val'Nur, Lord of the Westmark? I
was forewarned a little as we came to the door of
the Old Armory.

I have never in my life been able to slip unno-
ticed into a room. Sidling and lurking were never
my strong points. I came in, the music faltered, a
hearty laugh broke off, dogs began to bark. There
were nine or ten people in a room that is still to
me the most beautiful room that I was ever in.
There were firebaskets in a long white marble fireplace and overhead golden candleracks. Two wide
balconies swung out over that courtyard where I
had seen the fires lit at New Year and the beggars
dancing. The vista of Krail, the lighted city, across

the river, and the river itself with its traffic of
ships gave the Old Armory a watery dimension. In
that room we were in another world, suspended
above the water, which rippled and reflected upon
the softly painted walls and made the river-spirits
and fishes painted upon the ceiling swim gently.

The musician at his lute blinked dark eyes at me
and went on playing; a young girl sat near him
tuning another instrument. Valko lorded it before
the fire, deep in conversation with an older fellow
in a black velvet scholar's gown and fluted white
Lienish collar. Knaar sat playing Battle with a
lady in a golden gown; his look in my direction
was fierce and irritable. Duro, his elder brother,
Valko's image, lounged in a deep padded settle
and played with the dogs, two setters and a
wolfhound.

My eye was drawn to the man who had been
laughing. He sat with his lady who was beautiful
as a rose, delicately flushed in a spreading layered
gown of crimson and white, her nutbrown hair
held with a net of pearls and rubies. He was darkly
handsome, with hair brown-black and a trimmed
beard; his arched brows and the proud arch of his
nose were features of Lien.

The lady in the gold dress rose up and swam
towards me through the luminous chamber. She
was younger than her lord by twenty years, tall,
oval-faced, with dark hair caught in a heavy knot
at the nape of a slender neck and fathomless blue
eyes. She was Nimoné, Valko's second wife, step-
mother of his two sons, the only member of his
family for whom Knaar had a good word.

"Yorath!" she said for all the world to hear.

"Dear Yorath, welcome to Krail! We owe you Knaar's safety, if not his life!"

She led me forward and presented the noble visitors from Lien: Lord Alldene and his lady. I bowed low. The lady looked at me over a fan of pink feathers and the lord smiled, showing his teeth.

Valko said to his scholarly companion, "Hem Yorath is one of our newest commanders."

I caught the odd half-squinting look of this man, Master Rosay, also of Lien, then met Duro, who grinned and gave me his hand. I stroked the dogs and received a curtsey from the pleasant-faced young girl with the lute, the Lady Merilla. Then I was able to return to the table with its gilded set of battle pieces on their board and sink down next to Knaar.

"Goddess . . ." said Knaar under his breath. "What a circus! How fares the rift?"

"You have visitors . . ." I murmured.

"Folk from Lien," he said. "The wife is pretty Who knows what they want from our noble house?"

I had a first inkling of what it was to be the friend of Knaar and the vassal of his father Valko. Knaar really did not know who these people were; his father had not seen fit to tell him. I knew them well enough by sight, though Hagnild had complained that his scrying stones were imperfect instruments. I had seen "Lord and Lady Alldene" seated in their throne room at Balufir, among banks of roses. I had seen "Master Rosay" at their side, very decent, belying a reputation for magic and intrigue. I could even guess at the identity of the young girl, Lady Merilla. I wondered if the party had come by land or by sea. Nimoné, seated beside the visitors, answered the question.

"And you were none of you seasick?" she asked, smiling. "You were proof against the ocean?"

"Master . . . Rosay provided cordials," said the Lord Alldene.

I basked in the golden ambience of the room and took in the royal guests: Kelen, Markgraf of Lien, Zaramund, his lovely consort, the Lady Merilla Am Zor, his niece, sister of the King of Chameln, and above all, Rosmer, the old fox of a vizier. Hagnild had his own vanity; he pretended that other magicians hardly existed. His own brother was the exception. Certainly he despised the state-craft of Rosmer and the markgraf and deplored their cruelty. But I knew that he was aware of Rosmer's workings in the art.

"What is the matter?" demanded Knaar. "Is my father up to his tricks again? Who are these people?"

I sighed.

"Find out who they are," I said. "I am sure your mother knows."

"She is a jewel," he said, "but a bad player of Battle. See if you can win with black from her position."

"I cannot concentrate. Your citadel and your family and your guests are too much for me."

Servants came bearing the sweet wine of Krail in crystal goblets. No table was set, so I thought we must be dining in another chamber. Then, as the talk grew merrier, Valko and Nimoné walked to a certain place before the windows accompanied by servants. Knaar gave me a grimace. Nimoné clapped her hands, once, twice, and there was a

faint rumbling beneath the floor of the Old Armory. A long trapdoor opened in the flooring and
slowly a table rose into view, laden with golden
dishes and steaming, fragrant food. The servants
steadied the table and its heaped platters, locked
it into place and drew up settles. Everyone cried
out with pleasure and applauded this wonder.

"It is like magic!" cried fair Zaramund.

"Hush, my lady," said Duro as we took our places.
"My brother helped design this table, and he cannot hear the word magic."

"Well, there is none in my table," said Knaar,
rising to the bait. "It is a matter of honest winches
and pulleys, not the so-called dark art."

"Who would say that magic is not honest?" asked
the markgraf softly.

I was close enough to Knaar, seated as we were
at the foot of the unmagical board, to give him a
warning kick. He became aware that the visitors
were observing him with amused interest and that
his brother had somehow begun to make a fool of
him.

"Not I!" I put in heartily. "A magician might be
listening! Don't you agree, Master Rosay?"

The young girl, Lady Merilla, laughed aloud,
and everyone joined in her laughter. Knaar glow-
ered a little but held his peace. When Rosay or
Rosmer answered me, I noticed the timbre of his
voice, not deep but resonant. He leaned out a little
and stared at me, holding up a single round eye-
piece of colored glass or gemstone.

"To be honest with you, Hem Yorath," he said,
"I believe magicians are always listening. Yet honest men have little to fear from them."

Renewed laughter. We ate and drank at the golden table in the golden room. Knaar said to me aside, "So that's it. I know who they are, and I know why they are here. The Lady Merilla, poor wretch, is being shown off to my vile brother."

I wondered that Knaar, who had had as much military training as myself, thought of such a peaceful explanation for the markgraf's visit. I saw Lady Merilla's possible marriage with Duro of Val'Nur as no more than a pretext. I believed Kelen and Rosmer would encourage Valko to make war with the Great King.

I felt a growing uneasiness all through the evening. My head throbbed, my skin burned; under my robe I felt a sharp pain now and then as if my silver medallion with the swan of Lien had become red-hot for an instant. Before we rose up from the table, the sky outside had darkened. A mighty thunderstorm broke over Krail; rain washed away our view of the city and the river; a thunderbolt crashed directly above our heads. Rosmer stood with Valko observing the storm. He turned again and looked at the company with his seeing glass raised. I felt his gaze directed upon me again, and I was afraid.

The evening that had begun so well was a discomfort. I escaped as soon as I could, when the first of the guests took themselves off. Knaar teased me for "going to bed with the women," but Valko approved of my going and named the seventh hour of morning as muster time for the troop. The small yellow-clad page was called again to lead me to my chamber. He trotted along sleepily, but at the door of my tower room he gave me a broad grin. The storm still howled over our heads.

"Your servant says, lord . . ."

"What then?"

"It is a night for witches!"

He grinned again as I took coins from my pocket and gave them to him, then ran off into the maze of dark and light corridors.

Ibrim sat before the fire in my chamber mulling a crock of wine.

"Witches?" I said. "What we have here is a magician. Perhaps the Eilif lords of the High Plateau are reaching out towards Rosmer of Lien."

Ibrim had a secret smile.

"I waited only to mull your wine," he said. "This *is* a night for witches!"

"You may sleep by the fire, man," I said impatiently. "No need to go down to quarters.

Still unsettled I turned to the tall bed and drew the curtains a little. There, deep in the featherbeds of Val'Nur, her only covering, the Owlwife slept. I watched her enchanted, certain that the stormy night *was* all her doing, that my uneasiness was merely a summoning to this great good fortune. I called her name softly, and she woke, smiling, and held out her white arms to me. When I turned my head, Ibrim had already slipped away.

I had gone early to bed. Between times we drank wine.

"Master Hagnild did not approve of your messenger," said Gundril, "but he trusted me with a reply."

I broke the seal of the letter and was disappointed to see that it was so short . . . a few lines of that cryptic scholarly hand.

"Serve your new liege of Val'Nur faithfully," wrote Hagnild, "and all may yet be well. Believe me I have taken your letter to heart and my loyalties are as divided as your own, but I must go on a little. You did right to send the Dolt and his lady to the Southland. When the world ends here, as it will do, sooner than you think, I will go to my old home where the waters meet."

There was a postscript:

"Beauty can be a sweet mistress, but beware of those with pretensions to magic. Your friends in Nightwood wish you well."

I showed the letter to the Owlwife. She smiled a little.

"He is the finest of men," she said, "but there is a sadness in him. He guards a secret."

"You can tell me no more than that?"

"I cannot look into his mind," she said. "I am only a changeling."

"You are flesh and blood!" I said. "You are no fairy woman of the Shee!"

"No, I am not," she said, "but I was raised by them. They are my people. I am a changeling *to them*. I was given into their care as a babe in arms. My magic is of their kind and has little to do with the things of this world of men and battles and kings and the sons of kings."

"Lady," I said, "I have seen you in the service of two mortal men . . . Thilon of Val'Nur and Huarik of Barkdon."

"I must go about in the world of men," she said seriously. "Sometimes I have an errand from the Eilif lords, sometimes, as with Huarik, I must earn my bread."

"What was the story with poor Hem Thilon?"

"He searched for a cure for his sickness," she replied, "and came upon a cache of jewels, ancient treasures of the Shee. I entered his service to get them back again. I tried to cure his sickness with all my art, but he was marked for death."

"Now what is your errand?"

"I am your leman, your lover," she said. "And I will be employed as your kedran messenger and scribe. But there is light magic at work, too. Perhaps I am meant to guide you."

We spoke of Rosmer, that dark magician, under the same roof, and of the Eilif lord whom I had met on the Green Fort, near the rift. So much talk of magic made me perplexed and uneasy. The Owlwife soothed my brow and wound me in her arms again; she was my perfect lover.

I woke in the stormy grey light of morning, and Gundril Chawn was dressed to go down to the quarters of our troop. There was still time for me to sleep. In these last morning hours, I had one of my strange dreams. I dreamed that I woke in my bed in the tower room at the citadel and the storm still raged overhead. I saw the hooded figure that haunted such dreams, and I heard my name called. Then, for the first time the caller came closer. I saw that it was a woman, an older woman with jewels glinting under her hood. I lay with a feather-bed drawn up to cover my nakedness and the strange woman looked at me with a wry smile.

"So I have found you," she said.

Her lips did not move, but I heard a voice and knew that it was her voice.

"You cannot speak," she said. *"You are dreaming. Take care, Yorath. Trust no one, light or dark. Beware of Rosmer, the old monster. Do not serve Lien. My lovely swans are flown. Oh child . . . we are both like the dead, you and I, the dead or the unborn.*

Who knows where we are hiding? I must leave you. It is difficult for me to reach so far."

The lady's voice had softened almost to weeping, but now she raised a hand and I heard the storm rage overhead. Then the dream became confused and sociable as my dreams often were. I was among a company of fine lords and ladies who resembled persons that I knew or half knew: Thilka and Strett of Cloudhill, Nimoné and Valko, even Gundril Chawn, Duro, Knaar and the officers of my company. When I woke, I hardly remembered my dream; it had swirled away and it returned in broken images and phrases.

Now the sunlight was streaming in through the widened windows of my tower room, and Ibrim had brought breakfast. I dressed and was armed and tried to cast away all the clinging threads of my dreams and even of my love-making. I felt a distaste for all softness, even the luxury of the citadel. I must be a soldier and nothing else. I went down and saw to the mustering of the company, who were alert enough but somewhat subdued by their surroundings.

Softness was not going to be a threat to us in Krail; after this welcome neither I nor my men set foot in the citadel for several years. On this day we were given our orders by a ferocious captain of the guard. We had a choice of lodging: a wing of the third barrack in the Plantation on the other side of the city or a certain untenanted place in the city itself, the Hunters' Yard, on the river bank. We had time to inspect this place before riding to the Plantation in time for our first parade.

We set out in good heart and crossed over the Moon Bridge, which led to the citadel, and entered

Krail with our banner flying. Citizens going to market gave us a cheer from the street corners. I remembered Krail a little, and we had a young guard to show us the way. We went down the river bank past the High Bridge and found the Hunters' Yard. It was spacious and well-built but fallen into disrepair.

I went in with my captains, Gorrie and Hallin, and Quartermaster Münch. The Owlwife came with a salute and asked that the camp-followers might be allowed to see the place. I watched the wagons come into the yard and saw the wives and servants get down, exclaiming over the big stone house, half-timbered in an exotic, almost Lienish, fashion, and over the stables, the barn, the well. I realised that it would be hard to budge them.

I wandered into the barn . . . a proof that Krail had once been a country town whose livestock had gone the way of its hunters . . . and heard a soft call. The Owlwife stood in shadow, and two large shapes rose up from her outstretched hands. There were a dozen owls large and small gazing mildly down on us from the rafters.

"This is a fine place," she said, smiling.

"I am being persuaded, I see that," I said as gruffly as I could.

I went back to Gorrie and the others and said, "Well, shall we take the Hunters' Yard?"

There was a chorus of agreement. As veterans . . . some had been in the king's longhouse since they were twelve years old . . . they hated all barracks. The company cheered when they heard the decision; we left the camp followers in possession and rode on through Krail two miles further to the Plantation. So the Wolves came to dwell in the yard of the Hunters' and we never regretted it except perhaps on cold winter mornings.

The size of the Plantation and the scope of Valko's military arrangements were greater than any I had seen and rivalled those of the Great King. Among the broad fields of corn and cotton, beside a string of small ponds, he had brought the Mel'Nir talent for practical building and military organisation to its finest flower. The rural setting softened the look of the barracks, storehouses, stableblocks of yellow stone and brick, but day and night long the air rang with voices of command, the thunder of hooves, the cry of trumpets.

The War Lord of Val'Nur kept a thousand mounted troopers under arms, trained four hundred more in his longhouse and was liege to two other free companies ... the Sword Lilies and the Eagles of Gath Gayan, each with their separate barracks. Separate, it was said, for different reasons. The stockades kept men out of the Lilies' domain, even if those tall, fierce girls could look after themselves, and stockades kept the Eagles caged. These birds, two hundred of them, had an evil reputation: they looked and behaved like brigands.

So it was that when we rode in and presented ourselves to the officer of the watch, he looked us over with a grin.

"By Old Hop," he said, "are these your wolves, Hem Yorath? I think we've got a wedding guard here!"

"Wolves are handsome beasts," I said, showing my teeth.

We put on menacing looks and came to the parade ground on our mettle. We were in time to join

in a mounted drill and acquitted ourselves well
enough. Before I went in with my officers to present ourselves at Headquarters, old Captain Hallin
said to me, "Ah, I know the smell of this place,
Lord . . ."

"What's that, Captain?"

"The smell of peace," he said. "Of the Long
Peace. These men are for spit and polish, for tax-
gathering and helping with the harvest."

"Is not peace better than war?"

"Truly," he said, "but when the peace is broken?
We learned more in six moons campaigning among
the wild tribes of the Chameln than some of these
men have in twenty years as troopers."

We had been yoked in our drill with one of the
spans of light horse: fifty men of a height and
weight to ride swift horses. Now their officer, the
obrist of our hundred, came forward and we saluted him. He was under six feet, dark, about forty
years old: Obrist Quent, Hem Quent of Quentlon,
an ancient family of the Westmark. He returned
the salute unsmiling; he stared up at me with an
expression of hatred and contempt that froze the
blood.

"You drill badly," he said in a harsh voice which
he kept just below the level of a shout. "Free company does not mean a herd of bullocks. Extra drill,
after midday mess, understood?"

Understood. I presented my two captains. He
made a slighting reference to their service with
the king and their defeat in the Chameln lands,
then led us further into the duty room. The captain-
general of our five hundred or ten-span sat in a
pleasant alcove made of screens working with his
scribe lieutenants.

"Yorath," screamed Quent, "Landless man. Last rank ensign, unranked leader of free company of the Wolf. Captains Gorrie and Hallin, discharged veterans of Balbank, reporting to Captain-General Flieth."

The captain-general was a tall and genial man, who smiled sunnily at me.

"Yorath," he said, "formerly of Cloudhill . . ."

"A hero!" cried Quent. "The Butcher of Silverlode."

"He lent Captain Knaar some service there," said Flieth. "We must give you some rank, Ensign Yorath."

I was made a marshall of the army of Val'Nur. It was a convenient catch-all rank that could mean anything or nothing: a marshall could be a head groom, the leader of a special mission or even a general's herald. It was a rank above that of captain but below that of obrist; I was slotted into place.

"Question for Marshall Yorath," screamed Quent at once. "When will he move his dirty cutthroats and their whores into third barracks?"

With some relish I saluted again and replied, "My company will not lodge in the barracks, Obrist Quent, sir. We have been given the Hunters' Yard in the city."

From beyond the screens I heard a sound of soft laughter, quickly hushed. The officers of the Plantation were listening to our ordeal.

"Carry on, Marshall Yorath," said Flieth, mild as ever. "What is the state of affairs in the rift?"

I told him briefly, and we escaped. In the duty room we were received decently and made welcome.

"A pack of doves," said a lieutenant, "not wolves. Why didn't you clout the little bastard, Marshall?"

"Surely that was what he wanted?" I grinned.

The bloody-minded Obrist Quent of the Ninth never altered; he was like a natural bane, a cold wind in winter or a blazing summer sun. He used the light cavalry just as ill. It took me time to realise how closely he worked with Captain-General Flieth. They were like a pair of clowns at a fair, one gentle and smiling, the other snarling and hitting about with a bladder.

The Free Company of the Wolf gained a reputation for good behavior; we were long-suffering and kind; we did our drinking and roistering in our own yard.

On the fourth evening as we rode back through the streets of Krail to the Hunters' Yard, I heard a voice somewhere between earth and sky shouting, "Yorath!" There, hanging from a rope at about eye level, was a creature that resembled nothing so much as a giant spider.

"Forbian!" I cried.

I reined in and held up a hand. The little man clambered down, and I put him on the front of my saddle.

"Well, boy," he said, "you've grown well and done great things. I see you are ready for more good advice."

A lame beggar, especially one as crooked as my poor friend, was a strange companion even for the leader of a free company. Yet the presence of Forbian brought us nothing but good fortune. Our doors were free of beggars; in fact they cleared away all our refuse. We learned the best markets for our supplies. I found out the most honest goldsmith and sold the emerald collar of the Duarings for a fine price and pleased the company with the division of the spoils.

I was soon able to ride to the northern part of the city and come to the swordmaker's yard, with others of my company who had leave. We came into the yard with some dash.

"Is Bülarn the Master about?" I asked the boy who ran to hold Reshdar.

"Nay lord," piped the boy, "he is dead two years, warriors guide him home. Here is the young master."

Arn stood at the door of the forge, changed almost out of recognition. He was like his father and like his uncle, both at once. He was so broad that he looked squat, and the muscles of his arms were like tree roots. He stared at me with a slow smile that I remembered, and I knew that he was seeing that image from the forest pool where we had made wishes. There stood a mighty warrior in black armor mounted upon a black charger.

Finding Arn again, married to his cousin, Bülarn's eldest daughter, and the father of twin sons, was as close to finding my own kin as possible. In my snuggery at the Hunters' Yard, I could sit down at table with my beloved Owlwife, my servant Ibrim and my ancient Forbian Flink, busy with some scribe work. Arn, my friend, would come bringing me swords, and we would talk of old times. Knaar often came swaggering in, complaining that I outranked him at the Plantation, that the Yard was shabby, that his brother was a fox.

We looked out at the river and the citadel. The caravel that had brought the royal visitors from Lien had sailed away with nothing settled regarding Duro's marriage, but a war with the Great King was certainly brewing. Ghanor and Gol and Breckan of the Eastmark were furiously recruiting and stirring up trouble on the borders of Val'Nur. The point was that no one had determined where these borders were. The Long Peace had produced a zone of land between the king and the war lord where there were free towns, some looking towards the Palace Fortress, some towards Krail as their natural allies.

Valko, the Commander-in-Chief, had us tightly in hand all through a mild winter. The first buds of spring had the forces of Val'Nur, the magnificent army, untried in battle, eager to ride forth. A pretext was soon found: Prince Gol seized a village on the northwest corner of the High Plateau to quarter his New Hundreds. We marched out of Krail to the sound of drums and trumpets and the golden sistrals or war cymbals shaken aloft. Fires were lit at night to the Gods of the Farfaring and to the Soldiers God, the Light-Bringer. This was the year 327 of the Farfaring, the forty-third year of the Great King's reign, known for battles on the High Plateau at Aird and at Goldgrave.

The Free Company of the Wolf was sent west into the gentle hills of the free zone. Quent kept his light horse to do great things upon the plateau and we went off in high fettle to garrison a villa at Selkray on the sea coast. The expected attack in our region never came; we spent the summer fishing and looking out from our tower. We sent demanding recall, fretting with inactivity. At summer's end, a town in the hills sent up signal fires and we raced to its defence.

It was a small and hard-fought action against a

troop of light horsemen and kedran with the banner of a hawk ... the crest of Hursth of Hurhelm in Balbank. There were more than double our number, but they were tired and we beat them easily, driving off some and capturing the leader on open ground. I went in and took him myself, for he was a brave and nimble fighter. His horse was a light, tough grey, his armor was unmarked, he had an empty shield. At last he leaped down, cursing horribly, and let himself be taken.

"I'm not going to fight you, Yorath, you bloody monster!" he shouted when his helm was off.

"Benro! Benro Hursth!" I cried. "Goddess, you're dead! You died at the Adderneck!"

"No," he said bitterly. "I disgraced myself. I escaped. What are you going to do? Kill me?"

"Don't be a fool. This is my free company. We'll have you for ransom."

So we had tasted blood and taken one rich prize, for Hursth of Hurhelm paid dearly for his son. When we sent word of the action, we were recalled although it was barely autumn. A dull campaign, said the company, but next year it might be better. Krail was dirty and disordered; the winter was hard; Aird had been an undecided encounter, Goldgrave a defeat. Knaar and Benro sat with me in the Hunters' Yard and made big eyes at my sweet Owlwife, and we did not once question the wisdom of campaigning.

"When will you learn?" asked Gundril Chawn, when we were alone, this winter or maybe the next. "The Long Peace is done. This is the beginning of the Long War."

I rode out with Benro when his ransom was paid and bade him farewell.

"Thanks," I said, "for not trying to escape."

"I gave my word." He grinned. "Knaar and I were the troublemakers at Cloudhill, Yorath, but there is one great difference between us. Remember it. I can be trusted!"

The Free Company of the Wolf was always on the edge of the battle. At Krisgar, also called the First Battle of Balbank, we were brought in late and helped turn the tide. At Donhill in '29 we rode escort to Valko Firehammer and his staff; we watched from a hill as our hundreds gained the victory. We saw Duro, a poor soldier; almost taken by Ghanor's light cavalry: Valko set his teeth and sighed and permitted us to rescue his son. I was put forward as obrist, but the promotion was not confirmed. At a duty conference in the spring of the year '31, I turned on Quent at last, and in his rage he said too much. He called the company cowardly dogs whose leader was protected by those higher up. My duty was read out again: the Company of the Wolf would go west into the Chyrian lands collecting taxes. I flew into a god-rage or pretended to, overturned the table, punched Quent to the ground and took my men back to Krail, snarling.

I waited, and about sundown Valko came to the yard alone with only one servant. I heard his limping step upon the stair, four years of war had left their mark. He came in, and we sat very quietly together over a goblet of wine.

"What is it?" he asked. "Are you short of money? Are the men giving you trouble?"

He heaved a bag of gold on to the table. "Extra payment," he said. "Perks. I have a fund for it."

"Let me fight, Liege," I said. "Let the wolves do their share. Why do you hold me back?"

He sighed heavily.

"I take little heed of magic," he said, "but I've seen and heard some strange things. I know that you are an orphan, raised near the Inland Sea by some old scholar. What do you hold from Rosmer of Lien?"

I was surprised and wary. "He is a powerful magician," I said, "and a man of intrigue. I would not trust him to serve any interests but his own."

"He looked at you," said Valko, "and told me your parentage. He suggested I keep you unharmed."

I could not speak.

"He swore," said Valko, embarrassed, "that you are the bastard son of Prince Gol of the Duarings, the royal house of Mel'Nir. Do you think that is possible?"

He paused and lightly twitched his left shoulder. "Taking everything into account . . ." he said.

I thought of Gol of Mel'Nir, as seen in a scrying stone or riding out to hunt or on the battlefield. He fought well enough. Hagnild thought better of him as he grew older. Was this a father?

"Yes," I said. "Yes, it is possible."

"Gol has no heir," said Valko. "He could marry again and sire many princes . . . but with the fortunes of war . . ."

"Lord," I said. "How would this serve Rosmer or his master, Kelen of Lien? What else did he want?"

Valko smiled and shrugged. "I can tell you that too," he said. "He wanted Balbank. He needs a foothold across the river in Mel'Nir. It is part of

his grand design for the expansion of Lien. I think
he will make the Markgraf Kelen into a king. It
would suit him very well if the Heir of Mel'Nir
was a young man in the service of Val'Nur, a
power friendly to Lien. Of course he has courted
the Great King and Prince Gol himself, but now he
looks to us."

"Well, the present Heir of Mel'Nir lives in the
Southland," I said. "Princess Fadola has a son,
Prince Rieth of Mel'Nir, four years old."

Valko chuckled.

"Poor little devil," he said. "I hope this prince
has more wit than poor Rieth of Pfolben, that
great donkey who trained with you lads at Cloudhill."

We both laughed sadly, thinking of Rieth, blond
and empty-headed, who had died at the Adderneck.

"You'll go to the west," said Valko. "It will not
be a soft duty. I'll dress it up for your company as
a secret mission. The Lord of Pfolben may be mounting an army against us. You must come round
from the coast and check the garrisons at our two
fortresses by the Southwood. Understood?"

Understood. I told no one but the Owlwife of
Valko's revelation. I had thought so long about my
parentage that it sickened me; I turned my mind
away from it. I knew that Caco had lied about
Nils, the soldier, and Vida, the lady of Lien. My
silver swan meant nothing. My mother was doubt-
less some lady of the court, even a country girl in
service at the Palace Fortress. I had the notion that
many had known my true parentage and laughed
behind their hands. I even saw a likeness to Prince
Gol in my own face.

*   *   *

The Company of the Wolf went dutifully into the west, into the Chyrian lands. We rode now into the poorest part of Valko's realm, a strange and savage country, flecked with the tall dolmen of an older time. The folk were dark, not really small-built like the folk of the Firn in the Chameln lands, but short by our standards. We rode among the hamlets and lonely farms like invaders, the giant tawny warriors who had come through the mountains. The ways were foul, the summer wet and cool; there were high tides flooding the coastal villages. We took what money we could from the wretched people and heard no word from Krail.

So having taken little enough part in Valko's triumphs, we had no part in his misfortunes. Duro lost four hundreds on the plateau and lost his own life with them. Everywhere the forces of the Great King found the best lie of the land, the best weather, the best forage, and it was said that the Duarings had come into their own. Valko came home lame before the summer was half done, carried in a litter.

We heard of all this furthest south in our ride as we came to the fringes of the Southwood. A crowd of ragged villagers poured out of the trees, and among them were two men from the southernmost fortress, Lowestell, sent to find help. The news from Krail was terrible, the news from Pfolben worse. The sleeping giant, the Southland, and its lord, had awakened. Lowestell had been stormed, its garrison beaten; the other fortress, Hackestell, was under siege. A mighty southern army ranged over the High Plateau in the name of the little Prince Rieth, the Heir of Mel'Nir. The Lord of

Pfolben, I recalled, had ever been a friend of the royal house. The Princess Fadola—my aunt, the Princess Fadola —had told me so at Silverlode.

I withdrew to the nearest village, a miserable heap of stones called Coombe, and sent my own scouts back into the coastal lands we had left. Taxes would be remitted, we would literally give back the small heap of coin we had just collected and pay more besides if forces could be levied to raise the siege of Hackestell. I woke early in the morning in my tent and heard a noise like the sound of the sea. I had almost a ten-span of men and women eager to fight for Valko of Val'Nur, with more pouring in.

We divided and disciplined our horde as best we could and armed them with whatever came to hand. The Chyrian land seems to have an old dark-green net of short grass stretched over handfuls of stones, right for throwing. I went out with Chyrian scouts, on foot, and they led me through bog and briar to an old scrap of wall on top of a low ridge, two miles from Hackestell. We could see the southerners camped round the outer walls of the fortress, an excellent encampment. We went closer still, crawling through a patch of heath on our bellies, and came so close that we could smell the food cooking, see the wives hanging washing on the bushes. There were lookouts posted, but clearly no one expected an attack from the south or the west. I judged that there were three hundred troopers besieging Hackestell.

I sent the better part of the company north again, by night, and on the first fine day for half a moon, they came riding down the high road in bright sunshine. The besiegers—bored as only besiegers

can be—brightened up and quickly came to horse.
The little troop of the Wolf cantered and challenged at a safe distance. The besiegers moved out
a little; the Wolves retreated. It could not go on
too long. Before the southern hundreds drew themselves up to charge these insolent troopers, I came
from behind a screen of brushwood, mounted on
Reshdar, with Chandor, my standard-bearer. Ten
of my men rode out from hiding. I gave a long
battlecry, and it was echoed by a thousand Chyrians. I charged down a long slope with my men
strung out among the horde. We swooped down on
the besiegers of Hackestell like the Dark Huntress
and her war-hounds. The savage looks and cries of
the Chyrians had alarmed my own Wolves. They
remembered the wild northern tribes of the Chameln
lands.

The southerners had no chance. They turned in
disorder, seeing an army rush down on them from
the west, and the main body of my troopers took
them in the flank. The men of Val'Nur within the
fortress, seeing this unexpected deliverance, did
what they could. They fired a few last arrows,
hurled stones from their walls, and at last flung
open their gates and rushed upon the foe. The
awful shrieking cries of the Chyrian horde turned
to songs of triumph. Hackestell was relieved.

I knew the commander of the fortress for an old
friend. It was none other than Trenk, the officer
who had served Knaar, at Cloudhill and at Silverlode. Now he was garrison captain of the hundred
men at Hackestell.

"Godlight, lad," he said to me after his formal
greeting, "you have more luck than the Shee. This
is an army . . ."

My troopers were engaged in saving the southern horses. The Chyrians were being driven back from their plunder and mayhem in the camp.

"An army to save Krail?" I asked.

Trenk had more news of the southern army; the besiegers had taunted the garrison with stories of its advance, but that had been ten days past. Now the host of Pfolben was out of reach; perhaps they had already attacked Krail. We sat down in Hackestell that night and held a council of war. We admitted two local leaders to our conference. One was a young priest-warrior, Druda Strawn, the other a retired kedran captain who had served in all the lands of Hylor. Emeris Murrin was a middle-sized, brown-faced woman of about fifty, and she had a keen military judgement.

We stared at the map and saw that the golden city of Krail with its citadel, its bridges, the outlying barracks, was a place almost to defy defence from within.

"Marshall Yorath," said Captain Murrin, "we see it wrong. The city was never meant to be defended. Only the fortress was built for such a pass."

What she said was true, and we had all become too much bound to Krail to see the truth. I thought of the wives and children left at the Hunters' Yard, even of the Owlwife who had special gifts for survival. Valko was a war-lord; he would stock and defend his citadel.

"We must save both the citadel and the city," I said. "If the southerners are within, we will drive them out; and if they are not yet come in, we will keep them out."

"Brave words," said Druda Strawn. He was tall

and thin with a dark skull face and lank black braids. He did not conceal his feelings of contempt for our council.

"You must walk on the high ground," he said, "as those others have done from the southland. It is the last stronghold of the light folk in all the lands of Hylor. They are strangers to you ... 'fairy folk' or the like, though in old time they saw the men of Mel'Nir enter through the mountains, and they talked with their kings and nobles. But you must not forget that the high ground is their land."

"We mean no disrespect to the Shee," I said. "Would they help us, Druda Shawn?"

He laughed. "They do not waste words on soldiers, Marshall."

"Druda Shawn," I said, "I am sure you are in better standing with the Shee than any here, but I spoke with an Eilif lord five years ago and it was in the Green Fort, far in the northeast, by the Great Eastern Rift."

He looked at me very closely then, his green eyes glittering.

"I will go up this night when the moon has set," he said. "I will commune with the Shee and ask them to show the lie of the land at Krail. Then I will bring word to this council."

Trenk was restless, even Kedran Murrin a little skeptical, but we let the young priest-warrior go out and climb the plateau, which lay only a mile or so away from Hackestell fortress. We hung about "waiting for the fairies," as my officers put it.

Answer was not long in coming. Druda Strawn rode back smiling grimly and began to place counters on the map. Here were the southerners: troopers, light horse, encampments ... he had been shown it very plainly. The army of the south, ten thousand strong, had divided above Krail on the plateau. Two thousand had invested the citadel and sent an occupying force into the city while the rest went on to seek combat in Balbank or to meet up with its allies, the armies of the Great King.

"Is the king's daughter with them?" asked Kedran Murrin. "Is the new prince there, the child?"

"I doubt that," I said. "For if Prince Rieth fail but one finger joint, Ghanor the King is likely to have him killed because of the old prophecy."

I saw that Druda Shawn looked at me more closely than ever. "The king is an old man," he said, "and cannot live long. Would you be bold to kill such a king if he came within your reach, Hem Yorath?"

"Ghanor of Mel'Nir is an evil old ruffian," I said, "but I do not fight with old men."

I turned to the map again.

"We will not disturb the Shee on the High Plateau after all," I said. "I think I see where we should come into the city."

"Wait!" said the priest-warrior, "there is more . . ."

He lifted up his round bronze shield, stripped off its woven cover and propped it up on a settle.

"Watch," he said harshly. "You must see all before the image fades."

Then he gestured, and the shield was like a mirror filled with whirling mist. When it cleared, I saw the city of Krail spread out before me, as if seen from the plateau. A fine day, the standard flying over the citadel . . . I saw the camp of the southerners and some movement on the city waterfront near the bridges. A normal traffic of boats on the river but no sign of fire or destruction in Krail itself. The image began to fade.

"Were those southerners unloading grain?" I asked.

Trenk smiled, my captains, Gorrie and Hallin, shook their heads, Murrin blinked sadly. No one had seen an image in the shield except myself and the priest.

"The Shee have done us good service," I said, "but they have the knack of making mortal men look fools!"

So we began the rescue of Krail while the army of the west sat down by Hackestell Fortress and feasted on the ample provisions of the southerners. Riders went out that night to the river Demmis; all produce, all traffic of fish, grain, fuel into Krail was stopped. We marched the horde by easy stages in a wide sweep to the northwest, training them a little as we went. I sent back into the Chyrian towns and villages not only the gathered taxes but extra foodstuff that had banked up in barges and fisherboats along the river. I bullied the riverboat captains and traders and scattered promises of payment in the name of Val'Nur.

We crossed the river many miles below the city and approached it from the west, through the rolling cotton fields that lay about the Plantation. Our excellent Chyrian scouts brought back word that the barracks was tenanted by wives and widows and by wounded men of Val'Nur, with only a few southerners patrolling at the entry to the city. The southern general, Egenar, had fallen into the same trap as we had done . . . his army still drew sustenance from the undefendable city across the river.

Our plan was to besiege the besiegers, and far off in Balbank an army of Val'Nur had turned home towards Krail.

We came in by night. We had sent no word into the city ... too many burgers seemed to be on good terms with the occupying force. When our cry went up, "A Rescue! A Rescue! Swords to Val'Nur!" the citizens either wisely kept their beds or rushed out and attacked the southerners. The garrison captain in the center of the city saw his danger too late and rushed to hold the bridges but in the light of dawn we secured them all. I had feared my Chyrian troops as much as the southerners, but days of good food and the awe they felt at entering the capital kept them from excess.

There was a spirited battle for the Hunters' Yard, where southern officers had been billetted. Our own folk turned up unharmed, camping in the barn with much of our treasure squirreled away. The true joy of a soldier's life is the moment when he gets down from his horse and takes his loved wife in his arms. I found the Owlwife there, in the owl-haunted barn, and as I held her close she whispered, "It has begun!"

Outside all the citizens of Krail were on the streets cheering. "Yorath!" came the cry, "Yorath! The Wolves and the Westlings!"

"Do you hear what those Westlings call you?" whispered Gundril Chawn. *"Ruada* Yorath ..."

"What does it mean?"

"Prince Yorath," she said. "It is the name given to princes of the blood."

So I was a hero in Krail and the leader of heroes. I can say that I trusted this acclaim very little, but I used it without scruple. In the service

of Yorath, his Wolves and his Westlings, the city
was brought to order, the wharves were tightly
held, good intelligence was brought in from east
and west. Across the Demmis loomed the citadel;
it had a patched look, for all the windows that had
made it a pleasant place had been bricked up back
to arrow slits. We knew who was within, from
Valko and his lady Nimoné to their servants and
the hundred men of the guard, all trained cross-
bowmen. The Sword Lilies were there too and a
remnant of the Third Hundred, "Valko's Own,"
the two regiments who had fought a rearguard
action against the southerners when the siege was
set down.

The southern general, Egenar, knew that his position had become more perilous with the loss of
the city and of the river traffic. He hurled all his
might, including his siege engines, against the citadel, to reduce it before the winter came or the
relieving army of Val'Nir returned. We looked on
helplessly. I rallied the Westlings and moved out a
little to the north, but the river bank was firmly
held. Sharpshooters with crossbows and the Chyrian
short bow on the Old Bridge and the High Bridge
did better.

The best help of all came from a bunch of irreg-
ulars who called themselves the Sewer Rats.
Forbian Flink brought me forty beggars or "veterans" from Darktown who claimed that they regu-
larly crossed the river swimming or on floats and
scavenged the sewers and the mudflats below the
citadel. They had plans. The southern camp was
bewitched: the siege engines burned where they
stood, fires broke out in the baggage wagons, the
pickets were loosed every night. The bane spread

into the unreaped fields beyond the Southern camp, which might have given them provisions. Soon they were in the midst of blackened wastes, the besiegers besieged indeed.

Far away in Balbank two armies of Val'Nur were still disputing the free zone with the armies of the Great King. In all the years of campaigning, little had been gained; thriving towns had been sacked, and the countryside stripped bare. Knaar of Val'Nur, for his father's honor, took a part of General Flieth's hundreds and was riding homeward over the plateau to relieve the citadel. He offered no battle to the southern army, clustered about Lort and the edges of the plateau. He came in time to chase Egenar, who broke off at last. The defeated general dragged the remnants of his siege army across the plateau, harried by Knaar's light cavalry. When the pursuit was broken off, Egenar's troops could not face the long way home. They went another way and fell upon the Great Eastern Rift and plundered it from end to end.

There was great rejoicing in Krail when the siege was lifted; the bridges were flung open, and the bells rang out from the garrison fort and the Meeting House. I rode over the Moon Bridge at the head of the Wolves, and the city and the citadel rang with my name. Valko, just able to sit a horse, came to meet me, and we rode in triumph through Krail. The wheel had come full circle: what I had begun at Silverlode, my care to save the rift, went for nothing. My act of mercy towards the Princess Fadola had raised up an army against Val'Nur.

Even the timing of this triumph was not good. Knaar arrived when the siege was over and was slighted by a quiet welcome. His brother Duro was dead, had died a hero. He was left with no one to hate unless it was Yorath, lucky Yorath, rumored to be a prince, who had stolen his father's good opinion. Everywhere he heard shouts for Yorath, his Wolves and his Westlings. I was indeed the hero of the hour.

CHAPTER
V

KNAAR SWIRLED THE GOLDEN WINE IN HIS CRYSTAL GOBLET and looked out moodily at the water. "This room reminds me of the Old Armory in the citadel," he said.

We were wintering out of Krail for the first time, at Selkray, that villa on the seacoast where my company had spent the first year of the war. The room where we were sitting looked out at the stormy western sea. The year was ending, the year of changes with the mystic number 333, and now we were both great men. Our officers sat at a respectful distance. Music played, two young girls in robes of painted tissue were dancing. Off in a corner a scrawny fellow was scribbling in a small Lienish book: Brother Less, the chronicler of great men.

"They are sisters," said Knaar. "Come Yorath, are you still such a bashful monster?"

146

Knaar had become more lecherous since his marriage. His bride was Sisgard of Quentlon, daughter of the fiery obrist, and she was at the citadel in Krail awaiting the birth of her first child. Knaar was Lord of Val'Nur. I wondered that I had ever thought him like his father. I had come to know Valko better after the siege was raised. I was a welcome guest in the citadel and helped the lord ride out in the spring on his last campaign. Things were going so badly for Val'Nur that there was no question of keeping me from the field whatever my parentage. It had been a year of splendid fights and splendid victories. I rode out as a General of Val'Nur and boldly quartered the prancing black horse of the Duarings upon my personal standard.

"I think you are still hankering after your jade," said Knaar, "your witch woman . . ."

"Always," I said lightly, taking a sip of wine.

For my sweet Owlwife had gone. I could have numbered the moons and days since I had last seen her. She had left me without a word; I did not know why she had gone. In the time that I had for reflection, I wondered if it was because of my many deeds of blood. I had done so many, had personally hacked to death so many mortal men, that the chroniclers had run out of words of praise. There was hardly a person that I knew, man or woman, who would not have excused these deeds and tried to turn me away from my morbid fancies.

By Andine in Balbank I had ridden down a child; I could still see the small broken body lying in the mud and the soundless scream of agony upon the mother's face. In the late summer of '32, after the Second Battle of Balbank, the master stroke for the forces of Val'Nur, I killed an old man. I came

round the side of a little hill, leading Reshdar in
the narrow way, separated for a moment from my
escort. A tall figure loomed up in my path: a party
of fugitives were hastening away from the edges of
the field. I saw this cloaked figure coming at me
with a roar, and I struck out with the flat of my
sword, tumbling the fellow down the rocks. His
hood fell back, and I saw with disgust that it was
an old man, his silver hair stained with blood . . .
Was it for these things, I wondered, that Gundril
Chawn had left me? Was it for my true parentage?
For now I knew all, I knew the truth, and the
Owlwife did not bide long with me after it was
discovered.

As I rode off to war again, in this same year '32,
with the ailing Valko, I stood in my room at the
Hunters' Yard and Ibrim helped me don my fine
new armor. Gundril was there and Forbian, perched
at his writing desk. As Ibrim tightened the neck
piece of my strip mail I was chafed by a thong; I
drew off the small pouch with Caco's amulet and
flung it to Forbian.

"There!" I said. "Some work for you, my friend.
Unfold my amulet so that it doesn't fall to pieces!"

I thought no more of it. I went into the field and
did great things and returned in autumn at the
summons of Nimoné. Valko had been brought home
again, now he was dying; Knaar was already at
his side. I made haste to the citadel, and Knaar
met me in the courtyard. He had a queer trium-
phant look; I had come too late. He did not even
bid me come in to give my condolence to Nimoné.
As I rode back with Ibrim over the Moon Bridge,
the palace guards had lit the death fire on the
highest platform of the citadel, and the trumpets

in the city were sounding a last wild call for Valko Firehammer. I came to the Hunters' Yard and greeted the wives and children of the company, all solemn for the lord's death.

In my room I found Forbian and the Owlwife sitting oddly still, as if they had hardly stirred in the moon since I left them. The lamps were lit; they had been waiting for me. I saw at last that their grave expressions were not only to do with the death of Valko of Val'Nur. Forbian pushed two strips of parchment along the table into the circle of lamplight.

"I made a transcription," he said dryly. "The old script is destroyed in places."

My amulet had been unfolded and delicately pasted upon a second parchment. The treasure that Caco had worn was in fact an official document from the Palace Fortress of Mel'Nir and it was one year older than I was myself. It was a safe-conduct:

"Let pass in all the lands of the Great King, Ghanor of Mel'Nir, Mistress Caco, widow of Yeoman Bray of Alldene in the Mark of Lien, waiting gentlewoman to Her Royal Highness the Lady Elvédegran of Lien, Princess of Mel'Nir, wife of His Royal Highness Prince Gol Duaring, Heir of Mel'Nir."

It bore traces of the royal seal and was countersigned by Pulk, a former captain of palace guard.

We sat quite still for a long time exchanging a few words. Did I understand? Yes. And was it possible. No, no it was impossible, but it had been done. Hagnild, the healer and magician from the Great King's court, had spirited away a marked child of the royal house, not to mention a waiting gentlewoman. I was no bastard. I was the true-born son of Prince Gol and of that young, golden-haired lady of Lien, the fair Princess Elvédegran. I drew off the silver swan that I wore and laid it on the table beside the safe conduct.

"You could be heir to half the world," said the Owlwife softly. "Kelen of Lien has no children . . ."

I saw that, too. The Markgraf Kelen's sisters, the three swans of Lien, had all married princes of other lands. The children of Hedris and Aravel, consorts of the Daindru, the Kings of the Chameln, were excluded from succession to Lien. Had any such provision been made for a male child of the youngest sister, Elvédegran? I shook my head as if to drive away a cloud of kinsfolk: Kelen of Lien, Aidris, the Witch Queen of the Chameln and Sharn Am Zor, her co-ruler, who was called the Summer's King, for his beauty and noble bearing.

"Yorath, Yorath," said Forbian Flink, with that contortion of his face that his friends knew for a smile, "I told you long ago to come to some kin . . . but I had not reckoned with all this!"

"What will you do?" asked the Owlwife, pressing my hand. "Surely you can use this knowledge to good ends. This war that presses so hard upon the poor dark folk, upon mortal men . . ."

"Valko is dead," I said. "Knaar will rule in Val'Nur. I must go back to my army in the field."

"Yorath . . ." she said.

I do not believe that I looked at her, but long afterwards I could recall how beautiful she looked, in the half light, in her green robe. At that moment there came a clash of arms and muted orders from below. I heard my name: "General Yorath . . ." and Ibrim looked in to tell me that the garrison obrist of the city and the city reeve waited below. I was the ranking officer in Krail, the victor of Balbank, and a great favorite with the citizens. I was required to light the mourning torches before the Meeting House. I went off and performed this sad duty and returned late to the yard after conferring with officers at the Plantation. The Owlwife came to my bed, but we spoke no more of my parentage or my soldiering. In the morning she was gone. I had neither seen nor heard of her again; I knew that she had returned to the Shee, her adopted folk. Once, as I rode on the High Plateau, I had gone out alone when the moon was high and cried out to her and to the Eilif lords to send me my love again, but I was given no answer.

In the winter Knaar was betrothed, and he married with great splendor at the New Year, 333, the Year of Changes. One other change was imminent: in the spring the Great King did not take the field, and it was common talk that he lay dying in the Palace Fortress. In the meantime Knaar drove the army of the south from the field, and I recaptured the free zone for Val'Nur. The armies of Prince Gol and his generals . . . one was Strett of Andine who had used his half-brother of Cloudhill so badly . . . did well enough, but we did better.

So between advance and foraging, between the hectic cry of the trumpets, the charging over bloody fields and the long exhausted silences of the aftermath of battle, the year went by. In the Maplemoon, as winter came down, Prince Gol sent messengers to Knaar of Val'Nur and proposed a truce. He would confirm this truce in the last moon of the year, in the Ashmoon. We were certain that this meant that the old king's death was upon us at last; Ghanor would breath his last as the year of changes waned. We waited with our escorts all winter long at Selkray villa, and now the Ashmoon was in its last quarter.

"He will call a truce for a year, half a year," said Knaar, motioning to the servants to refill our glasses. "What will you do with yourself, Yorath?"

"Take a long furlough," I said. "Look over the manor at Demford."

I was not telling the truth. I planned to seek out Hagnild and to search for my lost love, the Owlwife. I planned to do great things; perhaps it was the wine or the death of the old king and the old year. The manor of Demford, west of Krail, was Valko's gift to me in his will, along with the deeds to the Hunters' Yard. The small Free Company of the Wolf had been disbanded; those not dead or retired from service formed my escort. Chandor, the standard-bearer, had gone home at last to the Eastmark. The Westlings, on the other hand, had added a five-span to Knaar's army.

"I always liked Demford," said Knaar. "It was part of poor old Duro's inheritance."

"Here's the night half gone and no messengers in sight," I said. "We're going stale here like two middle-aged generals."

"Speak for yourself!" said Knaar. "What we need is a fool. You have that fool, that deformed dwarf back in Krail . . ."

"The trouble with Forbian is that he is no fool," I said, yawning. "I'll check the lookout before we take our walk."

"No hurry," said Knaar.

I stood up and stretched. The dancing sisters, who were crouched by the musicians awaiting fur-

ther orders, cowered and fluttered their eyelashes.
I looked around for Ibrim, but he was not there. I
had sent him back to Krail two days before with
my good Reshdar, who was ailing: the fodder at
Selkray did not agree with him. I had ordered
Ibrim to look in at the Hunters' Yard; I still hoped
for news of the Owlwife.

I drank a round with the officers; it was a sign
for them to dismiss if they had no duty. I went up
alone to the low tower and found that besides the
two watchmen, Brother Less, the scribe, was there
before me. We leaned on the parapet and looked to
the northeast, to the downs flecked with snow and
the road the messengers must follow from the Palace Fortress.

"The year is going, Brother," I said. "Have you
found your enlightenment?"

"No, lord," he said in his papery voice. "No,
lord, it may never come in this world. The Lord of
Light grant it to me in the next."

"Tell me, Brother Less," I asked, "is this Lord of
Light, whom you honor, the same as the Light-
bringer, the Soldiers' god?"

"Yes, lord. He is Inokoi, the Lame God, and he is
worshipped in the land of Lien."

"Well, I have had my enlightenment," I said. "If
there is a truce, I will do all in my power to extend
it. I will try for peace."

He stared at me in the half darkness.

"Lord," he said, "General Yorath, that is enlightenment indeed!"

I went down feeling less heavy in mind and
body. Knaar was waiting in his cloak on the ter-
race of the pleasant garden room; a servant swung
my own cloak about my shoulders. We wandered

off on our nightly walk. It was Knaar's own way of keeping his health in the languid routine of the winter quarters. We walked as we always did up to the clifftop and peered down at the seals who lived among the rocks. A pair of servants paced after us. The night was crisp; the grass under our feet was heavy with frost, and snow lay in the hollows about the villa. We stood on one headland and less than a mile away there was another with a good road linking them. We usually walked about halfway down this road to a certain standing stone and then turned back.

This night we had hardly reached the stone when there came a sound of running footsteps.

"What's that?" said Knaar.

The man pounding along from the next headland was a stranger in servant's dress; the two men with us, both from Knaar's escort, drew in closer.

"Help!" panted the man. "The wagon will go over the cliff!"

"A wagon?" I asked.

"Slid on the frosty ground . . ." he gasped. "There is a lady in it . . . hanging by a thread . . . it will go down! In the name of the Goddess, lords or whoever you be, help me!"

"Come on then," I said, "we'll help, man! What lady is this?"

The man reached out and plucked Knaar by the sleeve.

"Oh come," he said. "She will not say her name . . ."

We were already running with the man and climbing the slope to the clifftop. I saw the dark shape of the wagon canted over the edge of the cliff. Before I reached it other dark shapes rose up: ten, twenty men, wrapped in their cloaks.

"A trap!" I said. "Here, Sergeant, give me your sword, I am unarmed."

"*I am armed*," said Knaar of Val'Nur.

He drew his hand from under his cloak and plunged a dagger into my side.

I felt the blade strike a rib, drew back with a cry of pain. I seized Knaar by the wrist, flung him aside and kicked down the sergeant as he came at me. I snatched up his sword and prepared to sell my life dearly. I was full of fear and rage, thinking of the trap that had been so carefully set by my friend, my own liege lord. I shouted aloud for help and heard how my voice rang out in the frosty night. How could my escort in Selkray villa not hear it? Had they turned against me, too? Now I was in among the crowd of assassins. Hacking and thrusting like a madman, and I had no breath to cry out. I slipped in the frost and thought of Huarik the Boar. I was no longer the young champion of Silverlode. I was more experienced, more dangerous, but I was older, and I had learned to fear death.

Knaar stood back from the fight, nursing a broken arm and taunting me through his own pain. A stream of unreasoning hatred poured from him, a resentment that had festered for years. I saw that he had raised up a horde of my own ghosts to fight me, for the smaller men who cut at me with long curved blades were Danasken assassins. I brought down two or three and now fought with my back towards the clifftop. The wagon had been hauled onto level ground. Yorath the Fool, the deformed fool, crowed Knaar, had been lured into the trap by a cry for help, by a lady in distress.

Now as the swordsmen pressed me close and I bled from many wounds, a tall man stepped from behind the wagon and called a halt. He was a warrior of Mel'Nir, tall as myself, but somewhat younger: a champion indeed.

"Know my name!" he cried. "Know my name, Yorath Nilson! I am the Lord Fibroll!"

The name meant nothing to me. The newcomer attacked, and I knew him for a swordsman less skillful than myself. He called to the Danasken to draw themselves away so that he might come to me, and as they moved back one fell down at my feet, a little man. I snatched him up in my left hand, lifting him high in the air by his bunched clothes. At that moment I remembered.

Whether from remorse or loss of blood, the world grew misty before my eyes and I set the man down again. I shoved him harmlessly back amongst his fellows instead of dashing him at the Lord Fibroll. I stepped back to the very edge of the cliff where they could not follow me. I thought of the rocks and the boiling surf that might lie below and saw again that old man I had slain in Balbank, his silver hair dabbled with blood. I lowered my sword.

"Hem Fibroll," I said, panting. "I remember your name."

"Let me come at you then!" he cried.

"No," I said. "I will not fight you. I will fight no more."

"Coward!" he cried. "Where is your honor?"

"Where is yours?" I asked sadly. "You have been drawn into treachery by Knaar of Val'Nur."

"You murdered my brother!" cried Hem Fibroll.

"I killed him," I said. "I flung him down and killed him in a fit of god-rage when I was sixteen years old. He had ridden down and killed an old woman, my foster-mother. I have long been sorry that I killed Hem Fibroll and his fellow trooper. Make what you will of that. I will fight no more."

I cast aside the sword that I carried, and we heard it fall into the water. Then I turned my face to the stars overhead and I cried out to the powers of earth and sea and sky.

"Hear me!" I cried. "See where I am! I am Yorath Duaring, true heir of the royal house of Mel'Nir. I am Yorath the Wolf, and I have cast away my sword!"

Then with the last of my strength I flung myself over the cliff into the sea.

The icy water took me, and I sank like a stone. I was so close to death from my wounds and from the freezing water that I seemed to be already in another world. Whirling dark shapes moved all around me, over and under me as I sank down, then raising me up again from the rocky floor of the sea. I saw the stars again and breathed and lost my senses.

I came to myself in a dream of soft arms that kept me from the cold and a swift movement through the water. I turned my head and saw a face next to my own: dark eyes, flowing hair, a smiling mouth. It was almost a woman's face, and the bodies that pressed against me, furry and soft, were like the bodies of women. I knew that I had fallen among the Selchin, the seal-wives, who live among the seals and share their nature. Now they bore me swiftly through the waters of the western sea. They did not speak, but their eyes were full of tenderness.

Daylight woke me, pressing upon my eyelids, which were gummed together with blood and sea salt. I moaned with pain. The journey with the seal-wives had ended, and my wounds were no longer numb. I pried open my eyes and could not see the sky, but I felt a cold wind blowing and I lay on stone. The least movement caused me pain. As I tried to turn on my side and draw my sodden cloak about me, a wound on my back opened and I felt warm blood gush out. I tried with my good left hand—for my right hand ached from gripping a sword, and a Danasken blade had given me a cut on the forearm—to press the cloak to my back and close the wound. The salt water had a sharp sting.

I saw that I was on the threshold of a very old stone tower, it was a ruin, tumbledown and deserted. White sand stretched out to meet the incoming tide, and I saw the marks in the sand where a whole troop of seal-wives had dragged a large, limp body up the beach to the doorway of the ruined tower. I saw grass growing beyond the tower and grey rocks; I guessed that I was upon some island in the midst of the western sea.

I was all alone; no sea birds flew by; the sound of the sea was muted. Against the tower grew a small tree, stunted and black, with a few dried leaves still clinging to its branches. I stared into the ruin and saw a wonder: a spring of water in a broken stone basin. Slowly and in great pain I dragged myself across the stone floor to the spring and drank and tried to bathe my wounds. A pale wintery sunlight shone into the round cell where I lay; I saw that the stones of the tower were hacked with runes and with script. I saw a string of runes and made out the name *Ross* and again *Ross Tramarn* and when I painfully craned my neck to see further *Ross Tramarn, Prince of Eildon*. I laughed feebly and wondered aloud that so mighty a prince had inhabited this desolate place.

I woke again and it was thick night. From being cold, now I burned with fever; I feared for my life, thinking of deadly wound fevers.

My mind wandered. A voice spoke to me in the darkness, a woman's voice, very clear and distinct: "Young lord?"

"Who speaks?" I demanded. "Are you the spirit of this place? Can you help me?"

"I am no more than a voice . . ."

"What place is this?"

"This is Liran, the Isle of Sleeps."

"Are we alone? Is there no one else?"

"Only an apple tree," said the voice, "and it is very stupid."

"I will die here, cast away . . ."

"No," said the voice, "you have been placed here by some magician. No one can die on Liran's Isle. The spring will help to heal your wounds; it has magical properties. Who are you, young man, to warrant such care?"

"I am Yorath, Heir of Mel'Nir," I said. "I am a prince, though I have hardly lived as one. I was a soldier. . . ."

"Tell me . . ."

I spoke of my life. The voice prompted me and laughed a little and sighed and wept as I did, telling of my life.

"You have done much for so young a man," said the voice. "How will you go on?"

"I will change my life or I will die," I said. "If I come off Liran's Isle, I will not be a soldier. I will not be a prince, a ruler of Hylor. I will seek out some place far from the haunts of men and live there simply as I once lived in Nightwood as a boy."

"Will you live alone?" asked the voice slyly.

"If need be," I said. "The Owlwife, my true love, has forsaken me."

"First, Yorath, you can help *me*," said the voice. "I have waited long ages, but now the time has come. Help me, and I will reward you."

"Spirit, I am very weak. How can I help you?"

"I am imprisoned here under a spell. You can set me free. I must change my nature."

"I will help you if I can," I said.

"I will trust you," said the voice. "Here is your reward. I will tell you a secret, and you must tell it to no one light or dark or the way will be lost again from that moment. You say that you would live far from the haunts of men; then this is the path to take. You will be healed, and when you are strong again you must journey into the Chameln lands. You must go into the northern mountains beyond Last Lake and travel northwest along a wide frozen river that edges its way down into the distant White Ocean. Go to the place where this river bends around a black rock. From the top of this rock you will see to the south a place where three fire mountains stand; one has crumbled away and the two others are almost burnt out. Find your way over the fallen mountain and there it lies . . . lost Ystamar, the Vale of the Oak Trees."

I felt at last a small stirring of my own spirit, a gleam of light in my darkness.

"I will do it!" I said. "Thank you, spirit. This is a rich reward."

"I hope you come to it," said the voice, "for now I will tell you the secret of Liran's Isle. The spring will help you to sleep, it will heal your wounds, but it will cause you to forget all that you have told me: your friends, your heritage, even your name."

I was very much afraid.

"This is a dreadful thing," I whispered. "In the name of the Goddess ... I must drink. I have already taken water from the spring. When will I forget?"

"Day by day," said the voice, "from the present to the past. Names will go first. You stumbled over a name or two in your story."

"Everyone does that ... forgets names ..."

"Who was that chronicler in Selkray, the one seeking for enlightenment?"

"I know the man you mean," I said, "but I cannot quite ..."

I saw his lean, dark face, I recalled our last meeting upon the watchtower of the villa, but the name had gone.

"I will go mad," I said. "I will lose my soul!"

"No," said the voice, "you will become very peaceful. And here is my second reward. I know how you can regain your memory. In the morning go to the apple tree behind the tower and strike down one of its magic fruit. Hide this away in your cloak. Tell no one you have it. When you have been taken from the Isle, you will one day find and eat the apple and you will remember."

"But if what you say is true, I will forget all about the damned apple!"

"No one forgets to eat and drink," said the voice. "You will eat the apple because you are hungry. It will keep fresh."

"Spirit," I said, "I do not doubt you, but I am puzzled. Prince Ross of Eildon was once on this island. Did he drink from the spring? Did you speak to him?"

"He was here seven years long," said the voice, "but it was before my time. Perhaps he bewitched the spring. The Princes of Eildon put me under a spell . . ."

"You have done me a great service," I said. "What must I do to set you free?"

"Go to the door of the tower," continued the voice evenly, "break off a branch of the ash tree that is growing there and cast it into the sea."

"Agreed," I said, "but will you not tell me your name even if I forget it again?"

"I am called the Alraune."

Then I saw that daylight was coming into the ruined tower. I was alone. Only the stunted black tree scraped against the stone in the morning wind.

My fever had lightened and many of my wounds were healing. I was still very weak and in pain. I heaved myself up, clinging to the basin of the spring and then to the wall of the tower. I came at last to the black tree.

"Alraune," I whispered, "which branch shall it be?"

There was no answer, but the branches twisted about and one offered itself to my left hand. I took hold of it firmly and stripped it off downwards where it joined the trunk. There was a shriek of pain and, shuddering, I turned and threw the branch down clumsily into the receding tide upon the sand. The waves washed over it and drew it down into the water. All at once the branch was gone, and a woman stood there with the waves washing about her ankles. She was slender and pale, with long hair of a greenish yellow. She flung out her arms and danced on the sands, naked except for her long, wild hair.

"Farewell!" she cried. "Farewell, Yorath! Farewell to Liran's Isle!"

Then she ran down into the sea waist deep, flung herself down into the cold grey water and swam off strongly to the northwest. I watched her until she was lost in the mist upon the surface of the sea.

When I turned back, I saw that the remains of the black tree had fallen down. I took it up and found that its roots had dried up, it was no more than a heavy, dead stick. I stripped off a few more branches, and using it as a crutch, I limped out and looked at the island. It was very small; the further shore was less than fifty paces behind the tower, and there in a patch of greener grass stood the apple tree. I limped painfully towards it, and as I came up it moved its branches. I stood on the thick grass and gazed up among the leaves.

"Mortal man," whispered the apple tree, "I am the tree of wisdom . . ."

"Tree of wisdom," I said, "where are your fruit? I cannot see them."

"They are very precious," said the tree.

"I do not think you have any fruit," I said. "The birds have eaten it!"

"Birds!" said the apple tree shrilly. "Look, foolish mortal! Behold! On this branch here!"

I lifted up my ash staff and struck down an apple and caught it as it fell. It was firm and golden green. I sank it deep in the pocket of my cloak, a roomy inner pocket where I had kept battle plans. As I limped away, the apple tree still preened itself and said, "I am the tree of wisdom . . ."

I sat by the spring in the tower and had to drink a little. I tried to turn my mind away from the throbbing of my wounds. I felt a sudden chill as if hailstones were sliding down my back. I turned my head and saw that a part of the wall had become smooth and black, like a dark mirror. A point of light shone in the depths of this mirror and there appeared the figure of a man. He was smooth-faced and pale, with long dark-red hair and a blue robe glowing with magic fire. I saw that the magician who had brought me to Liran's Isle was Rosmer of Lien.

"General Yorath," he said, his voice full of concern, "I heard your cry for help and had you brought to this island."

"Master Rosmer, I owe you my life."

"Highness," he said earnestly, "I saw from the first that you bore the aura of the Duarings, the royal house of Mel'Nir. Lately I have discovered even more . . ."

"Master Rosmer," I said, "I will not lie to you. I have reason to believe that I am the Heir of Mel'Nir, only true-born son of Prince Gol. Do you see this silver swan that I wear?"

He peered out of his mirror and gave a sigh.

"So it is true," he said. "Hagnild Raiz has pulled off a master stroke. You are the child of the Lady

Elvédegran, the youngest sister of my liege the Markgraf Kelen. You are not only the Heir of Mel'Nir, you may be the Heir of Lien."

"How can this be?"

"The children of Queen Hedris and Queen Aravel, the consorts of the Daindru, the double rulers of the Chameln lands ... they are barred from succession to Lien. You are not, poor fellow."

"Master Rosmer, I beg you to bring me off this island."

"A boat is already on its way, Highness, with as much wind as my magic can raise up to fill its sails. It will take several days. Rest and heal your wounds with water from the magic spring."

"A magic spring?" I asked. "I hope it has no evil working!"

"None at all, Highness Yorath," said Rosmer. "There is also food on the island."

"Magic food?"

"No," he said, smiling. "A sea chest of sailors' provisions in the ruins of this tower. I will look in again."

His image wavered in the dark mirror, and then he returned and said, "Highness Yorath, who attacked you last night?"

"Knaar of Val'Nur," I said, "and some hired assassins. I seem to remember another man, a lord. It is all very cloudy."

Rosmer smiled again and faded from view. I went into another part of the ruined tower and found the sea chest of sailors' food. It was well-preserved but salty. After a meal of salt pork and black bread, I had to take another drink of the spring water.

*   *   *

Rosmer, the man in the mirror, came back now and then. I had been doing some fishing with tackle from the sea chest, and I had lit a small fire to cook the fish. I felt very peaceful.

"I think you have done a lot of soldiering," he said cheerfully. "Can you tell me your rank?"

"Ensign," I said. "I think I made ensign at that place in the east, the horse farm. Did I tell you of that time?"

"Yes, you did. And you came to the city in the west of Mel'Nir . . ."

"Yes, a fine place. I think it is called Krell, Krall . . . you know the place I mean. Good sir. I must tell you that I have wounds that will not heal . . . this one on my leg. I have been injured in some battle, and I need a healer."

"You will come to one. I am sending a boat for you. In the meantime drink from the magic spring. It has healing properties."

I slept deeply and had no dreams. I wandered all over the small island. When I came near to the green tree behind the tower, it drew up its branches and cried out, "Go back! Go back! I will not give you any!"

I could see no fruit on the tree.

A man appeared in a dark mirror. I asked him to tell me his name again, and he said it was Rosmer.

"Tell me," he said, "What is your name?"

"Yorath, of course!"

"What land do I come from, Yorath?"

"I'm sorry, Master Rosmer, but I don't know."

"And what was your native land?"

"That's easy," I said. "I am a man of Mel'Nir."

"What is the name of the old magic kingdom of the west?"

I shook my head.

"Do you remember a woman called Gundril Chawn?"

I was suddenly less peaceful. I felt a pain in my head.

"I feel that I should remember her," I said. "I am sick. I am still in pain. Did you say something about a boat, Master Rosmer?"

When he had gone, I sat looking out at the sea and thought of the name Gundril Chawn and found myself weeping. A picture formed in my aching head: a bird with yellow eyes flew through a dark forest. I strove in vain to remember the name of this bird, of any bird.

"Young man!"

A man in a blue robe stared at me from a dark shining place on the wall of the tower.

"Young man, what is your name?"

"Sir, I cannot tell you. I have lost my memory."

"Can you remember anything at all?"

"Yes," I said. "Yes, I am sure that once I lived in a dark wood, a forest, with a man and an old woman. I had a friend, and we climbed trees together."

"Nothing else?"

"A woman. I think I loved a woman. I long to remember her."

"Tush . . . the world is full of women," said the man, smiling. "I have come to help you, my friend. My name is Rosmer . . . can you remember that?"

"I will try."

"A boat is coming for you. Go out and wait on the beach."

I did as I was told. I sat watching the sea, and

presently I saw a ship with yellow sails that stood off the island. A boat was lowered with three men, and they brought it to the beach.

"Lord of Light," said an ugly man in a sea cloak, "this fellow's a monster! Hope he is quietened down."

"Come now, friend," said one of his companions. "Step into the boat. Master Rosmer—you know him, eh?—he bids us bring you off this island."

"Thank you," I said.

I limped down with the aid of my staff, wrapped my cloak about me and stepped into the boat.

My memory did not return, but once I began to drink the stale water aboard the caravel instead of that sweet, treacherous spring water on Liran's Isle I was much more myself. I could learn the names of persons, places and things and not lose them from one day to the next. I lost the uncanny feeling of peace that I had experienced; I strove to recall more of my past.

The captain of the caravel, a man named Adrock, treated me well. He had the third mate, who acted as healer and barber, take a look at my leg wound.

"Nasty," he said. "I can do no more than put a dressing on it, soldier. You must get it seen to when we make port."

Straightaway when I was on board the ship, I began to dream again. I had two dreams. In one I roamed a forest, hunting, and came home to a brown house and sat down to supper with the man and the old woman. The second dream was puzzling. I came riding up to a bridge over a river, and at the other side of the bridge stood the cloaked figure of a woman. She called to me, called a name. At last I heard the name and tried it out. By the time the caravel reached Balamut and set sail inland for Balufir, I had a name for myself. I felt as sure as I could be that I was called Yorath.

The river Bal was a wide and placid river, not quite like the river in my dreams. I stood on the high bridge of the caravel with Captain Adrock and saw the snowy fields and white-roofed towns of the land of Lien. On the right bank there were fewer settlements; a watchtower rose up here and there above a manor house.

"That land is called Mel'Nir?" I asked.

"That's right, lad."

He gave me a strange look but all the sailors did this and some raised their voices whenever they spoke to me as if I were stupid or hard of hearing. I was becoming shrewd; I checked the name of Mel'Nir because I had heard the men calling me "the Melniro."

"I think I am a man of Mel'Nir, Captain," I said.

He laughed. "You are that, lad." And he explained.

"The men of Mel'Nir are tall and strong and have your coloring," he said. "Anyone would know you for a Melniro."

We came in sight of the city of Balufir, spreading far and wide over the downs and crowding down to its river harbor with a forest of ships' masts. The caravel turned out of the main stream and sailed along a still, deep channel. Frosty sedges covered the banks; I stood with the captain again and he said, "In summer there are swans all over these pastures. Now they are flown to the Burnt Lands to escape the winter's cold. Look there, we're coming to it: there is Swangard."

It was a building hard to describe even if one had not lost a few words. I wondered why it had a large moat with no less than four drawbridges and why it stood upon a flat plain or piece of parkland. It was all of white stone, but in this cold season it looked almost blue. It was a long, rather low building with fanciful towers on its four corners and, in the center, a taller tower.

"What is it?" I asked. "Would it be called a palace? A fortress?"

"To tell the truth," said the captain, "folk around here call it 'The Folly.' A markgraf built it about two hundred years ago as a residence, shall we say, for his wife."

"A residence?"

"She lived there," said the Captain. "He kept her pent up because he was jealous. But he did not want to be too hard on the lady, so he prettied up the place, as you see."

"Who lives here now?"

"Why it is a Hermitage of the Brothers, the servants of Inokoi, Lord of Light, bless his name."

The caravel dropped anchor. I bade farewell to the captain, and in the dusk of a winter's day I got down into the ship's boat again and was rowed to a jetty. A pair of soldiers in bright blue livery bearing the emblem of a silver swan were waiting beside two brothers in brown robes. When I had clambered ashore, they led me up to a third man who stood apart. He wore a pointed black hood, edged with white, and a long black tabard, embroidered in silver, over his brown robe. As we came up to him, the brothers kept plucking me by the cloak and whispering, "You must kneel, you must bow the knee, it is the Harbinger . . . it is the Brother Harbinger . . ."

I saw that this was an older man, with a long, set face.

"I beg your pardon, sir," I said, "I cannot kneel. My leg is injured."

He looked up at me with an expression of cool interest.

"What is your name?" he asked sharply. "Do you know your name?"

"I think my name is Yorath, Brother," I said. "I have been wounded and I have lost my memory. Did Master Rosmer send you? He promised that I should come to a healer."

"I am a healer," he said. "Come into the Hermitage."

He led the way unsmiling, and the two soldiers and the brothers came after us. We trudged from the jetty to the edge of the moat, a long way over the frosty ground, then crossed a drawbridge and came into the outer court of Swangard.

In contrast to the chilly approach from the river, this place was warm and busy. There was a forge and a stable and living quarters around the thick walls. The brothers went about in their brown robes, bowing the knee to the high-ranking Brother Harbinger. I saw a few poor folk waiting to be fed at a kitchen and even a man selling hot chestnuts.

We came to another wall, a high white wall, and one of our soldiers lifted a heavy bar that locked a tall gate. Inside the wall was a neglected garden straggling around the base of the inner tower. Other guards, still in the blue uniform with the emblem of the silver swan, lifted the bar on the outer door of the tower. We went in and began to climb a broad staircase. I had to rest on the first landing my leg was troubling me so much, and the Brother Harbinger looked back impatiently. At the top of the stair was a guardroom and another barred door.

The rooms at the top of the tower were reassuring, for they were well-furnished and spacious. A small fire burned in a pleasant room with blue hangings, and beyond this bower was a bedchamber. The two brothers who had come in with the Brother Harbinger busied themselves with hot water and instruments. I was undressed and washed and my wounded leg was attended to. It was a long and painful process. I cried out at times, and one of the assistants soothed me and fed me mulled wine. At last I was put into a clean, soft bed-gown and given a bowl of broth.

When he had washed his hands again, the healer came and spoke to me.

"I am Jurgal," he said, "Brother Harbinger or First Teacher of this foundation. I must tell you, sir, that we have saved that leg just in time. Judging by the scars and bruises on your body, you have taken enough wounds to kill any normal man, even a giant warrior of Mel'Nir."

"Is that what I am?" I asked. "A giant warrior?"

"A soldier, certainly. And you remember the name Yorath?"

"I believe that is my name."

"Where were you before you came here?"

"I was on an island. The caravel *Goldbarsch* took me off and brought me here. I knew I was coming to meet a Master Rosmer, whom I understand is vizier of the Markgraf of Lien. Before that I remember nothing except a little of my childhood."

"You learn quickly enough," said Jurgal, "and you reason pretty well."

"Good Brother Jurgal," I said, "you have dressed my wounds ... for which I thank you heartily. You are a healer and a man of holy life. If you know who I am, why I have been brought to this place, or anything of my past history I beg you to tell me in the name of Inokoi, the Lord of Light. Try to understand my dreadful uncertainty ..."

I watched him very keenly. I saw by the light in his eyes that he did know something and by the way he dropped his gaze from mine that he would not tell me. I tried to search the faces of the two assistant brothers, but they were gazing raptly at Jurgal, their Brother Harbinger.

"You must try to sleep now, Lord Yorath," said Jurgal. "Master Rosmer will visit you soon."

I was left alone. I heard a noise of bolts and bars as the guards let out the brothers and then made the doors fast again. I wondered why the healer had called me Lord Yorath ... was it a slip that showed my true rank? I remained awake for a long time simply trying to remember; I did this very often from this time forward. I tried to remember by an act of will and by daydreaming, stringing idle thoughts together. I heard light footsteps come and go beyond the door of my bower; there were other chambers in the top of the white tower.

It seemed to me that I was in an unusually comfortable prison. I thought of the captain's story of a Markgrafin of Lien, two hundred years ago, who had been pent up in Swangard. Even as I thought of this tale, a woman, not far away, began to wail and scream and weep. Was this a madhouse? How did I know that there were such places?

I chased after a single image, a grating where madmen stuck out their hands, thin filthy hands. Fools Tower? Fools Keep? And at last I had it: Fools Fortress, not the true name of the place. I lay back afraid; I was completely delivered over to the mercy of my fellow men, and I began to doubt this mercy. The wailing woman who shared my tower was quiet at last, and I was able to sleep.

CHAPTER

VI

My PEACE HAD GONE. I SPENT DAYS AND NIGHTS IN A torment of anxiety and restlessness. I wracked my brains, listened like a madman indeed to all that went on around me. When my leg was mending, I limped about staring greedily from every window that I could reach at the world outside. The Brother Harbinger, who came to dress my wounds again, asked me many questions to determine the limits of the strange cloud that lay over my mind. To fill up the empty spaces left in my mind and to comfort me in my distress, he decided, naturally enough, to convert me to his religion.

On his third visit, he brought from under his fine embroidered tabard a small book bound in grey leather in the style of Lien.

"You think, Yorath, that you are still able to read?" he asked.

He gave one of his rare smiles, glancing at the four young callants who had accompanied him.

"I think so," I replied.

"Read to me from this book!"

Upon the cover of the book there was a sun symbol and the words *The First Book of Matten*. Inside there was a longer title that said: "The First Book of the Wanderings of Matten Seyl of Hodd, nobleman of Lien, and his Blessed Meetings with Inokoi, The Lord of Light." I read this out and then came to the famous opening passage of the Meetings; the callants all mouthed the words as I read. They knew this first book off by heart.

"I walked through a marsh and could not find a dry foothold. I fell into the morass. Wherever I looked there was ooze and mud. Tall reeds shut out the light. I saw a Lame Man in the marsh who held out his hand to me and set me upon a firm path.

"He said, 'Matten, you see that this marsh is wet and foul. Its green places breed pestilence. Yet see where the sun dries the marsh and sends light to drive away the mists and the darkness. Follow me into the light.'

"I followed the Limping Man along a firm dry path and we came out of the marsh. In the light of the risen sun I saw that this man was not of flesh and blood. He was of the spirit. I trembled and cried out: 'Who are you, Lord?'

"And he replied, 'I am Inokoi, the Lord of Light. Look now on this ugly marsh which we have left behind us.'

"I turned and looked at the marsh and saw that it was the world in which I lived. I saw that there were those who could never come out of the marsh, for it was their nature to breed and to brood in darkness and foulness. I saw many of my brother men who could seek the light and find out the spirit. I knew that the spirit was the better part of a man, his true nature. Therefore I cast aside all the foulness of the world. Just as the mud upon my hands and feet dried up and fell away in the sunlight so the evil that clung to my spirit fell away in the light of the living truth declared to me by the Lame God."

The Brother Harbinger and the callants all looked at me expectantly as I came to the end of the first passage of the *Book of Matten.*

"What do you feel, dear brother?" whispered one of the callants.

"I am a little afraid," I said. "I do not like to think of the world as a foul and ugly place. I know I am thrown upon the mercy of the world and the people in the world because I am wounded and have suffered some kind of brain-shaking."

This answer disappointed the callants. Jurgal, the Brother Harbinger, said to me:

"You are not 'in the world.' You are here with us."

"Brother Jurgal," I said, "I believe I am in a prison."

"Your wounds are being healed," he said calmly. "Keep this holy book, and it will heal your spirit. We will speak further."

So I read *The First Book of Matten:* the young nobleman's short and simple account of his six meetings with the spirit-being who called himself Inokoi. I read of Matten's worldly life, which he had cast aside, and wondered if I had done the things that he had done, namely, "consorted with women of little worth" or "drunk wine day long and night long and eaten rich food in a beastly manner" or "given out gold for luxurious trappings, toys and unhealthy amusements."

I wished that I knew when Matten had lived, how his story fitted in with the history of Lien and of Mel'Nir. I wished for a history book, a book of battles and kings and queens and their legends, set out with quaint pictures drawn about the letters and in the margins, a book . . . *yes, I remembered* . . . a huge book with its wooden covers bound in brown fur . . .

I tried to discuss *The Book of Matten* and the teachings of Inokoi with Jurgal, the Brother Harbinger. We touched upon the need for holiness of life and upon the need to heal the world, to "drain the marsh." We spoke of *The Second Book of Matten*, also called *Hiams the Healer*. It tells of Matten's friend and spirit-brother Hiams, founder of the Brotherhood. He too had been granted, at the end of his life, a vision of the Lame God. He beheld the six orders of creation, which Inokoi showed with the aid of an ear of wheat: kings and noblemen, priests and scholars, soldiers and merchants, farmers and handworkers, women, beasts.

I asked when Matten had lived and what had become of him. The Brother Harbinger smiled again.

"Matten is not dead," he said. "He has gone on his last pilgrimage."

"You mean he has died and become a spirit?" I asked.

"No," said Brother Jurgal. "He set out on a pilgrimage from First Hermitage at Larkdel on the river Bal at dawn on the first morning of the Birchmoon in the year two thousand and three of the Annals of Eildon, as time is reckoned here in Lien. He gave a large life-stone to Brother Hiams, our first Harbinger, and set out to wander the lands of Hylor. He believed that the Lame God would go by his side and watch over him. The light in his life-stone, preserved in the sanctuary at Larkdel, has never gone out. He was then thirty years of age so we call the year of his departure the thirtieth Year of Matten. In Hylor there are too many ways of reckoning the years; Matten was born in Hodd exactly two hundred and twenty-five years ago come the fifteenth day of the next Hazelmoon."

Brother Jurgal rose up and looked about at my bower, where we were sitting, and gazed a moment from a window with white-painted iron bars beyond the mullioned panes. He confided to me another great mystery of the followers of Inokoi, which touched upon the very tower we were in. It was called Ishbéla's Tower, for the markgrafin who had been imprisoned here at Swangard. She was a lady of Hodd, the mother of Matten. When she was widowed of the Lord of Hodd, Matten's noble father, she had so seethed with lust that she had caused the markgraf of that time to marry her and then to shut her up. So it was that the struggles of Inokoi against the foul influence of the Marsh-Hag, his greatest enemy, whom he always defeated, were mirrored here in the history of Matten, the pure and penitent youth casting aside the toils of his evil mother.

Without quite knowing why, I felt uncomfortable with Brother Jurgal's religion. Yet the image of Matten wandering the world pleased me.

I could look through a grating in the door of my

bower onto a corridor. I saw two old women who carried food and linen to the madwoman; Brother Jurgal would not tell me the name of the woman who shared my tower; he twisted his lips in disgust when talking of any woman. I saw another woman, a lady-in-waiting in a Lienish gown. She was fine-looking, a proud, plump beauty. I wished that she might come to wait upon me; I longed, in fact, to consort with her. It was a thing that it would be very pleasant to relearn with such a teacher. With or without my memory, I knew that the holy life of the brothers was not for me.

Rosmer came in seven days. He stood before me, a neat, balding gentleman with an odd half-squinting look. He was plainly dressed in a scholar's gown of black velvet and a white fluted Lienish collar. He looked not so different in his dress from Jurgal, the Brother Harbinger. Yet he was clearly a man of the world, a man from Balufir, the noisy, colorful, luxurious city that the brothers talked of in whispers.

"Do you know me?" he asked.

"Yes, Master Rosmer," I said, "but I think that when I last saw you . . ."

"Yes"—he sighed—"I had my hair and a blue robe. Vanity . . . pure vanity. I hear from the Brother Harbinger that you are making good progress."

"Master Rosmer," I burst out miserably, "I am in prison!"

"It is a hospital," he said mildly. "You are not healed. Tell me, what do you know of yourself?"

"What do you know of Lord Yorath?" I demanded angrily. "I am under an evil spell! Is this your doing?"

"Believe me, I saved your life . . ."

"For what? To be pent up in this prison like the poor Markgrafin Ishbéla? I will die here. I will fall into a melancholy fit . . . you will be to blame."

"Do not give way to such doleful dumps," said Rosmer. "I am not to blame for your misfortunes."

"Who then?" Will you say it is the work of the Marsh-Hag or my evil mother?"

Rosmer laughed aloud, then primmed up his mouth.

"The Lord of Light is not the best medicine for a man with no memory," he said.

He snapped his fingers, and the guards brought in baskets of good things.

"See what I have brought you," he said. "Books, fruit, wine . . ."

There was even a vase of roses, yellow, white and red. They were the loveliest flowers I had ever seen; they filled the room with their perfume.

"These are from the Markgrafin Zaramund's own winter-garden," said Rosmer. "You can see Alldene, the royal manor, from the window of your bed-chamber."

"I am a soldier, a man of Mel'Nir," I said. "What have I to do with the rulers of Lien?"

"You are our guest," said Rosmer. "What will make you more comfortable? Will you have music? A walk on the roof? It is too cold to go down into the garden."

"Who is that other poor prisoner, the woman who weeps and cries out in the night?" I asked.

"Alas, it is the Lady Aravel," he replied softly, "the Markgraf Kelen's only surviving sister. Queen Aravel, the widow of Esher Am Zor, a former King of the Chameln lands, and mother of the present

King Sharn. There is a double sovereignty in those lands, the Daindru, and Sharn rules with his cousin Queen Aidris . . ."

"The Witch-Queen!" I said. "I have been told by Brother Jurgal that there is a witch-queen in the Chameln lands."

"I am sure she dabbles in magic," said Rosmer dryly.

"Master Rosmer," I said, "I have no company here. I see a lady who passes by to serve that unfortunate Queen Aravel . . ."

"I think I know the lady that you mean."

Rosmer did his best to cheer me. In the evening of a long winter's day, a key turned in my door and a new gust of perfume filled my bower.

"Great Goddess!" said a sweet, bold voice. "I knew it at the first . . . you *are* a conjuring!"

She was a sight to make a Hermitage of brown brothers roll in the snow. A woman no older than myself, tall and full-breasted, with a low-cut Lienish gown, golden-brown hair caught up in a jewelled net, and a lovely, plump, smiling face.

"I have the advantage of you, Lord Yorath," she said. "I have seen you before, but I am sure you will not remember. I am called Zelline of Grays."

She carried a ribboned lute.

"Master Rosmer thought you might like to hear some music," she said.

"Lady Zelline," I said, "you are the most welcome sight that I remember!"

She sank down before my fire and played on the lute very skilfully. I asked her, first of all, where she had seen me.

"I know that you have lost your memory," she said, "but my first sight of you, Lord Yorath, will bring you little help. It was a fleeting glimpse we had of each other. It was—how the time flies—eight years ago in the citadel of Krail, the city in the west of Mel'Nir. You strode down a passage-way after a little scrap of a page dressed all in yellow. You were on your way to dine with the lord of the citadel, Valko of Val'Nur. I was a wait-ing woman in attendance on the Markgrafin Zara-mund, my cousin. I was with another girl, and we saw you pass by and could not believe that anyone could be so tall and strong!"

She fluttered her eyelashes, and I was almost overcome, not only by her divine presence but by this mysterious flood of information. She played more music, and I questioned her further.

"You really have lost your memory," she said. "I thought you might be foxing to deceive Rosmer. Poor boy, I can give you little help. You had newly arrived at the citadel, and yes, you were the friend of the younger son of Val'Nur, a dark boy named Knaar. You had both been in some bloodthirsty scrape up country, and you had just ridden in at the head of a free company of soldiers. Rosmer was in our party, of course, as well as Kelen, the Markgraf Kelen, and poor Zaramund and that wicked girl, Merilla Am Zor; after all our trouble to find her a husband, she ran away. She rode off one day when we returned to Lien, took her younger brother, Prince Carel, and a musician, and went into the Chameln land to her brother King Sharn. I expect *he* has married her to some savage chief-tain."

I shook my head sadly.

"I wish I could remember all these people . . ."

"It was a happy time," said Zelline wistfully,

"because Zaramund still hoped to bear a child, the heir to the land of Lien. Indeed she became pregnant for the last time when we returned from the Westmark of Mel'Nir. She lost the child at the new year. All hope was gone. Since then she has lived in fear . . ."

"The markgrafin? What is she afraid of?"

"That she will be put aside by Kelen, her husband, so that he can marry a new wife. He must have an heir. Zaramund's life is ruined: she has lived like a queen, she is a famous beauty, she had Kelen's love, for many years . . . but now . . ."

Zelline spread her hands.

"And you, Lady Zelline?" I asked.

"I have been married too, since that journey to Krail," she said. "I have two sons, my two dear boys, but poor old Fernan, my Duke of Chantry, is dead. I am a widow. I am, believe it or not, a Dowager Duchess . . ."

She looked at me with a gleam in her eye.

"Do you suppose Rosmer means us to marry?"

"Lady," I said, "you are a wonderful match . . . but what am I?"

"Rosmer would hold no one in Swangard who was not highborn." Zelline smiled.

I took the opportunity to kiss her hand, her smooth shoulder.

"Who knows if we are suited?" I whispered.

"One more song . . ." said Zelline.

She sang a ballad that was sad and sweet: "The Three Swans of Lien." It woke strange echoes in my reeling brain.

"It is no song for this tower," said Zelline. "Queen Aravel is the last swan of Lien."

"Once I had a silver swan, an amulet," I said. "I wonder what has become of it?"

The fire was dying; we could hear the wind howl about the white tower and see flurries of snow blown against the mullioned window panes.

"Oh my lord," said Zelline, "we are alive and warm, even in this melancholy place. I have been sent to cheer you."

So the fair Zelline became my lover. We clung together while the storms of winter raged around the tower. There were consequences of this attachment. I lost the sympathy of the Brother Harbinger completely, and I began to see the new religion that Rosmer himself was spreading throughout Lien for a narrow and twisted dogma. I understood that the Marsh-Hag was an insulting name for the Goddess, the benign spirit of the natural world. On a less exalted plane the love—even if it was a fleeting love—that Zelline and I felt for one another renewed my strength. I knew that Zelline, my splendid lover, was a creature as unfree as myself; the Duchess of Chantry was another vassal in the continual game of Battle Rosmer played with living men and women. Far from being content to stay in the tower at Swangard, I knew now that with or without my memory I must escape and throw myself upon the mercy of the world again.

Rosmer visited me several times; he was interested, he said, in my sad case. We walked upon the battlements of the tower with the guards, and he pointed into Balbank and spoke quite openly of his grand design for the expansion of Lien. Even now I cannot tell what plans he had for me: whether he could have restored my memory by his craft, whether he would ever have attempted to reveal my parentage or bring me forward as the heir of Lien.

We sat in my bower and gazed into a small

silvered mirror mounted upon a stand. Rosmer would tap upon the glass or place a token—a coin, a leaf, a twist of wool—on the table before the mirror. Then faces would appear in the glass; living faces, although some of those we saw were long dead. It was a demonstration of magical craft to equal any that I ever saw, but he set little store by it. It was simply a test of my memory or a game he played for interest and amusement. I saw a handsome man, hawk-faced, richly dressed, and another, somewhat older, with ruddy curls and a beard. The first was a stranger, the second I believed I knew. I had the sensation of discomfort, of yearning in my head that suggested a hidden memory.

"Kelen," said Rosmer, "the Markgraf. And Valko of Val'Nur, your liege lord."

He rewarded me with scraps of information, even with tales from the past told from his own peculiar perspective.

"Now see, now see . . ." he whispered.

A golden locket lay open before the mirror: it was filled with fine curls of hair, children's hair. Three young girls were shown in the mirror; they were taking turns to brush each other's hair. They were all beautiful, the youngest was hardly more than a child.

"The swans," said Rosmer. "The swans themselves. Hedris, Aravel and Elvédegran. Their lives were pure misfortune. They were ill-starred, endowed with beauty and rank and not much else. Perhaps, who knows, Elvédegran might have shown . . . Ah, it is too late. See, here is the Old Pen, the Mother Swan: Guenna of Lien."

The woman in the glass was darker than her daughters and, like them, very beautiful.

"A proud spirit," said Rosmer, "humbled at last. The most intelligent woman I ever knew, but *she* knew her worth far too late. Ungovernable. See here . . ."

A coin lay before the mirror. A strange man appeared; he had a piercing dark glance, blunt features, fair hair streaked with grey.

"I do not know him," I said.

"A magician," said Rosmer shortly. "A good healer as well. Once he cut me for the stone, eased my agony. Now behold: a face from Mel'Nir!"

An old man glared from the mirror; he had a terrible face, bloated and cruel, with hooded eyelids, down-curving lips. I gasped aloud.

"I know him!" I said. "I have seen him in a glass or a scrying stone, seated upon his throne. It is the old King, the Great King, Ghanor of Mel'Nir."

"Dead at last," said Rosmer. "It was long prophesied that he would die at the hands of his own kin, the Duarings."

"And was the prophecy fulfilled?"

"Who can tell?"asked Rosmer with his sideways look. "He was brought home to his Palace Fortress sorely wounded after the Second Battle of Balbank. He lay dying for more than a year."

"Who is the new king?" I asked. "Is he called Gol."

"You have that from the books," said Rosmer, "not from your memory."

He sorted through the pile of leather bound books that he had provided: a history of Lien and its neighbors, tales of Eildon, books on horsemanship, dancing, gardens, a book of strange beasts, a book of verses. He laid it before the mirror.

"Hazard," he said. "Robillan Hazard, one of our

poets. He and his fellows are part of the glory of Lien. But he came to grief . . ."

The poet had a wise, whimsical face. His hair, his brown moustaches, even his eyebrows all turned upward, but his wide grey-green eyes were melancholy.

"For all his masques and revels and tales of magic," said Rosmer, "he was a great purveyor of *discontent*. What was it that he said: 'the world's a prison . . .' No, I remember."

He recited softly

"I brave the streets, the marketplace, the fair,
Or seek some wilderness, the world forsaking,
In company I feel I am alone,
Alone, in solitude, I am not free.
My sternest jailer is my own despair,
The darkest prison of my own making."

I could not hold back; I laughed and groaned, impatient at the foolish poet.

"Oh you may protest," said Rosmer, "here in this fine . . . hospital. Hazard has come to understand captivity very well."

"He is in prison?"

"No longer," said Rosmer. "He had a taste of the wells as they are called, the dungeons of the Blackwater Keep, in the riverside district of Balufir. But now he is free and gone into Athron, so I am told."

He brought it out in a very matter of fact tone, but I thought it likely that the poet had been one of Rosmer's victims.

The vizier took more wine and bade me stoke up the fire. Then he sighed and murmured and tapped on the glass impatiently. A woman appeared, sweet-faced, with long blonde braids.

"Who knows this lady now?" he said. "It is Ishbéla, for whom this tower is named, the mother of Holy Matten."

"I cannot love the Lame God," I said warily. "I do not know what to make of the brothers and their religion."

"Most men and women lack virtue," said Rosmer. "A priesthood is an excellent thing. It will spread over the land and promote order. The Druda, the priests, of Eildon wield great power."

Then, having settled Lien under the yoke of the Brotherhood, he revealed another terrible thing. He showed yet another beautiful woman in the glass; he summoned her up with a red rose petal.

"Fair Zaramund," he said. "I have been very patient, but now the day is done, the time of roses is at an end. There . . . I am quoting Hazard again. A poem for the old Markgrafin, Guenna. They come and go, these women, like roses, like field flowers . . ."

Zaramund's image wavered and dissolved and was replaced by the image of a young girl. She was fresh-faced rather than beautiful, with light blue eyes and smooth brown tresses.

"A field flower," said Rosmer. "A daisy or a cornflower. Fideth of Wirth, daughter of a bumpkin knight with some distant connection to the Markgraf's own family. A country cousin."

I asked no questions, but it was easy to read some sinister significance into all the dry utterances of this man. My loss of memory, the cloud that lay over my mind, made me the prey of strange imaginings. I was uneasy in Rosmer's presence because of my plans and my hidden thoughts.

The task I had set myself, of escaping from
Swangard, was a formidable one. I was still well
guarded, and I saw that this was because of my
size and strength. I played the gentle giant; I af-
fected a limp and clung to my ash staff. I was
smiling, docile, stupid with my jailers. In secret I
exercised and trained my muscles, slackening with
inactivity.

I looked out undaunted from the top of the tower
at the garden, the high inner wall, the courtyard of
Swangard and the four drawbridges. The northern
bridge was never raised, it was rusted into place
and used as an ordinary bridge leading to a crossroads. Just where this bridge gave onto the courtyard, there stood the forge and the stables; I must
either have a charger that could bear my weight
or a two horse cart. I planned to go some way
westward along the bank of the Bal then abandon
my stolen horse or cart, swim over the wide river
and regain the land of Mel'Nir.

I watched covertly but eagerly as the spring
came to the garden of the tower: sooner or later I
would be taken down and allowed a walk in that
untended patch of green with its ruined flowerbeds
and untrimmed fruit trees. In the north there was
one tree I thought might bear my weight half way
up the wall. It was an old apple tree, once trained
against the wall but now gnarled and drooping.

The choice of a time was more difficult. Rosmer
of Lien must be far away, that was certain. I feared
his magic more than I did the guards and the
brothers. I stared at the courtyard and the northern gateway and observed the traffic that passed
in and out on different days. Firstday, Fastday and
Thirdwatch were too quiet and Midweek was too

busy, for it was market day. Fiveday and the Longwatch, the two days that ended the week, at least in the Mel'Nir reckoning, were better for my purpose.

As time wore on into the Willowmoon, the courtyard around the northern gate lost its wintery aspect. Beggars came and sat in the sun; the brothers cast off their gaiters for sandals; carts with spring vegetables arrived. Travellers went about again, and sometimes stayed at the Hermitage. I became aware of two new men at the forge, helping the aged Brother Smith and his two callants. One was a thin brown-skinned man who sometimes stood for a long time watching the tower. Once as I strolled upon the roof with my blooming and beautiful duchess, I believed he raised a hand in salute. The other farrier was a massive fellow who drove a cart with two fine large horses, both large enough to bear me comfortably. Still I watched and became used to seeing these two men and a certain lame beggar, horribly twisted, who sat minding a little hand cart full of clothesline props and wicker baskets.

I walked in the garden at last with my four guards, stalwart men of Lien; all went well and I was never more quiet. I managed to show that I was relieved to return to my bower and tired by the effort of walking so far.

The brothers who came to bring me food and act as my servants changed from week to week. A certain Brother Lee stood before me one morning; he was thin-faced, dark and very nervous.

"Steady, Brother," I said as he spilled my morning milk.

"Lord Y-Yorath?"

He fixed his eyes upon me with a beseeching look, and as I stared back at him he lowered his eyes sadly.

From Zelline I learned that the court would go on a progress to Nesbath, a town on the Inland Sea, the Dannermere, so that the Markgrafin Zaramund might take the waters. Rosmer, of course, would go with them. Zelline herself planned to go on this spring journey, but the poor madwoman, Queen Aravel, became ill and the duchess stayed to attend her. It was a duty she never shirked, although the poor woman was a violent and difficult patient.

On the first day of the Longwatch that ended the Willowmoon, Brother Lee brought my food at midday. He said, "You will walk in the garden today, Lord Yorath."

I made no reply. The frightened fellow became even more bold.

"You have friends," he whispered. "You might . . . go far . . ."

"Brother," I said, "I cannot tell friend from foe."

We were interrupted by Zelline, Duchess of Chantry, billowing into the room in her new spring mantle. The brother at once fell silent and averted his eyes while Zelline kissed my cheek.

"I travel to Nesbath to join the court," she said. "The poor lady is recovering, and she has others by her."

She bustled to and fro in both rooms snatching up her lute, a book of music, a box of sweetmeats, a scarf. I saw a feather fan that she had let fall beside a chair and carried it after her into the bedchamber. Zelline was searching for a brooch.

The fastening had broken during a roof-top walk, and she had slipped it for safekeeping into the pocket of one of my cloaks.

"There, your silver swan," she said. "These pockets are a treasure trove."

She flung the swan medallion onto the quilted bedcover. I picked it up and stared at it before slipping it over my head. Why did I have a swan of Lien?

"Come, what a boy you are Yorath," said Zelline, laughing. "An apple in your pocket!"

She threw it across the room, and I caught it. It was a fine golden green apple; I could not remember putting it into my pocket. Zelline gave a glad cry; she had found her pearl brooch. I bit into the apple.

My memory returned; I filled up with the memory of my whole life as a cup is filled at a spring. No time had passed but I remembered all my life to that time. I remembered all my training, my soldiering, how I had served Strett of Cloudhill and Valko of Val'Nur. I remembered how I led the Wolves and the Westerlings and became a great man, a general, and how I was struck down by Knaar, my friend, on the cliffs at Selkray. I remembered my lost love, the Owlwife. I remembered Hagnild and Caco and Arn, my boyhood friend. I remembered who I was by birth: the Heir of Prince Gol of Mel'Nir; the Heir of Lien.

I bit the apple again for good measure and remembered still more. I remembered all that had passed on Liran's Isle as my memory faded, all that the Alraune had said.

"Goodbye, my dear!!" cried Zelline. "I must fly away!"

I took her in my arms and kissed her.

"Good-bye, dear Zelline!"

Perhaps a crumb of apple remained upon my lips.

"Take care," she whispered, fingering the silver swan that hung around my neck.

Zelline swept out of my chambers, and I heard the guard at the head of the stairs lift up the beam of the door for her. I stood at the window of my bedchamber in Swangard, that royal prison, and looked at the north gate. I saw the brawny smith, the dark man, the crooked man. I called softly:

"Brother Less . . ."

He stood in the doorway staring at me.

"Brother Less," I said, "the spell is broken. I am myself again."

"Praise the Lord of Light, he whispered. "Lord Yorath . . . Prince . . . we have not much time . . ."

We heard voices beyond the barred outer door: the second guard had come up the stairs. In a few moments they would come and fetch me for my walk.

"The signal!" said Brother Less. "If I give the signal from the window, Lord, then a ladder will come over the wall by the bent tree yonder."

"Give the signal!"

"The guards?"

I picked up my ash staff with a sigh.

"I will take care of them."

He came past me, drew out a red scarf and waved it through the bars before the window. I slung on my old army cloak and went to the table in my bower. I had half of my apple left. I cut away the core and slipped it into my pocket. I divided the rest into a smaller and a larger portion and wrapped them in a napkin of linen. When Brother Less came to stand nervously beside me, I placed them in his trembling hands.

"Brother Less," I said, "I have no idea why you should do all this to save me. I hope you come to no harm."

"Lord," he said, "it is for the records, for the truth. I saw . . . I heard what was done at Selkray. I was a witness."

"Then for the truth do one more good deed," I said. "Here is the magic fruit, the apple from Liran's Isle that has restored my memory. I charge you to bring this larger piece to Aravel of Lien, the poor madwoman who is pent up in this tower, my mother's elder sister. And the smaller piece is for you, for your enlightenment."

He took the napkin and folded it into the sleeve of his robe. We heard the beam lifted.

"Stand in the doorway of the bedchamber!" I ordered.

I might have ordered the poor man to look afraid, but he did this anyway. I stood against the hangings on the left of my doorway. The young guard came in calling my name, seeing only Brother Less with a look of terror on his face. When he was in, I tripped him and caught him behind the ear with the ash staff. The second guard was unable to draw back; I struck him, and he fell in a heap across his companion.

I ran out and through the door at the top of the stairs and let the beam fall to lock it behind me. The staircase was dark. The lower door was ajar, and I could see the uniform of a third guard waiting on the threshold. I went very swiftly down the staircase clinging to the wall where I could not be seen. Then I limped painfully on my staff to the door and came out into the spring sunshine.

"There we are, Lord Yorath," said the third guard cheerily. "Where's your escort then?"

I stood aside to let him peer into the building, then whirled about, kicked him firmly on his broad rump and sent him sprawling through the door. I had the door shut and barred and I rushed at the fourth guard with upraised staff. He was standing half turned aside on the path. He swung up his pike with a look of fear; I struck it aside and felled him with a blow to the wind and a blow to the neck.

I raced through the tower garden until I came to the bent apple tree. A whistle sounded, and there was Forbian Flink perched on the top of the wall. He played out a sturdy rope ladder fastened on the other side of the wall. I scrambled up and over.

"Come then, Forbian!"

He clung to my shoulder, and we scrambled down on the other side. The ladder was attached to Forbian's upended handcart, and Ibrim held it fast. He smiled fiercely, and we had time to clasp hands before we ran to where Arn Swordmaker stood with the horses ready: two brown chargers; one for me, one for himself; and a swift red steed for Ibrim. We leaped into the saddles and went thundering over the northern drawbridge out of Swangard.

CHAPTER
VII

WE TURNED TO THE WEST AND WENT GALLOPING ALONG a good road beside the river. Ibrim had taken the lead, and we rode on and on, slackening our pace for passersby and market carts. We exchanged only a few greetings and followed Ibrim as he went deep into the Lienish countryside, down leafy lanes, through villages, across patches of untilled common land. We had put twenty miles between us and Swangard before we drew rein. There on the edge of a small wood, we dismounted and led our horses into the trees.

"Our first camp," said Ibrim. "Welcome, dear lord. Welcome back from the dead!"

We all embraced and clapped shoulders and shouted with laughter. Then we made camp and watered the horses at a brook before we sat down beside a small fire and I told my story. I recounted what had happened from the time I set out on my walk with Knaar of Val'Nur to the present time when, a few hours past, I had eaten the apple of wisdom from Liran's Isle. But I kept to myself certain things that the Alraune had told me and certain of my own thoughts.

At last I said, "Now my dear friends, I owe you more than I can ever repay. Pray tell me how you came here and found me."

Ibrim took up the tale.

"I brought your steed Reshdar back to the Plantation, and he was very sick as you recall. The sergeant horse doctor cured him and turned him out to pasture. He told me plainly that the poor animal had been poisoned, and I had a first thought of treachery. I wondered who would do such a godless act as poison a horse.

"I returned to Selkray in two days and found all in an uproar. General Yorath had been lost in the sea, fallen to his death from the cliffs trying to assist a traveller with a wagon that had come off the icy road. Lord Knaar was tireless in his search for a body along the seashore and clamorous in his grief for his lost friend and liegeman. He has never swerved from this, Lord. He has treated your soldiers well, held to your wishes for the Hunters' Yard, declared a day of mourning for you in Krail.

"I was stunned with grief, and I rushed down to the seashore with the other searchers and sat there mourning for my master. It came to me that you were not dead. I have a touch of the sight, as you know, from my ancestors in the Burnt Lands. I knew that you were not dead, and I had some half-formed suspicions of the manner in which you had fallen from the cliff. I sat upon the shore alone and prayed for Ara, the Great Mother, to enlighten me.

"After two days and two nights I was enlightened. First there came Brother Less down from Selkray villa. He told a strange tale. He had been standing alone on the tower the night you were lost; the two guards were suddenly called below to quell some fight in the duty room, but he remained on the tower. He saw you walk out with Knaar of Val'Nur and before that he had seen a few of Knaar's soldiers leave the villa with a wagon. He was too far away to see or hear all that passed, but it seemed to him that there was a fight on the further headland. He heard a voice crying out, your voice, crying for help. Even as he plucked up courage to go down and alert your escort, there came the alarm from Knaar himself and his servants. You were lost . . . plunged into the icy sea. He watched all that was done and kept his own counsel. He saw the wagon, the few travellers who said it was theirs. He saw nothing of this Hem Fibroll or his assassins, but I had already seen, among the things brought up from the strand by the searchers, two broken Danasken blades, which I thought came there by chance.

"Brother Less did not dare tell his tale to anyone but myself. Suspicion weighed heavily upon us. Yet we could not tell your escort and set them against the power of Val'Nur, against Knaar who is their liege, too. I sat by the sea and prayed still for guidance. One morning a seal-wife came up out of the sea and looked into my eyes and showed me a certain pool among the rocks. I gazed into this pool, and it became a mirror and in it I saw a woman's face."

"A woman?" I asked.

"A lady, I should say," said Ibrim. "She is dark, and neither old nor young. She is a mighty sorceress. I do not know her name. She spoke to me saying: 'Ibrim, your master, the Lord Yorath, is not dead. I will see that you find him, but now you must go back to Krail and wait at the Hunters' Yard. Tell his trusted friends Forbian, the beggar, and Arn Smithson of Nightwood. Bring the scribe, Brother Less, if he has stomach for an adventure to put in his chronicles.' "

"Well, Ibrim did as he was told," said Forbian. "He came to the Hunters' Yard where there were all long faces, believe me, and mine among them, mourning for your death, Yorath. I had taken out your testament, leaving the yard for a home for the veterans, widows and orphans of the Company of the Wolf. I did not know what to believe when Ibrim brought this tale of sorceresses and seal-wives. We went to fetch Master Arn Swordmaker."

"I was about to set out on a journey to the north," said Arn. "I had said farewell to my wife and my boys and girls and left the yard in care of my first apprentice. I meant to seek out Master Hagnild in Nightwood and tell him of your death. The Great King had died soon after New Year, and the truce had settled upon Mel'Nir. I was inclined to believe Ibrim's tale, for I recalled how we had done magic by a pool in the forest, long ago. I believed always, my friend, that you were of noble birth and it had long been rumored that you were the son of Gol, the new King of Mel'Nir. It seemed to me that powerful forces might be ready to save you."

"We sat in the Hunters' Yard every night and peered into a mirror as the lady had instructed me," said Ibrim. "On the last day of the Tannen-moon, the message came. The lady greeted us from the mirror and spoke again: 'Lord Yorath has been brought into Lien from a magic isle in the western sea. He is in the power of a magician, Rosmer, the Vizier of the Markgraf of Lien. Rosmer will keep him pent up and helpless, but he will not kill him, for Yorath is the Heir of Mel'Nir and of Lien, the true-born son of King Gol and his first wife, the Princess Elvédegran. This is where you will find the Lord Yorath.' "

"Then we saw that white prison, Swangard," said Forbian, "a place neither palace nor fortress. We saw that it was a hermitage of the brown brothers. And the lady said: 'You might bring Yorath out of this place when Rosmer is away from the city, from Balufir. None of you are known in Lien. Go to Swangard and spy out the tower. If you do bring him out, I will show you where to go. Let Forbian copy this map.' So I fetched parchment and quills, and a map of Lien was in the mirror. I sat and copied it as quickly as I could. Then when it was done, the lady said again, 'Good Luck . . . you will be rewarded!' We have heard no more from this lady, but here is the map showing exactly where we must go."

"We left Krail separately and secretly," said Arn, "and travelled together to Lort where we knew poor Brother Less was hiding himself. We persuaded him to join us. He did it for the truth, so he said, and for the saving of a prince of the blood. He agreed to travel to the Hermitage and go into it, for he is, after all, a follower of the Lame God, though he was trained at another foundation."

"I hope he comes to no harm on my account," I

said. "I cannot see that any will blame him for my escape."

"Now you know all, Lord," said Ibrim. "We were set back by your sickness, the spell you were under, but, praise to the Great Mother, you have been released."

"The point is this," said Forbian, "do we go on as planned? Do we trust this lady? She has served us well so far . . ."

"Is it a trap?" asked Arn. "Should we go back to Master Hagnild? Should we cross the river and return to Mel'Nir?"

"No," I said, "we will go on. I do trust this lady. I have seen her in my dreams. I think she must be some kin of mine who knows the ways of Lien."

So we rode on, following the map, through the beautiful land of Lien between the two rivers. Now that my memory had returned, I found that I was faced with all my old cares again and with new ones besides. I yearned more than ever for my lost Owlwife and counted the moons and days that we had been parted and wondered if we would ever meet again. I puzzled over the treachery of Knaar of Val'Nur. But one thing was certain, my face when I saw it in a forest pool, was that of a bearded man. I had been denied the privilege of anything but moustaches for more years than I cared to remember, but now I was not a soldier any longer.

We were riding through a well-ordered, thickly populated country with fine towns, decent villages and elegant country houses among the trees. For all that, we found it a finicking small place for those who have lived in the broad countryside of Mel'Nir, and we crossed it in a week at the narrowest part. I began to understand Rosmer's grand design better; for all its order and high living, Lien was too small, too full of people. The spring weather broke—I thought I recognised the lady's work—and we rode on through heavy rain and windstorms. If there was any pursuit, we never heard of it.

We came at last to the river Ringist, the border with the Chameln land. Over the swift-flowing river there loomed the dark trees of the Great Border forest, clothing the slopes of the mountains. We passed a town called Athery and saw a Chameln town across the river in the rich mining district called the Adz. Still we followed the map and came to a place where the Ringist plunged through a gorge; there was a wooden bridge over the river, just as I had seen in a dream. We were instructed to cross this bridge, but on the other side there was no sign of the lady. We rode on through the dripping trees of the border forest.

"This is better," said Arn. "We're safe in the forest."

"It smells of home," I said. "Of Nightwood."

But Forbian shivered and moaned and said that he preferred the city. Ibrim allowed that he liked to be able to see further ahead: the High Plateau and the Eastern Rift had always pleased him.

"At least I have come on a journey," said Forbian, from his place on the front of my saddle. "I never thought to travel the world or come into Lien."

We followed the river and saw on the other bank, in the neat fields, a large white building, which was a foundation of the Moon Sisters. The map was nearly at an end, but we could not guess our destination. We turned up a narrow stream that ran into the Ringist. There was a clearing or what had once been a clearing, now thick with underbrush and nettles and young trees.

I saw tracks at the base of a tree stump and said, "The Kelshin know this place."

"Not the Kelshin," corrected Forbian. "Those others . . . what are they called? We have come into the land of the Tulgai."

Behind the trees there was a ruined building of some kind; I saw the corner of a grey wall. It was raining steadily as we came to the oak tree marked on our map, a spreading forest giant. We sat in our saddles with a sense of disappointment; no one stepped from behind the tree to greet us, no Tulgai swung down from its branches. Ibrim gave the signal as he had been instructed: he rapped three times upon the trunk of the oak with his sword hilt. Nothing happened. I moved my horse closer, bent down and struck the trunk three ringing blows with my ash staff.

There was a sound like the rending of the air overhead or like a chord of music. Before our eyes the scene was changed: the clearing was green and filled with sunlight. It rained still among the trees and across the river, but here was another magic place where the weather was a matter of craft. We rode forward amazed. There between two wooded hills was a small keep with towers and turrets, the same that I had once seen in the forest pool.

I led the way across the green fields; at a path to the keep we got down and led our horses. Music sounded, like distant trumpets, I thought they were calls of the house of Lien. So we came to the open door of the keep, and at the top of a stairway stood an old man and an old woman welcoming us into the house.

"Come in," they said softly. "Come in, Prince Yorath . . ."

The old man came down and took the horses, and three or four servants in hooded tunics ran up to help him lead them to the stables. We followed the old woman into the hall of the keep, which was cool and shadowy. We could hear music, the laughter of children, the clash of pots and pans in the kitchens. The old woman took our cloaks and bustled us further into the pleasant hall, rather bare of furniture but painted in friendly colors. There were flowers and leaves arranged in the long fireplace. A door opened, and the silver trumpets sounded faintly. The lady came forward to welcome us.

She was of middle height with brown-black hair threaded with grey and dressed in Lienish fashion under a silver net. Her gown glittered as if green light was trapped in its folds, but I saw that she used little magic on her face: she had an ageless beauty. She looked at me with an expression of great tendernes.

"Dear Yorath," she said, "welcome to Erinhall. Good Ibrim, Arn Swordmaker, Forbian, you have served your friend, Prince Yorath, most truly. Pray you, let me speak to the prince alone. Go with Mistress Bowyer to your chambers, and soon we will all sit down to dinner."

When we were alone, she smiled and said, "Do you know me?"

"I have heard your voice in my dreams, lady," I said, "and I have seen your likeness once in Swangard, but I can hardly believe . . ."

There was no sound to be heard now, a silence had fallen on the keep. Far away I thought I could make out the footsteps of my friends mounting the stairs. The lady said, "I am Guenna of Lien. I am your grandmother."

Her eyes had filled with tears. I took her hand, and we sat down together. She held up a silver medallion, a swan of Lien.

"Mine was the first one," she said, "and I gave one to each of my daughters. Hedris gave hers to her daughter Aidris, the Queen of the Firn in the Chameln lands; and Elvédegran, your mother, wife of Gol of Mel'Nir, placed hers upon your breast."

"Grandam," I said sadly, "I come from Swangard, and there is a lady there . . ."

"I know," she said. "My daughter Aravel is confined in that place. Who knows what became of her silver swan? Her son Sharn does not have it, nor her daughter Rilla, nor the youngest one, Carel. Alas, Yorath, there is no magic in these poor silver swans. When I gave them to my three girls, I could do no more magic than conjure up a few pictures in a wishing well."

"But now, Lady," I said, "I think you must be a mighty sorceress. This is a magic place."

"Erinhall was built by a Lienish nobleman, one of the Denwicks, as a hunting lodge," said Guenna. "He had the land from the Daindru, the twin rulers of the Chameln lands, in payment of a debt. When I first saw it, years ago, it was in the midst of a small overgrown park, but the building itself was sound, more or less as you see it now. The first magic that I learned to perform had to do with the hiding of this place. The real Erinhall stands in a clearing. Passersby on the river and in the forest and even those who might look from afar through scrying stones see only ruin standing in a wilderness. If anyone chanced to come through the forest, they would be prevented by strong barriers. The Tulgai, the small folk of the forest, keep me supplied with game, which they leave by the Boundary Oak."

"I saw Erinhall," I said. "I saw it in a wishing pool in Nightwood. I had wished to come to some kin. Raff Raiz, my friend, had us all make wishes that day."

A man gave a gentle cough somewhere in the shadowy hall.

"Come then!" said Guenna of Lien, smiling. "Yorath, I cannot entertain you in royal state, but I have another guest who has come to welcome you."

A man in a robe of white wool came slowly towards us. For a moment I thought it was Hagnild, but then I saw it was a younger man, his hair grey-blond, his features more rounded, his expression stern, his dark eyes piercing. It was Jalmar Raiz, Hagnild's brother, the father of my two friends, Raff and Pinga, with whom I had spent one magic summer.

"I bring you greeting, Prince Yorath, from Aidris Am Firn, Queen of the Chameln lands, sharer of the double throne of the Daindru," he said formally.

I asked after his sons at once, and he told me that Pinga waited for him in Achamar where they served Queen Aidris. Raff Raiz had become a merchant adventurer in the lands below the world. I found him less easy and pleasant than Hagnild.

"Master Raiz is a healer," said Guenna, "and he has come here with great speed and secrecy. Yorath, let him examine you."

"Surely," I said, "but I am sound in wind and limb, Grandmother."

"I hope it is so."

She left me alone with Jalmar Raiz, and I asked

at once, "Master Raiz, why does my grandmother live in this exile?"

"She hides from Rosmer, her sworn enemy," he said bluntly. "She watches him and thwarts his plans if she can."

"I have heard Rosmer speak of her as if she were dead," I said. "Is that what he believes?"

"He believes that she is incurably crippled and living in that hospice of the Moon Sisters across the river," said Jalmar Raiz. "People from the court at Balufir bring offerings to the banished markgrafin on feast days. They see a pitiable old woman, half blind, unable to move or speak. I do not know how this working is done. Most likely it is a real invalid with the looks of the markgrafin put upon her by magic."

It was a gruesome picture.

"Who knows all this?" I asked.

"Very few. Even I did not know it until I had served Queen Aidris for several years. King Sharn has had some encounter with his grandmother."

"But the members of this household . . . the servants?"

"There are only two living servants," said Jalmar Raiz with a grim smile, "the old man and his wife. The markgrafin is also attended by wraiths . . . by her own conjurings."

"She has risked discovery on my account," I said.

"You are the Prince of Mel'Nir," he said. "You are the only grandchild that this poor lady has seen in the flesh for some years and a child long believed dead, the child of her beloved youngest daughter. And more than all these things, Yorath, you are the Heir of Lien."

A silver trumpet sounded, and the old steward, Master Bowyer, begged leave to show me to my chamber. Jalmar Raiz accompanied me and found that in spite of my "assassination," my sojourn on Liran's Isle, and my imprisonment in Swangard, I was indeed perfectly fit. The Brother Harbinger had done good work. Jalmar Raiz questioned me shrewdly as he poked and prodded as if to make sure that my wits were sound.

So there began for me and for my friends a marvellous strange time in Erinhall. We dined to the sound of music; we were surrounded by the sights and sounds of a great house. The hooded wraith servants were all about us, and there were other wraiths. One might see children playing upon the lawns, peacocks in the orangery, even hunters riding home. In the great hall there were sometimes lords and ladies dancing in fantastic costumes and gilded masks. When I appeared, silver trumpets sounded, and the dancers bowed to me. I lived the life of a prince in exile, a prince of shadows.

I sat with Guenna of Lien in a kind of indoor garden, and she questioned me very closely about my imprisonment in Swangard and my conversations with Rosmer. I found it more difficult to answer than I expected; we were too far apart, in age and in the kind of lives we had led. I told her of Rosmer's words when he showed the image of the Markgrafin Zaramund, and then the image of the young girl, Fideth of Wirth, a distant connection of the house of Lien.

"What does it mean?" I asked. "I did not mark his words much at the time, but since I regained my memory . . ."

My grandmother was tense and excited.

"He will put her aside at last," she said. "My son's wife is barren, poor creature. I remember when she was a tiny girl, five years younger than your mother, Elvédegran. She has been markgrafin, the flower of the court, for twenty years, and now she will be put aside for the young girl, Fideth of Wirth."

"Why now?" I asked. "Is there a reason?"

"I can guess," said my grandmother, smiling. "Perhaps it is more apparent to a woman. Fideth is pregnant by the Markgraf Kelen, and she is a young and unspoiled girl of good family. Kelen . . . and Rosmer . . . are sure that she will bear Kelen's child."

"What will become of Zaramund?" I asked.

"She will be proclaimed 'barren and unfit for marriage' by the Royal Council," said Guenna. "It is a brutal proceeding, but there are worse things. It makes no reflection on her virtue. Kelen might have done this long ago, but he loved his wife and he feared her family, the Lord Merl of Grays and his sons."

"Grandmother," I said, "Rosmer would do nothing . . . worse?"

"So you have learned to fear him?" she said. "I do not believe that he would do the lady harm after so long."

She rose up distracted and walked among the dwarf trees in their tubs, touching the leaves, then went up to her tower room where she kept her scrying stones and worked her magic.

There were more common occupations for us at Erinhall: Arn and I did handwork, repairs about the house; Forbian did his copying and illuminat-

ing; Ibrim caught fish in the stream. My grandmother, when she summoned me every day, spoke
of the land of Lien. She was patient when I spoke
of Mel'Nir and of my life, but I wondered if it truly
interested her. She would beg me to explain a
certain military action, to play out a battle for her
on a tabletop in one of the lower chambers with
scores of battle pieces: king, queen, vizier, rider,
tower, soldiers. She followed very well, but the
true details of even a small encounter sickened
her.

One day I took up the figure of a vizier and said,
"In Mel'Nir he is called a general, except in the
Chyrian lands where he is a druda or priest."

"So it is in Eildon," she said. "And in the Chameln
lands he is a shaman, and in Athron the magician."

"Grandmother," I said. "What of Rosmer?"

She did not look at me, but took up another
vizier from our little plan, a black piece.

"He was my husband's advisor," she said, "and
mine too when I was left a widow with four young
children. I would not be ruled by him. I saw the
danger too late; I thought it was a matter of mere
intrigue. Rosmer stole away the heart and mind of
my son; he forced me to leave my throne; he sent
away my youngest child to the Palace Fortress of
Mel'Nir, where she died. He is suspected of com-
plicity in the murder of my elder daughter and her
husband, the King and Queen of the Firn, and he
sent assassins to kill their daughter Aidris. He has
driven my daughter Aravel mad. One day, if he
does not find me out before that time, I will cause
him to be killed."

We heard the sound of music, the voices of children playing, the splash of falling water. Guenna

gestured impatiently, and all was still. She rose up, and her sleeve swept aside the pieces in our battle plan on the tabletop.

"I am tired of the second battle of Balbank . . ."

When she had gone, Jalmar Raiz stepped out of the shadows.

"Perhaps the markgrafin should have an interest in such an important battle," he said softly.

"Master Raiz," I said, "I have told you what I know of Rosmer's grand design for the expansion of Lien. I wonder about my grandmother's design. I hope she has no plans to bring me forward as Heir of Lien."

"I am not privy to the markgrafin's designs, Highness," said Jalmar Raiz, "but if I had to stage your restoration, it would begin with your recognition by your father, King Gol. Hagnild would bring you to him. The Palace Fortress is already a happier place, although the old king's death was announced but three moons ago. If Gol were to acknowledge you as his heir, all else would follow. You might, if you chose, denounce your murderous friend Knaar of Val'Nur and spread dissension among his armies. A number of your old comrades in arms would return to your wolf banner; you would have at least an escort, at most a small army. At this point Rosmer would begin to make overtures to you again . . ."

"After my escape from prison?"

"He saved your life, Prince Yorath. He has a respect for the blood royal. He is dazzled by the prospect of a common heir for Mel'Nir and for Lien."

"There will be a new markgrafin and a new heir, a true heir of Lien!"

Jalmar Raiz laughed and flicked his fingers; a wraith appeared with wine and glasses.

"If life were as certain as that," he said. "Children, infants, are as frail as snowflakes. You are a healthy young man. Rosmer would suggest a meeting, as I said, and you would agree, relying upon a heavy magical protection woven by Hagnild, the Markgrafin Guenna and myself . . ."

"Is he then so dangerous?"

"Do you doubt it? I think you know of his special talent. He is indeed the eater of souls. He works upon the mind, the desires, the hidden fears of his victims. He is very smooth and modest. You yourself find it difficult, Prince Yorath, to bring all his images together: the sorcerer in his blue robe, the kindly gentleman in black velvet, the intriguer who might imprison and torture men and women at his will . . ."

"That is true," I said. "But if I did come to a meeting with Rosmer?"

"You would kill him," said Jalmar. "At once and with the combined working of at least two gifted magicians. You would puncture his hide with a silver knife, stick him with alder stakes, cut him to pieces, burn his divided corpse to ashes and scatter them into the sea."

I laughed aloud and took a gulp of the wine.

"Do you hear yourself, Master Raiz?" I said angrily. "Three magicians who can people the world with their wraiths, turn the weather, sour the milk, bring plagues of boils, speak over hundreds of leagues—*and I must kill this man!* I must stab him treacherously to death as Huarik and his men served the rift lords at the Bloody Banquet of Silverlode, as Knaar of Val'Nur served the late General Yorath at Selkray!"

"You do not understand," said Jalmar Raiz.

"No, I don't," I said, past caring. "I will have this out at once."

I raised my voice and shouted, "Grandmother!"

Jalmar Raiz was very angry; he frowned and started up from his chair. The markgrafin swept back into the chamber to the sound of silver trumpets. She wore a long pale robe that trailed along the floor and a tall silver coronet. The shadowy room gradually filled with light, with globes of light that clustered about the walls.

"Master Raiz," she said coldly, "you are too much of a mountebank. No wonder Yorath shrinks from your Masque of the Death of Rosmer!"

"Grandmother," I demanded, "what are *your* plans for me? Are they so different?"

"Let Raiz finish," she said harshly. "There *is* a point you do not understand."

"As the Heir of Lien and of Mel'Nir," said Jalmar Raiz, still pale with anger, "you possess the blood of the Duarings and of the Vauguens of Lien; you also have the Eildon blood, through the markgrafin's late husband, Prince Edgar Pendark. There is a touch of light in your dark and mortal blood, as there is in Rosmer himself. You might become the chosen instrument of the sacrifice of Rosmer. You would perform a just punishment."

"No," I said heavily. "No, I cannot . . ."

"*Yes!*" cried Guenna of Lien.

She raised up her hands, and all the light surrounded her; she was a creature woven of silver fire. She began to chant, to call upon the powers of earth and air, upon the Goddess herself, in her avatars as the Spring Maiden and the Dark Huntress. She gave thanks for her powers and for my coming, the chosen instrument, the Heir of Lien, the heir of her pain and the healer of her sorrow. Part of her fiery aura came to me and shone about me.

"As the fire lies about you, Yorath," intoned Guenna, "so does your destiny. You cannot escape the duty of the blood. You know, deep in your heart, that you must rule. You have been a natural leader all your life . . ."

I rose to my feet and let out a parade ground roar, *"Stop this!"*

The magic light flowed away from me. I saw dark shadows upon the pale wall: an enormous man, a giant, stood over two figures who cringed away from him, one of them a woman. I sat down again, striving to control my god-rage. I stared at the dusty floor of the chamber.

"Grandmother," I said, "I beg you to think of my life in Mel'Nir. You see me, what I am: a soldier, a 'giant warrior.' I have led the life of a soldier, I have killed men and horses; I have waded through blood. Now the killing must have an end. I have cast away my sword; I will fight no more. Do not tell me my duty. I will not rule, neither in Lien, nor in Mel'Nir, which is my own country. I will hear no more talk of destiny, of royal blood, of blood sacrifice, of the chosen instrument. I have already performed such a deed, and when I think of it my soul revolts . . ."

"What deed?" demanded Guenna. "Yorath, dear child, what is this wild talk?"

I could not look at her.

"After the Second Battle of Balbank," I said, "I led my horse around the side of a little hill. A party of fugitives were making their escape along the same path. A tall man in a cloak ran at me; I struck him with the flat of my sword, tumbled him down upon the rocks. Then his hood fell back, and I saw that it was an old man, his silver hair all dabbled with blood . . ."

Jalmar Raiz gave a cry.

"Yes!" I said. "You knew it, Master Raiz. A few moments ago you taunted me with the importance of this battle."

"No," he said. "No, I swear it! I meant only that the battle was important for Val'Nur: it won the civil war for the Westmark."

"An old man!" whispered Guenna.

"So destiny was fulfilled," I said. "I blamed myself for striking down an old man, and I blame myself now even more, whatever his deeds. This was Ghanor of Mel'Nir, the so-called Great King. This was my grandfather."

Again there was a silence. Jalmar Raiz said at last: "What will you do, Prince Yorath? You will find it hard to escape your destiny."

"I will return to Mel'Nir, to Hagnild," I said, "and I will speak to my father, King Gol. I will ask that the truce be extended into a lasting peace. Then I will travel into the Chameln lands to Achamar and visit my cousins, the Daindru, Aidris and Sharn, if they will receive me. I will go further into that wild country and find out some place far from the haunts of men and live there simply as I did in Nightwood as a boy."

It sounded as simple and foolish as a boy's plan, Guenna put in softly.

"I make no empty promises," she said. "If you decided to make yourself known in Lien, to go to the court and support my interests there, then I could summon a companion for you. I can bring back your love again, the Owlwife, Gundril Chawn."

Her face was like a mask. She spoke a little grudgingly, and I knew the reason. The Owlwife was not a princess or a lady of high estate; she was no suitable mate for the Heir of Lien.

"No!" I said sharply. "Grandmother, I beg you not to summon her. She can find me out if she will."

The markgrafin turned away with a sigh and drew herself up as if she would sweep proudly from the room. Yet when she had gone a few paces, she uttered a loud cry and pressed her hands to her heart. Jalmar Raiz was at her side before I was, he supported her and gave her a sip of wine. Guenna's eyes were wild; she said in a hoarse whisper, *"Zaramund!"*

Then, clutching at my arm, "The tower room! At once!"

I lifted her up at my side with an arm about her waist and ran up the staircase with Jalmar Raiz pounding after me. I glanced back and saw my companions, Ibrim, Arn and Forbian and the two old servants crowded at the foot of the stairs.

We came into the tower room, which I had never entered; and at first I saw no more than a hundred lights of different colors—red, gold, green, blue—gleaming like eyes. Then Guenna, with a gesture, sent the hanging on the windows flying back so that the room was lit by the afternoon sun. I saw that the lights came from scrying stones and mirrors ranged everywhere about the room.

The markgrafin went at once to a group of stones upon a covered table with a green cloth and spring flowers before the stones. She gazed into a stone, and Jalmar Raiz was bold to go to her side while I hung back by the door of the workroom. They stared and whispered together, then Guenna sank into a chair, clasped the arms with her ringed hands and stared into nothingness.

Jalmar Raiz said, "There has been an accident at Nesbath. A pleasure boat sank in a sudden wind squall upon the Dannermere. The Markgrafin Zaramund is drowned, along with her father, the Lord of Grays and his two elder sons, Dermat, the Heir of Grays, and Tammis."

"Zelline?" I asked, suddenly afraid. "The Duchess of Chantry . . . ?"

"She was not aboard," said Jalmar Raìz.

He went about to certain other stones and watching places in the room; the tragic accident was known in Erinhall long before the news spread over the land of Lien. The markgrafin and her father and brothers had gone down to their death in full view of the Markgraf Kelen and his court, including of course the Vizier Rosmer. I felt a choking pang of fear and sorrow for all those in that pleasure boat, drawn under by their fine clothes, struggling in the dark water.

There was no doubt in Erinhall that Rosmer had killed Zaramund and her kinsmen by magic and by treachery: a squall of wind and a disabled boat. At least one other person shared this belief from the first. Garvis of Grays, a courtier, youngest son of his unhappy line, saw his father, his brothers and his sister, the Markgrafin, sink to their death. He trusted those about him so little that he left at once, and secretly, and went into hiding. He was now the Lord of Grays, his father's only surviving son.

In her tower room Guenna sat motionless in her chair, and suddenly she looked very old. I went and knelt by her side and took her hand.

"Grandmother . . ."

"Zaramund!" she said, very low. "He loved her. As long as she lived, I felt there was still some hope for him. Now he is lost utterly. That my son Kelen, my dear son, my first-born should lend himself to such a deed . . ."

"Are you sure?"

"He is lost," she said. "He is Rosmer's creature."

She leaned against my shoulder and drew herself up from the chair. Approaching the altar table with the scrying stones, she reached for a vase of wild roses, simple flowers from a hedgerow.

"The time of roses is at an end . . ." said Guenna of Lien.

She held the roses aloft with a cry, and the room became dark except for snapping tongues of flame. She cried out loudly in a strange tongue, not Chyrian but the Old Speech of the north. I could not understand her words, but it seemed to me that she uttered a curse.

From that hour, following the death of Zaramund, a curious bane spread over all the land of Lien. Every rose and every rose tree sickened and died. The rose gardens of the palace at Balufir became a blackened waste; the Wilderness, that lovely park, became a wilderness indeed. The fields of roses grown for their attar were lost, together with every solitary bush, every rambling rose, and every wayside briar. This blight fell heavily upon the folk of Lien and brought the death of their markgrafin into every house. It was rumored from the first that Kelen and his vizier, Rosmer, had had a hand in the death of Zaramund and the Lords of Grays. Rosmer had overreached himself at last. When, in six moons, the Markgraf Kelen wed Fideth of Wirth, with little pomp, shortly before the birth of her son, the folk of Balufir pelted the poor bride in her litter with blackened rose leaves.

Now Guenna, who had uttered the curse, took to her bed in Erinhall and would not be comforted. The house was still; all the wraiths had faded away, all the noise and bustle of a great house had been hushed. I gave word to my friends, and we prepared to depart.

Jalmar Raiz said, "Will you go then?"

"It is for the best," I said. "I do not want to raise false hopes. May I speak to my grandmother?"

"She has asked for you."

Guenna lay in the depths of a curtained bed, yet her hand upon the covers was still firm, her face still beautiful. I felt sure that she looked nothing like the poor invalid in the house of the Moon Sisters. We talked in low voices, though there was no one to overhear us.

At last I said, "I must leave Erinhall, Grandmother. I will go home into Mel'Nir and ask King Gol for an extension of the truce. For peace."

"We might have returned, you and I, Yorath," she said.

"No, Grandmother," I said. "I have not been trained to rule. I am not a prince. Forgive me."

"I give you a blessing," she said. "Go well, Yorath."

I felt a dull anger and helplessness that I had hardly felt in my life before. I was tormented by Guenna's lonely life and I could not, no, I would not help her. As I walked down the stairs, the wraiths were coming out again; I heard the children shout and play on the lawn. I looked from the tall window over the stairs and saw them. The tall brown-haired boy ran ahead of his sisters in their absurd Lienish gowns: Kelen, Hedris, Aravel and, ah ... there, stumbling over the grass, running, smiling, the youngest, Elvédegran.

When we rode off soon afterward, Jalmer Raiz came to my stirrup.

"Let Hagnild send to me a moon or so before you come into the Chameln land to visit the Daindru," he said. "You will be awaited at Radroch Keep upon the plain."

I bade him farewell, and we rode off across the park and turned into the forest at its eastern edge. Ibrim gave a low cry, and we saw that the park had gone. There was only a mass of tall weeds and thorns to be seen and, far off, the corner of a ruined wall. Following our map still, for it showed all of Lien, we crossed the Ringist again. We travelled through the province of Hodd, and it was a melancholy journey. Under a summer sky the roses were dying, and the folk were mourning for the Markgrafin Zaramund. We went on quite unremarked until we came to the river Bal and forded it at a place called Lesfurth. So we came into Balbank, in our own country, and the land was at peace.

CHAPTER
VIII

"COME THEN," SAID HAGNILD.

We tied up our horses outside the second postern gate, which was open and unguarded. It was midsummer, and the royal parkland was wonderfully green. The Palace Fortress was no longer the frowning, dark place that I remembered: it had been painted, plastered, refurbished and planted with banks of flowering trees. Banners hung from its parapets; ladies upon palfreys and children on their ponies rode out into the meadows. Now Hagnild led me swiftly up a little winding stair into a small tower room with one round window. It had been unused for many years except by Hagnild himself; the servants were afraid of the room. There was a table with his books, and on the window embrasure above the couch a bowl of fresh flowers, placed there by the Princess Merse herself, for Hagnild, her true servant, and for Elvédegran, who died there.

I had been told the story of my birth by Hagnild several times since I returned to Nightwood. Each time he gave the sad tale some different color: sometimes it was more dramatic, sometimes more matter-of-fact. When we came at last to this quiet room, there was little more to be said.

"You may think," said Hagnild, "that the people of the palace were very simple and superstitious not to question the fact that Caco, the waiting-woman, was 'carried off by the demon,' and indeed they were. But there was no search for her because Prince Gol believed he had killed or injured her in his god-rage, that she had been whisked out of his sight."

I asked a few questions, and then we fell silent. I was still amazed to see how old Hagnild had become; age had fallen on him like a cloud of dust. Of all the magicians I had encountered, he looked most like a magician: tall, thin, white-haired, fine-featured. He sighed now and took another look at the Dannermere where swans were sailing.

"Remember this," he said. "Your mother died in childbirth. That was the great battle that she lost, that I lost, for I was her healer. Gol was a clumsy and arrogant young husband, no match for a young girl from Lien, gently bred, but he was no monster. If she had lived, she would certainly have made a better life, even here, even with the old king upon the throne."

I might have added that I was the monster, that Ghanor would not have let me live . . . and with good reason. The threads were tangled; I let the matter rest.

My life had been set in order; I felt sometimes as if Yorath the Wolf had never existed. I had spoken four times with King Gol and believed we had reached some kind of understanding. Certainly the King's Peace would be reestablished. In the chronicles there was the true tale of Knaar of Val'Nur's treachery, and we had held it over his head. He had been sent a letter in my own hand and knew that I lived. As it was, General Yorath would remain dead, and in Krail he would be remembered with other heroes.

My companions had gone. Arn had returned to the Swordmaker's Yard and Forbian had gone with him; I trusted both of them to keep silent. Even Ibrim had left my service at last; he had ridden off over the High Plateau to the Danasken communities in the southeast to take himself a wife. All three of my friends were richer than they had been: the Lady of Erinhall had given them each a bag of gold. "And not fairy gold, at that," as Forbian had said, biting a coin to test it.

Hagnild opened the inner door of the tower room, and we wandered out onto a broad landing. We could look down into a courtyard where certain ladies of the court were taking the air. Destiny had struck again, and in a way that pleased me, for it had nothing at all to do with doom or darkness. King Gol, on a progress through the Eastmark, had been taken with a widowed lady of great beauty who was visiting her kin. She was a suitable match; and since she would bear no children, the right of Prince Rieth, Fadola's son, would not be challenged. Soon the king would be married to the Lady Nimoné, widow of Valko of Val'Nur. There she sat in the courtyard with Merse and Fadola and their attendants.

Princess Gleya, that unmarked child that I re-

membered from the scrying stones, was far away.
She had not lacked for suitors at the Hanran estates near Cayl, but Merse, her mother, had sent
her even further from the war that engulfed Mel'Nir.
At eighteen she was married to Prince Borss Paldo
of Eildon; she had crossed the seas to the magic
kingdom in the west.

I looked down again from an arrow slit of the
Palace Fortress, and below me in the summer
meadow, I saw a young boy upon a black pony. He
was about seven years old, tall and well-grown,
with red-gold hair: Rieth, the Prince of Mel'Nir,
the pride and joy of the whole court. Hagnild reported that he was healthy, straight, and of normal intelligence, giving the lie to any forboding
that might have arisen on this score. Baudril Sholt
and the Princess Fadola had a fine son.

Now Hagnild came to my side, and we both
looked down at the little prince handling his pony
skilfully and laughing into his father's face. I
glimpsed another life, one that had never been
possible for me.

"Ah, Goddess," said Hagnild, "the poor Duarings.
They deserve a respite from the tyranny of the
blood. And their greatest treasure has been denied
to them."

He laughed softly and blinked and patted my
arm. "I kept it for myself," he said. "Come, Yorath."

So we went down the winding stair again from
the tower room and returned to Nightwood. The
house in the wood had not changed; Finn and
Erda were still hale and hearty at the smithy,
aided by certain of their children. A widowed
daughter came to keep house for Hagnild.

There was another member of this household,

quite unexpected. When we first came—Arn, Forbian, Ibrim and myself—returned from our adven-
tures in Lien, something worried at our ankles and
bounced about before the hearth.

"A dog?" I said. "A hound puppy, Hagnild?"

"Look again!" he smiled.

I caught up the soft white bundle, and it whined
and panted; its eyes were green-gold.

"Goddess!" said Arn. "A white wolf cub!"

"Your brother Till shot the mother wolf," said
Hagnild, "and brought me this fellow because of
his white coat. I call him Zengor."

It was a royal name of Mel'Nir, a King of the
Farfarers who had come through the mountains.

"Can a wolf be trained?" I asked, setting the cub
down again.

"Try your hand, Master," said Ibrim. "I have
heard of great cats trained to hunt in the Burnt
Lands."

I trained Zengor; Hagnild had asked me to delay
my journey a little, to stay with him. All the rest of
the summer I wandered Nightwood with the white
wolf cub, and he proved himself as strong and
clever as any hound. He grew amazingly, a mighty
silver wolf, with no vices and a hundred endearing
tricks. I put a broad green collar on him in the
winter so that a hunter would not take him for a
maurauder. In the spring Hagnild and I sailed to
Nesbath with Zengor and came to the old home of
the Raiz family with some secrecy lest Rosmer
should be watching.

There I felt a stirring of hope, a longing for my
new life. I set out walking along the Nesbath road
on the first day of the Willowmoon. I had my
heavy cloak, my ash staff and a blanket roll; Zengor

walked by my side. The weather was clear and cool, with a few shoots of green showing at the edges of the road. We walked for four days and came through a place between two high cliffs where the road widened out and then became very narrow. To right and left rose high ridges clothed in loose pine, and on the edges of the road there were flattened places where new trees had been planted, row on row. I have never known a quieter place than the Adderneck Pass. I stood still and heard nothing but the wind in the tops of the trees, higher up on the western ridge. I shut my eyes and could not help but think of the ring of metal, the screams of men and horses, the arrows that flew out of the dark, the fires that were lit.

Zengor whined suddenly, and I opened my eyes. It was a place that lay heavily on the spirit of any passerby. Zengor growled softly, and I told him to be quiet. I saw that we were not alone. Twenty paces away there was a young man in a russet tunic; he came forward with a smooth, almost jaunty step that I remembered.

"Yorath Duaring!" said the Eilif lord, with an inclination of his head.

"Lord . . ."

"Will you walk all the way to Chameln Achamar?"

"I do not think the Chameln have horses large enough to carry me," I said, smiling.

"Go well," he said.

I remembered how I had been too proud to question this fairy lord. But now I was not too proud.

"Good sir," I said, "can you bring word to my lady, Gundril Chawn, the Owlwife? I long for her return."

"How long since we met, Yorath Duaring?" he asked.

"Eight years, nine . . ."

"Has it seemed long to you?"

"Yes," I said. "Very long. I am growing older."

"You have far to go."

I saw that he would give me no better answer.

"Farewell, Lord," I said.

I turned and walked on through the Adderneck, through the narrows, where so many brave men had died, and out again between two high bluffs on to the plain. Ahead lay a broad new road to the town of Folgry and the hills beyond, the central highlands; to the east I could see the Dannermere. All about me lay the plains, a boundless expanse of grassland, silvered in places as the wind swept over it and bent the grasses. I set out to the northeast across the plain, for I thought I could see Radroch Tower where Jalmar Raiz had said I would be awaited. I let Zengor run ahead and enjoy the freedom of the plain. It was like no other place that I had seen; there were larks overhead hovering and singing, and Zengor flushed out a hare that bounded away. It was the year 335 of the Farfaring, and I had left the land of Mel'Nir.

II

I walked on and came closer to the tower, which was old and grey and built in another fashion from the towers and keeps of Lien and Mel'Nir. I came past an empty sheepfold on the plain, stopped at a half-grown pine tree and called Zengor. I rested in the shade of the tree; the tower showed no signs of life, there were no banners hung out. I sat down on the ground and watched the plain. A party of riders approached from the east, along one of the wide roads of beaten earth that crisscrossed the plain.

As I watched, dreaming, three riders broke away from the group and began to cross the plain. They rode at breakneck speed in a wild tearing fashion, bent low over their horses' necks. The size of the plain was deceptive, and the distances hard to judge, but I saw that these were small horses, the leading horse white, the others grey, and that they were indeed riding straight for me, where I stood. I leashed Zengor and stood up. On and on they came, these Chameln riders, and the two greys swung out to either side.

The rider on the white horse came on, slackening speed at last, and cried out, "Yorath!"

She was a small woman, fine-boned, though she rode like a demon. Her clothes were richly embroidered, with splendid boots and long, fine leather trousers. Her horse was a white mare, not much larger than Prince Rieth's black pony, but tough and spirited. I saw that her companions were kedran, on grey horses just as small . . . the Chameln grey. I walked slowly towards horse and rider and had hardly to lift my head to her as she sat in the saddle. Her face was strange and fine, a northern face with high cheekbones, a radiant, pale skin, a pointed chin: her eyes were green as emerald. I saw Aidris, the Witch-Queen of the Chameln.

"Dan Aidris!" I said, bowing my head.

We stared at each other, two creatures so unalike that we might not have been of the same race of mortal beings. Yet around her neck she wore the swan of Lien, as I did.

"Welcome, cousin," said the queen. "Welcome to the Chameln lands!"

We exchanged a few words, talked of simple things: the countryside, the weather, the queen's white horse, who was called Shieran, daughter of Tamir, a famed white stallion. I told her of Zengor, my companion. I felt an immediate love and liking for this Cousin Aidris and believed that she had the same feeling for me.

I went with the queen to Radroch Tower, a nobleman's hunting lodge, and the next day we set out for Achamar. I was given a brown charger to ride, one of the new breed called Lowlanders, from the horse farms about Radroch, horses bred from the captured chargers of Mel'Nir. We did not go through the hills of the center, but took a wide sweep across the plain to the east and came in sight of Chernak, where Sharn Am Zor was building his new summer palace in the style of Lien. The king came out to meet us with his fair consort, Danu Lorn, and his court, a large and brilliant company. So I spent one day with the Daindru, the rulers of the Chameln lands. I saw that Sharn Am Zor was indeed handsome as a god; we were the same age almost to the day, but he seemed to me much younger. He was clean-shaven, and I felt myself a great bearded bear by comparison.

The Daindru were not troubled by problems of succession. Aidris and her fierce-looking consort, Danu Bajan, a chieftain of the Nureshen, had a son and two daughters; Sharn and his lady had a daughter and a son. All these royal children, together with the children of other noble families, were spending the spring and the summer at a manor called Zerrah. Jalmar Raiz, as tutor to the Heir of the Firn, Prince Sasko, was at Zerrah too, and Pinga with him, so that I did not meet my old companion.

I came on to Achamar with the queen and her escort and found it a marvellous city, not so dear to me as Krail, but old and strong and full of wonders. Nevertheless, I spoke at last to Aidris and excused myself from further attendance at court. I asked for a guide into the north and a safe conduct through the land, if that was needed. In the last week of the Willowmoon I left Achamar for the northern tribal lands, and my guides were Ivan Batro, Bajan's nephew, of the Nureshen, and his servant Amuth.

We left the city early in the morning, and the queen came down to the courtyard by the northern gate of the palace to bid me farewell.

"I know where you are going," she said, ruffling Zengor's mane. "I heard it once in Athron and did not understand."

"You were in Athron more than ten years ago, Cousin," I said. "Who could have told you?"

"The Carach tree." She smiled. "I asked the way to a certain place whose name I will not speak. The Carach tree replied: 'No one knows where it lies, but the Wolf and the Wild Swan.'"

Then she stepped up onto the mounting block and placed around my neck a large glittering green stone edged with runes worked upon gold, a jewel of the Firn.

"It is your safe conduct," she said, "and it is a scrying stone. We will see each other. If you come into the northwest mountains, called the Roof of the World, find out a tribe called the Children of the White Wolf. Commend me to their Chieftain Ark and their Spirit Maid, the Blessed Ilda."

"I will remember!"

So we moved on through the streets, chill and misty at this hour, and came out through the northern gate of Achamar: two men of the Firn on their grey horses, one man of Mel'Nir on a brown charger, and Zengor, the white wolf, running ahead. We passed along broad highroads through the cornfields and came to the plains again. We rode on and on across the seas of grass, camping at wells and sheepfolds, and came at last to the first lodges of the Nureshen.

We were greeted by Batro, father of my guide, and his mother Ambré, sister of Bajan. I had a fine guest lodge all to myself and was an object of some curiosity. I went out among the pleasant lakes and groves of trees that were before my door and tried a bathhouse on the lake shore. The lands of the Nureshen and the other tribes, east and west, are fine and rich with teeming fish in the lakes and rivers, berries and fruit, plots of rye, and herds of deer. Yet I could not linger; my journey had only half begun.

I had a map from Aidris Am Firn, and I asked for another. At night in my lodge I heard the sound of a drum, and presently there were voices at my door: a shaman had come with a map. He was a tall man for these parts and past middle age, with his glossy black hair threaded with grey and worked into a plait that hung past his knees. It was a mark of holiness. He offered me no name, but we sat down together and he unrolled his marvellous map.

It was two yards square and mounted upon leather. The mountains and lakes and forests had been worked out of leather and colored and glued to the map so that it was like a model of the countryside. There were the two great systems of mountains, one in the east and one in the west. The eastern chain rose in the northeast of the Chameln land, around a mountain province called Vedan, home of the Aroshen, an ancient tribe whom the Nureshen regarded as primitive and quarrelsome. It reached its highest point beyond the tip of the inland sea, the Dannermere, then went on, past the area of this map, down the Eastmark of Mel'Nir. The western mountain chain formed the border range with its thick forest, dividing Athron from the Chameln lands and stretching down into Cayl and Mel'Nir. This chain was highest in the northwest: the mountains rose up and marched across the roof of the world. Ramparts of peaks and valleys threaded by rivers of ice ended in a patch of whiteness, the distant north where no mortal man had ever been.

Between these two chains of mountains, east and west, there stretched a rising plain shaped like a river itself and this was called the Boganur, which might mean the "hard northern ground" in the old speech of these parts. It was a hunting ground for the tribes; a hardy breed of fur-trappers lived there and even wintered there in caves and ice huts. I saw a small tarn called Last Lake and beyond it a camp on the Boganur. Near this camp was a valley that led to a river of ice and further northwest was a mountain with a scrap of red wool on its crest. I asked if this was a fire mountain.

The shaman, who knew the common speech, answered that it was and pointed to other warm places. Here was a lake with boiling pools at its edges and here another fire mountain that had destroyed a village with its lava stream a hundred years ago. I still peered into the northwest and marked my own map to correspond with the shaman's map. I saw certain camps or villages marked in the mountains not far from the fire mountain, Egilla, that had first caught my eye and asked if these places were inhabited by a tribe known as the Children of the White Wolf.

"That may be what they call themselves," said the shaman. "We call them Garmicha, the children of Garm."

"Who is this Garm?" I asked. "Is it some god?"

"It is a giant," said the holy man. "He is a half-god, a hero, and some say that he lives among those mountains and that while he lives there the winters will never be too hard for mortal men to bear. The word has been taken into the old speech, sir, to mean giant. Have you not heard of the Morrigar, the giant-killers?"

His smile was positively sly. I knew who the giant-killers were very well: the men and women of the Great Ambush who had killed so many men of Mel'Nir at the Adderneck Pass.

Now I knew at least where to go. I bade farewell to my kind hosts of the Nureshen and to my good brown steed, for large horses were not used on the Boganur. I set out with a family of trappers for Last Lake. It was another strange country in which I found myself, beautiful at this time of year, with wild flowers and the white and purple heather. It swarmed with life: snow birds, in brown and white plumage, rose up clumsily at our approach. Small deer and the fierce wolf-cats, who preyed on them, whisked away into the stunted firs. I walked and was sometimes carried on a pony sledge. We came upon trappers with a team of dogs drawing their sledge, and the first whiff of Zengor almost drove them mad. The white wolf loved this new country. He brought me game, and in the night he howled at the moon like a true wolf.

"Peace," I said. "Hush, Zengor. Do not run off to the wolves."

The journey to Last Lake took many days. It was still very cold in the northern spring weather; the trappers told me that summer was coming, but I did not think it would be a true summer for me. I had a fur blanket, which I could use as a cloak, two pairs of boots from the Nureshen, and all that I needed to make camp. I bathed one last time in the manner of Mel'Nir, immersing myself in the waters of Last Lake; I understood why bathhouses full of dry heat were popular in this country.

I would not stay, but moved on alone with only Zengor for company and set my face towards the northwest. I found the camp marked on the map, a few wretched huts, deserted. I had provisions and even a bow, although I am not a good shot with this queer little tribal weapon. Zengor brought me snow hens, and I had some lucky shots at the hares. We worked our way steadily through the valley that led to the river of ice.

I saw no one. The slopes of the mountains were bare and stony, patched with hard, yellowish snow. There were few birds and beasts in the valley and

on the river of ice. Zengor shared my dried meat
and fruit porridge. Then we noticed a slight warmth
in the sun ... summer was coming, even to this
icy place. I found the going hard, on the ice itself
or on the edge of the river, strewn with boulders.
We came to a patch of scrub and feasted on a snow
hare, our first meat in many days. Far off, on the
river bank, I saw a tall, pocked stone, a black rock.

I was lonely and the way was hard. I saw no
sign of the Children of the White Wolf. At last the
black rock was reached, and I climbed it with
Zengor whining at the base. It was near evening or
what passed for evening in a land where the sun
never set. Fingers of light came through the mountains to the west, and when I looked over the ice
river I had a shock. A giant figure was poised in
the air against a cliff. Garm had come out of his
lair. I raised a hand, and the mist giant raised a
hand. It was my own spectre that I saw.

I stared until the landscape blurred but could
not see the fire mountain. Then the sun went a
little lower, and I glimpsed a smudge of cloud or
smoke. There was only one peak in a dark ridge. I
realised at last the madness of the whole journey.
Had the Alraune really existed? Was she some
conjuring of my brain? Had an evil spirit played a
trick on me to lead me into the wilderness?

In the morning we went on, and for the first
time the sun was warm. We made better time and
came to a place where the ice river curved away to
the north to seek an icy sea. I could see the fire
mountain plainly now, a broken volcanic cone,
and when at last I came to its base, it was clear
that there had once been three of these cones. Now
two were worn down to heaps of rock and rubble,

the size of a high ridge; perhaps an earthquake had brought them down. The remaining mountain smoked dangerously through its crest and through side vents. The ground seemed to move under our feet. Scrub pines and bushes flourished in the sandy, sulphurous warmth of the place, and a jet of steaming water came up out of the ground almost at our feet and then fell away again.

"There is nothing for it," I said to Zengor. "We must go over the wall!"

It took me more than a day to climb over the stony barrier. We spent one night on a ledge and went on as the sun began to climb. From the top of the broken cones, I could see nothing but frowning masses of rock, impassable ridges, and to the north and west, snowy summits. We scrambled down into a narrow valley absolutely dark and full of ashes and crept forward hardly able to breathe. Zengor whined and protested. The valley led nowhere. We came to a wall of solid rock.

I lit a torch to see the face of the rock before me; it was patterned by wind and weather, and glassy in places as if it had been hardened in fire. Nothing grew on this wall, but I saw a scrap of brown lichen. I touched it, and my hand shook. It was caught right in the wall as if it grew from the rock, and when I tugged to draw it out it broke away. I held in my palm half of a dried oak leaf. I planted my torch in the ashes and began to feel the rock wall with my fingers. I pushed on it. I spread my arms wide and lay against the wall and pushed with a gentle, even pressure. Zengor who had been watching his foolish master suddenly let out a howl and began to dig furiously in the ashes at the base of the wall.

There was a low rumbling like distant thunder; the wall began to move. A huge slab of rock pivoted and swung me along with it. I had only a moment to step back and seize my belongings. Zengor raced through the opening in the wall, and I stumbled after him. The rock swung shut behind us. I stood half blinded by the light; it was the light of the sun, but it came to me as a blaze of pure green: green of the thick grass; the reeds that grew by the purling stream; green of the foliage of the oak trees, saplings, young trees and trees so old that they might have been planted in the morning of the world, here in lost Ystamar.

III

I had come for the third time in my life into a magic place and I made it my home. The oaks of Ystamar are wise, but they do not speak: I believe they have accepted me. I have explored the valley, but it still holds many secrets. I know many paths in and out between the frowning ridges, but I do not think that anyone can enter this place unless it is permitted. The valley has its seasons; the oaks lose their leaves in autumn and stand bare in winter; but the winter is mild, with a few light falls of snow. Beyond the valley the winter is unbearably harsh, a long night, lit by the fires of the Goddess, the fiery curtains of the northern lights, which I see over the northern mountains. When the blizzards rage, birds and animals come to take refuge in Ystamar. I thought at first that I should not kill game or fish for my food, but I could not keep this rule. I am a flesh-eater, like Zengor.

I set to work in that first summer and built myself a house out of stone and clay. I built it beside a huge hollow oak in which I had been sleeping, and when I woke up one morning, I found that a "dead" branch of the tree had swung round in the night to make the roof of my house. I thatched and daubed this branch into place and used the tree's mighty hollow trunk as one room of my house. I added other rooms and lined the house with reeds.

On the banks of the stream I planted the core of the apple from Liran's Isle, and it grew and thrived. Emboldened by this I thrust my good ash staff into the ground. I was loath to lose it, but there were many staffs of oak for me to use if I needed them. After sometime, I saw that the ash staff had been wakened to life again and had taken root.

I made a calendar out of a slab of white stone embedded in a hillside on the north side of the valley. I scratched the days deep in the stone and colored them with charcoal. I made a writing ink and filled up with about half of my life the book of blank pages that Hagnild had given me. Then I set about making more paper to write the rest. I tried for a kind of woven reed paper that Hagnild had showed me, and in the end I had something very like it. I made clumsy clay vessels but could not fire them and simply dried them in the sun.

Zengor roamed the whole of the valley and was happy. In the first winter we heard wolves in the distance, but I do not think any came into the valley. I mused on his life as I did on my own. He was not a true wolf, his nature had been changed because he had been tamed. I could not tell what my true nature was. I was very lonely at times, at others very contented, as I had been on Liran's Isle without my memory. In the second spring I decided to revisit the world.

I studied my map, went out of a certain way between the rocks on the west side of the valley and strode off through the mountains towards a marked camp. The going was heavy, but I was in good training. I passed through a long valley and came over the shoulder of a mountain, sinking into last year's drifts. I came round a cairn of stones, and there they were: three shaggy, stunted folk with bow and spear. They stood stock still when I appeared. Zengor ran towards me down a steep bank, and I was afraid of their spears. I raised a hand and called to them in my few words of the Old Speech.

"We come in peace!"

Their reaction was strange. One turned and ran, one flung himself face downwards into the snow. The third remained upright, but his spear fell from his hand. I leashed Zengor, then walked closer. Slowly the fallen one, who was a young boy, raised himself up, clinging to his comrade. They stared at me as if their black eyes would never shut again. I said *"Peace,"* to them again, and the man who still stood whispered, *"Peace."*

"I seek Ark, Chieftain of the Children of the White Wolf!" I said.

"Ark." The man nodded. *"Ark is our Chief . . ."*

He pointed in the direction in which the third hunter had run off, shook his dazed companion and hurried away with gestures to me to follow.

They kept a good distance ahead but kept looking back as if to make sure I had not vanished. We came to the place marked on my map, and it was a large village, almost a town, with leather tents and storehouses of stone. The place was in an uproar; the people ran about like ants, and a word grew out of the murmuring and crying: Garm ... Garm ... Garm.

The chieftain was coming to meet me. He was thickset and ferociously ugly, distinguished from his fellows by an air of command. The people thrust back against the tents at his word, and he came on alone so that we met in the middle of the village beside a rough well.

"Ark?" I said. "I bring greeting from the Queen of the Firn in the Chameln lands."

He bobbed his head, turned and called up a younger man and presented him to me ... his son Kizark. This fellow had the common speech better than his father.

"I am called Yorath," I said, "and my tame wolf here is called Zengor."

"Do you live in the mountains?"

The question came from Ark.

"Yes," I said. "I live alone. I am a hermit."

They whispered together.

I said, "I am not Garm. I am a mortal man."

"You are a giant, Lord," said Kizark boldly.

"I am a man of Mel'Nir, a distant country," I said, "where many men are of my stature."

"Did the queen send greeting?" asked Ark. "She came into my tent once in the land of Athron. I took her for a highborn maid of the Chameln, but now I know it was the queen."

"She sent greeting," I said, "and a greeting to the Blessed Ilda, your spirit maid."

"Alas," said Kizark, "the spirit maid has left us these nine years past . . ."

He laid a hand on the only spirit tree in the village, and we raised our eyes. The thick stripped trunk of fir was unusually decorated—it was not strung with teeth and claws or painted in red or green. Its whole length was inlaid with flat pieces of pearly stone broken only by fine pelts of ermine. At the top there hung an immense fall of light golden-brown hair, the hair, I realised, of the Blessed Maid herself. The spirit tree, glittering in the snowy light, seemed to me a marvellous thing to have been wrought by these folk in memory of their priestess.

"The most beautiful spirit tree that I ever beheld," I said.

Kizark and his father cast their eyes down and smiled modestly. I was invited into Ark's lodge. I had long pondered, in my secret valley, over what I should bring out as a present or to trade. It could be nothing that gave away the nature of my retreat. I had found a treasure in a certain cave, and now I brought it off my shoulder and gave it to Ark: about twenty pounds of rock salt. It pleased him and his wife—a thin, knowing woman—very much indeed.

"What do you need, Lord?" asked Kizark. "We are not rich, but the Goddess has spared us for another season."

Zengor sat by the fire in Ark's lofty pine-smelling hall, and children came to feed him scraps of meat. I drank a fiery spirit made of berries and the milk of the mountain sheep and sat companionably with

Ark and his family. There were young women in
their best clothes who came to serve us at dinner,
and it was made clear to me that it would be no
breach of hospitality if I were to take one to my
bed. I was tempted, after so long, but I was still a
bashful monster. It seemed just as polite to get
drunk ... as evidenced by the other men round
about slowly rolling from their settles to the floor
... so I remained drinking round for round with
Ark. When we were both ready to sleep, he said to
me, smiling:

"You *are* Garm, my friend, although you do not
know it ..."

"How can that be?"

"The Goddess sends a messenger ... "

He meant, perhaps, an avatar. We rolled off to
our places by the fire and slept. Next day I wondered how Ark and I could have spoken so well
together when drunk.

I was fast friends with the chief and his family
after this first meeting, and I stayed three days in
the village. Then I turned my face back into the
mountains and took up my pack, laden with dried
meat, cheese, dressed leather and leather-working
tools and certain herbs from Lia Arkwife's garden.
I thought I might have to dismiss my followers,
but they left of their own accord, bidding me farewell at just that point in the road where I had first
appeared to them. I unleashed Zengor, and off we
went through the melting snows and came safely
home to Ystamar.

I thrived on my hermit's life ... or so I told
myself ... and worked hard all over the valley.
Once in every season I gazed into my green scrying
stone and greeted Aidris, the Witch Queen. In that

second autumn a female wolf came limping into the valley, and Zengor ran off with her to a den on the south side. I called her Vyrie, after Zengor's queen. She was a little, fierce grey she-wolf, never tamed, but her two cubs would come close enough for me to feed them. The winter was mild as usual, but any plans for a spring visit to the outer world, to Ark's village, were spoiled by my own careless-ness. I came down heavily as I moved a boulder, and for a moment thought my right ankle was broken. It was a sprain, no more, but it kept me hobbling for many days.

In the last days of the third spring, just as the valley was at its most beautiful, I became aware of the snow owls who flew about by day. There had always been one or two, now there were more, gliding in pursuit of hares or floating low over the grass in the twilight. I was turning the soil for a garden beside a great oak and saw three of these yellow-eyed birds sitting above me. I remember speaking to them familiarly as I did to all living things in the valley. I heard Zengor give his sharp wolf cry, not quite the barking of a dog, and thought that he had caught a snow hare.

The oak tree overhead began to "speak"; all its leaves vibrated and rustled, and the movement was taken up by other trees nearby. I laid aside my mattock impatiently and came out of the shadow of the trees. All the oaks of Ystamar were speaking. I walked slowly towards the northwest-ern tip of the valley where Zengor still raised his voice. It came to me that he was near the path through the rock walls that I called archway. The sun was in my eyes, and as I raised a hand to shade them, there was a flash of sunlight upon glass or metal. High up, where a stone arch gave on to a path down a grassy hillside, the dried bed of a stream, I made out moving shapes.

I called to Zengor to be still, and I watched them come down the hillside. It was a dream, it was an awakening. What Yorath was it who had lived so long alone, who had gone about in the world without his love? A tall dark-haired woman came on with sure unwearied steps and turned back to give her hand to a sturdy boy. He hurried on and ran past her and came running and sliding the last few yards until he drew up shyly, almost at my feet. I saw that he was tall for his age and straight, with fair skin and tawny hair, a boy of Mel'Nir.

"There now," said the Owlwife to the child, leading him forward. "Did I not tell you he was the tallest man in the world?"

I looked at Gundril Chawn and saw no trace of the years in that loved face. I looked down at the boy, who stared with his mother's clear brown eyes.

"What is your name?" I asked.

"Yorath," he said.

I knelt down to him and said, "I am called Yorath, too. I think you must be my boy . . ."

Then he came into the crook of my arm and let me embrace him.

"Is that your dog?" he whispered.

"It is Zengor," I said. "He is a white wolf. Go and speak to him. He is quite tame."

He ran a few steps towards Zengor. I stood up and took the Owlwife in my arms. It was five years and three moons since we had last seen each other in the Hunters' Yard in Krail, at the time of the death of Valko Val'Nur. Now we stood in Ystamar, our magic valley, and watched the child and the white wolf run to the banks of the stream while the welcoming snow owls glided overhead.

We have been granted years of peace and contentment far beyond any dreams I might have had as a warrior in Mel'Nir. My son tells me that there is a girl child who comes out of a certain ash tree by the stream and an apple tree that speaks in a baby voice. The Owlwife brought silver seeds out of Athron, and now a Carach tree is growing. I feel no wish to return to the world, but the world changes; the last word in the chronicle is never set down.

IN THE FACE OF MY ENEMY

Joseph H. Delaney, co-author of *Valentina: Soul in Sapphire*, is back with his most ambitious work yet—a massive volume that is awesome in scope and stunning in execution.

The time is 18,000 years in the past. Aged and ailing, tribal shaman Kah-Sih-Omah has prepared himself to die, seeking final refuge far from the lands of his people. The time of his passing is near when alien beings chance upon him. As an experiment, they correct his body's "inefficiencies"—then depart, leaving behind something that could not be, but is.

Kah-Sih-Omah finds himself whole again, and accepts this as a gift from the gods. Accordingly, he returns to his people, overjoyed that he may once again protect and lead them. But he is met with fear and rejection, and must flee for his life. Soon he discovers the incredible abilities with which he has been endowed, and embarks on a centuries-long journey that takes him across much of Earth, as well as to other worlds. During his travels, he struggles with the question of why he was granted strange powers and an extended lifespan. The answer awaits him in the far future . . .

In the Face of My Enemy is a book rich in characterization and historical background, and one which is guaranteed to intrigue readers. A map tracing Kah-Sih-Omah's travels on Earth highlights this fascinating saga.

Available November 1985 from Baen Books
55993-1 • 352 pp. • $2.95

To order by phone: Call (212) 245-6400 and ask for extension 1183, Telephone Sales. To order by mail: Send the title, book code number, and the cover price, plus 75 cents postage and handling, to BAEN BOOKS, 260 Fifth Ave., Suite 3S, New York, N.Y. 10001. Make check or money order payable to Pocket Books.

**For
Fiction with Real Science In It,
and Fantasy That Touches
The Heart of The Human Soul . . .**

Baen Books bring you Poul Anderson, Marion Zimmer Bradley, C.J. Cherryh, Gordon R. Dickson, David Drake, Robert L. Forward, Janet Morris, Jerry Pournelle, Fred Saberhagen, Michael Reaves, Jack Vance . . . all top names in science fiction and fantasy, plus new writers destined to reach the top of their fields. For a free catalog of all Baen Books, send three 22-cent stamps, plus your name and address, to

*Baen Books
260 Fifth Avenue, Suite 3S
New York, N.Y. 10001*

KILLER STATION

by Martin Caidin

A giant space station orbiting the Earth can be a scientific boon ... or a terrible sword of Damocles hanging over our heads. In Martin Caidin's *Killer Station*, one brief moment of sabotage transforms Station *Pleiades* into an instrument of death and destruction for millions of people. The massive space station is heading relentlessly toward Earth, and its point of impact is New York City, where it will strike with the impact of the Hiroshima Bomb. Station Commander Rush Cantrell must battle impossible odds to save his station and his crew, and put his life on the line that millions may live.

This high-tech tale of the near future is written in the tradition of Caidin's *Marooned* (which inspired the Soviet-American Apollo/Soyuz Project and became a film classic) and *Cyborg* (the basis for the hit TV series "The Six Million Dollar Man"). Barely fictional, *Killer Station* is an intensely *real* moment of the future, packed with excitement, human drama, and adventure.

Caidin's record for forecasting (and inspiring) developments in space is well-known. *Killer Station* provides another glimpse of what *may* happen with and to all of us in the next few years.

Available December 1985 from Baen Books
55996-6 • 384 pp. • $3.50